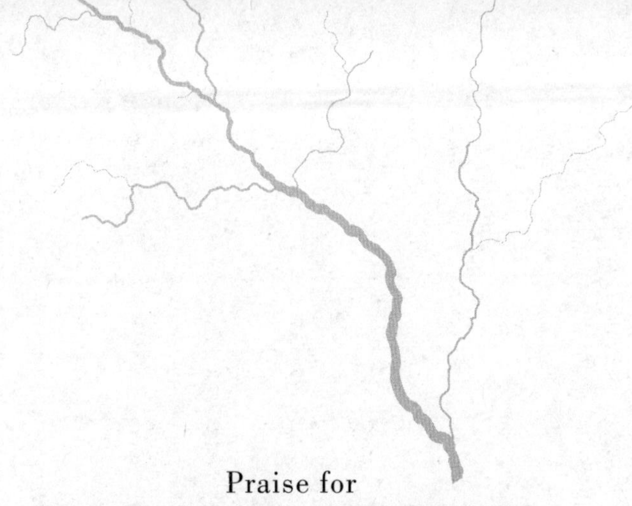

Praise for
THE MICHAEL VEY SERIES:

"Highly recommended. Michael Vey is thrilling storytelling, full of twists, action, intrigue, and outstanding characters. I wouldn't be surprised if Michael Vey sweeps the world."

—JAMES DASHNER, #1 *New York Times* bestselling author of the Maze Runner series

"My kind of book—fast, funny, and strange. Once Michael's astounding powers are revealed, the shocks keep coming chapter after chapter."

—R. L. STINE, #1 bestselling author of the Goosebumps series

"Michael Vey is one of the most original thrillers I've come across in years."

—VINCE FLYNN, #1 *New York Times* bestselling author

ALSO BY RICHARD PAUL EVANS

MICHAEL VEY
THE PRISONER OF CELL 25

MICHAEL VEY
RISE OF THE ELGEN

MICHAEL VEY
BATTLE OF THE *AMPERE*

MICHAEL VEY
HUNT FOR JADE DRAGON

MICHAEL VEY
STORM OF LIGHTNING

MICHAEL VEY
FALL OF HADES

MICHAEL VEY
THE FINAL SPARK

MICHAEL VEY
THE PARASITE

MICHAEL VEY
THE TRAITOR

BOOK NINE

RICHARD PAUL EVANS

MERCURY INK SIMON PULSE

NEW YORK LONDON TORONTO SYDNEY NEW DELHI

This book is a work of fiction. Any references to historical events, real people, or real places are used fictitiously. Other names, characters, places, and events are products of the author's imagination, and any resemblance to actual events or places or persons, living or dead, is entirely coincidental.

SIMON PULSE / MERCURY INK
An imprint of Simon & Schuster Children's Publishing Division
1230 Avenue of the Americas, New York, NY 10020
First Simon Pulse / Mercury Ink hardcover edition September 2023

Jacket designed by Tiara Iandiorio
Interior designed by Mike Rosamilia
The text of this book was set in Berling LT Std.
Manufactured in the United States of America
2 4 6 8 10 9 7 5 3 1
Library of Congress Control Number 2023940687
ISBN 978-1-6659-1955-5 (hc)
ISBN 978-1-6659-1957-9 (ebook)

To Boyd Evans

MICHAEL VEY
THE TRAITOR

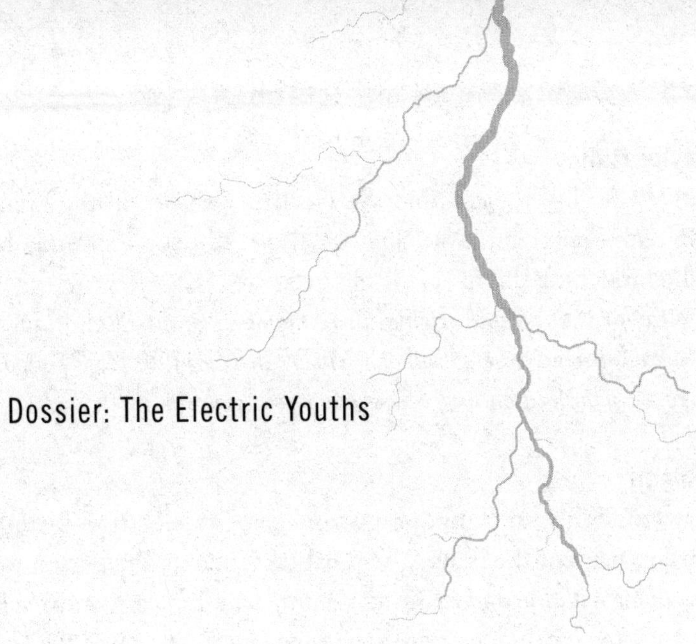

Dossier: The Electric Youths

Michael Vey

Power: Ability to shock people through direct contact or conduction. Can also absorb power from other electric children as well as through conduction from other sources.

Michael is the most powerful of all the electric children and leader of the Electroclan. He is steadily increasing in power.

Ostin Liss

Power: Not an electric child.

Ostin is highly intelligent, with an IQ of 155, which puts him at the same level as the average Nobel Prize winner. He is one of the original three members of the Electroclan and Michael's best friend. Ostin and McKenna are a couple.

Taylor Ridley

Power: Ability to scramble the electric synapses in the brain, causing temporary confusion. She can also read people's minds, but only when touching them.

Taylor is one of the original three members of the Electroclan. She and Michael discovered each other's powers at Meridian High School, which they were both attending. She is Michael's girlfriend.

Abigail

Power: Ability to temporarily stop pain by electrically stimulating certain parts of the brain. She must be touching the person to do so.

Along with Ian and McKenna, Abigail was held captive by the Elgen for many years because she refused to follow Hatch. She joined the Electroclan after escaping from the Elgen Academy's prison, known as Purgatory. She is currently missing and is believed to have been abducted by unknown Glows.

Bryan

Power: The ability to create highly focused electricity that allows him to cut through objects.

Bryan is one of Hatch's Glows.

Cassy

Power: An extremely powerful electric, Cassy has the ability to freeze muscles from a distance of more than two kilometers. She also has the ability to cause mass heart attacks.

Cassy was rescued by the voice before the Elgen knew of her existence. She was raised and trained in Switzerland by the voice.

Grace

Power: Grace acts as a "human flash drive" and is able to transfer and store large amounts of electronic data.

Grace was living with the Elgen but joined the Electroclan when they defeated Hatch at the Elgen Academy. She has been working and living with the resistance but has not been on any missions with the Electroclan.

Ian

Power: Ability to see through electrolocation, which is the same way sharks and eels see through muddy or murky water.

Along with McKenna and Abigail, Ian was held captive by the Elgen for many years because he refused to follow Hatch. He joined the Electroclan after escaping from the Elgen Academy's prison, known as Purgatory.

Jack

Power: Not an electric child.

Jack spends a lot of time in the gym and is very strong. He is also excellent with cars. Originally one of Michael's bullies, he joined the Electroclan after Michael bribed him to help rescue Michael's mother from Dr. Hatch. Currently embedded with the Chasqui and believed to be a traitor.

Kylee

Power: Born with the ability to create electromagnetic power, she is basically a human magnet.

One of Hatch's Glows, she spends most of her time shopping.

McKenna

Power: Ability to create light and heat. She can heat herself to more than three thousand kelvins.

Along with Ian and Abigail, McKenna was held captive by the Elgen for many years because she refused to follow Hatch. She joined the Electroclan after escaping from the Elgen Academy's prison, known as Purgatory.

Nichelle

Power: Nichelle acts as an electrical ground and can both detect and drain the powers of the other electric children.

Nichelle was Hatch's power over the rest of the electric children until he abandoned her during the battle at the Elgen Academy. Although everyone was nervous about it, the Electroclan recruited her to join them on their mission to save Jade Dragon, and she has become a loyal Electroclan member.

Quentin

Power: Ability to create isolated electromagnetic pulses, which lets him take out all electrical devices within twenty yards.

Quentin was once the president of Hatch's Glows, poised to be in power, just below Hatch.

Tanner

Power: Ability to interfere with airplanes' electrical navigation systems and cause them to malfunction and crash. His powers are so advanced that he can do this from the ground.

After years of mistreatment by the Elgen, Tanner was rescued by the Electroclan from the Peruvian Starxource plant and was subsequently staying with the resistance so he had a chance to recover. He was killed in Tuvalu during the battle of Hades.

Tara

Power: Tara's abilities are similar to her twin sister Taylor's in that she can disrupt normal electronic brain functions. Through years of practicing and refining her powers, Tara has learned to focus on specific parts of the brain in order to create emotions such as fear or joy.

Tara is Taylor's twin (they were adopted by different families after they were born) and was raised by Hatch and the Elgen until she left them to join her sister.

Tessa

Power: Tessa's abilities are the opposite of Nichelle's—she is able to enhance the powers of the other electric children.

Tessa escaped from the Elgen at the Starxource plant in Peru and lived in the Amazon jungle for six months with an indigenous tribe called the Amacarra. She joined the Electroclan after the tribe rescued Michael from the Elgen and brought them together.

Torstyn

Power: One of the more lethal of the electric children, Torstyn can create microwaves.

Torstyn is one of Hatch's Glows and was instrumental to the Elgen in building the Starxource plants. Once Quentin's right-hand man, he is currently working as a drug trafficker.

Wade

Power: Not an electric child.

Wade was Jack's best friend and joined the Electroclan at the same time he did. He died in Peru when the Electroclan was surprised by an Elgen guard.

Zeus

Power: Ability to "throw" electricity from his body.

Zeus was kidnapped by the Elgen as a young child and lived for many years as one of Hatch's Glows. He joined the Electroclan when they escaped from the Elgen Academy.

PART ONE

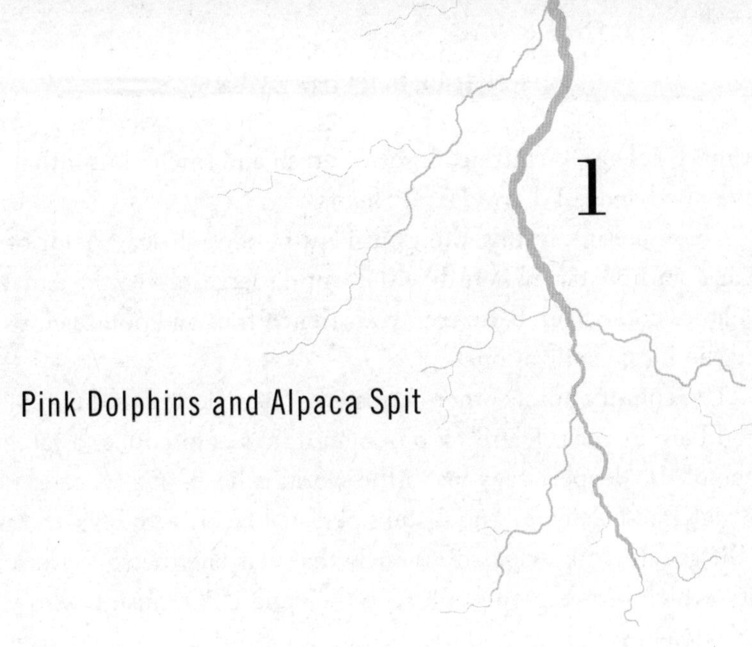

1

Pink Dolphins and Alpaca Spit

My name is Michael Vey, and I'm back in Peru.

I hate Peru. I've got good reasons to hate the place. The first time I was here, my mother was being held captive in an electrified cage, the Elgen tried to feed me to rats, and one of my friends was killed. And, as thanks for saving their country from Elgen tyranny, the Peruvian government put us on their Most Wanted terrorist list. So, yeah, not my favorite place. I'm sure there are a lot of great things about Peru. Especially when they think you're a tourist instead of a terrorist. I know because Ostin once went off on one of his diatribes and told me more about the country than I ever wanted to know.

For instance, Peru is home to most of the world's alpacas. If you don't know what an alpaca is, it's basically a miniature llama that isn't secretly plotting to kill you. Alpacas couldn't kill you if they wanted to. They're smaller, softer, and gentler than llamas, and their primary defense is spitting. Sure, it's green and smells, but if that was my only defense, I'd avoid street fights.

There are interesting things in Peru besides alpacas. A lot of big things start or started here, like the world's largest river, the Amazon. Potatoes come from Peru, ergo your french fries and potato chips. So did the Incan civilization.

The country boasts other curiosities. The tallest sand dunes in the world are in Peru. There's a mountain that's colored like a rainbow. One of the deepest canyons in the world is here—it's twice as deep as the Grand Canyon. And Ostin's personal favorite, the Nazca Lines, giant geoglyph drawings of animals that can only be seen from the air—which begs the question (cue the eerie UFO music), who were they drawn for?

Peru also has the world's most expensive coffee. It's called Coati Dung Coffee. It's exactly what its name says it is—coffee made from beans that have been eaten by a jungle beast called the coati (basically a raccoon with a bigger nose), then pooped out. The local Peruvians collect the beans, wash the poop off them, dry them in the sun, and then sell the coffee for around sixty-five dollars a cup. That's almost a thousand dollars a pound. I swear I'm not making this up.

In addition to the coffee-eating coati, Peru's got a whole slate of weird animals the rest of the world doesn't have, like pink dolphins, glass frogs, wood-eating catfish, hairless dogs, and penguins, which probably got stuck on an iceberg a thousand years ago, floated to Peru from Antarctica, and liked the neighborhood, so took up residence. I'm probably not making that up either.

But, like I said, I'm not here as a tourist, and I didn't come for the dung coffee. I came to rescue Tara and Jack from the Chasqui, a break-off band from the Elgen with another megalomaniacal leader. At least that was our intention. Now Jack claims he's one of them. What am I supposed to do with that? Could he have been brainwashed like in *The Manchurian Candidate*? I don't know, but Jack's the most loyal person I know. I'd trust him with my life. At least I would have. Now I don't know. He's just not one I would ever think could be a traitor. So, here's the dilemma we're wrestling with: Is it worth risking all our lives to save Jack from himself? And is that even possible?

I know that the last time I wrote, I said that I was bored and wished something exciting would happen, but boring suddenly doesn't seem so bad. Now I just wish people would stop trying to kill us. If I'm going to die, I'd rather do it in the comfort of my own home, not travel all the way to some piranha- and bug-infested jungle to be un-alived.

Like I said, I hate Peru.

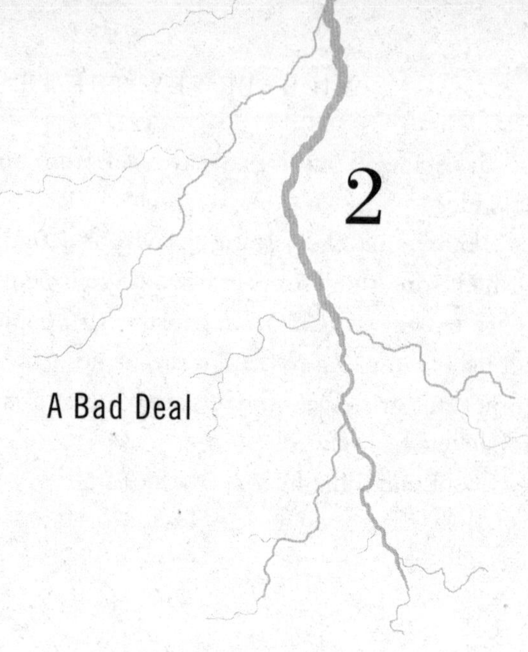

2

A Bad Deal

"You were right," I said to Taylor, sliding the satellite phone back into my pocket. I was with the rest of Alpha Team and the Electroclan near the entrance of Jacinta's zoo, about to head back to Alpha Team's compound, when the phone had rung.

Taylor looked at me blankly. "What was I right about?"

"That dream you had last night."

"You mean about Jack?"

I nodded.

Johnson turned back from the front seat. "Who was that, Michael?"

"It was Jack."

Ostin leaned forward from the back seat. "Why would the Chasqui let Jack talk to you?"

"Because Jack *is* a Chasqui now. He's joined them."

"This just keeps getting better," Johnson said.

"That's impossible," McKenna said. "Jack would never do that."

"Nothing in the realm of human choice is impossible," Ostin said. "As Einstein is said to have said, 'The difference between genius and idiocy is that *genius* has its limits.' In Jack's case, statistically speaking it's unlikely he'd join the Chasqui but not impossible."

"Yeah, got it," Taylor said, annoyed at Ostin's diatribe. "Where is he, Michael?"

"It sounded like he was in a helicopter." I looked at Johnson. "He says they want to do a swap. Taylor for Tara."

"What?" Taylor said.

Johnson shook his head. "That's never going to happen."

"That's what I told them."

"Them?"

"Jack was with the Chasqui leader, Amash. He said they're waiting for us."

"That is not good," Jacinta said.

"It might be good," Ostin said.

"How could that possibly be good?" Taylor asked.

"Because it means they think our focus is on saving Tara."

"It is," Taylor said.

"No, our first mission is stopping the Chasqui from killing a hundred thousand people by burning down Arequipa." He looked at Johnson. "Sun Tzu said that the whole secret of war lies in confusing the enemy so that he cannot fathom our real intent. While they're guarding Tara, we destroy their bats. When they respond to our attack on their bats, we free Tara."

"So you're a tactician now too?" Johnson asked.

"War is just math," Ostin said. "I'm a mathematician."

"War *is* math," Johnson said. "It's also art."

"War isn't art," Taylor said. "It's horror."

"I never said it was beautiful," Johnson said.

Taylor breathed out heavily. "So what do we do about Jack?"

PART TWO

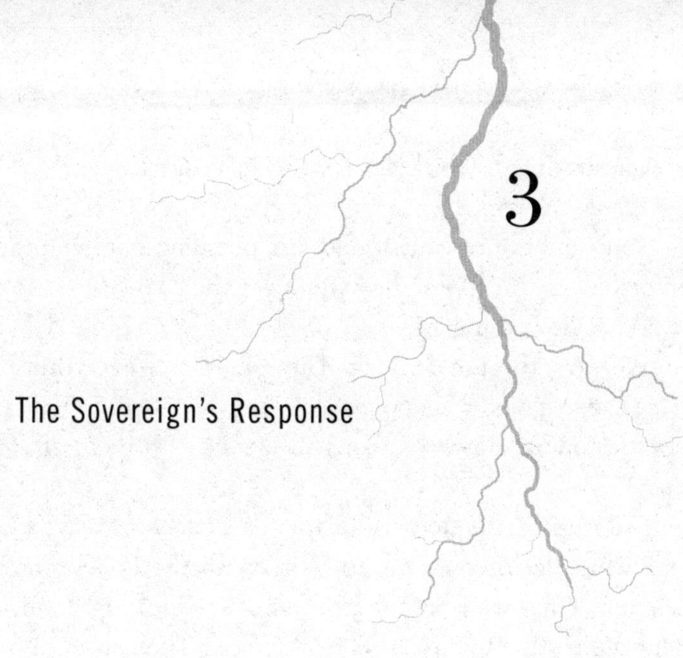

3

The Sovereign's Response

Jack handed the phone back to Sovereign Amash, who had been staring at him intently during the call.

"I take it Mr. Vey wasn't eager to make the trade."

"No, sir," Jack said. "Michael's not going to do anything to endanger Taylor. He's in love. He'd protect her with his life."

"Young love," Amash said, a dark grin crossing his face. "So full of hope." He turned to Jack. "When you attacked the Starxource plant, how did you come in?"

"On the river."

"How did you get into the plant?"

"Back then the Elgen raised bulls to feed to the rats in the Starxource plant. We got one of the bulls to charge the fence and damage it, knowing it would set off an alarm and the guards would come out to investigate. When they did, we jumped them, put on their uniforms, and took their truck back to the plant."

Amash smiled. "You electrics are clever, aren't you?"

"We do our best."

"You can be sure your friends are planning to rescue their friend. Unfortunately for them, they won't get the chance."

"What do you mean?"

"We own the jungle, Jack. The jungle and everything in it. We know everything that happens."

Jack nodded slowly. "What will we do with them after we catch them?"

"I suppose that's up to your friends. First thing, we lock them up for a while, let them come to terms with the hopelessness of their situation. Then we start the process of reeducating them. We teach them the truth. Our truth. They'll join us. They always do. You'd be surprised how easy it is to indoctrinate *Homo sapiens*. Especially the ones who think they're smart."

"What if they don't believe us?"

"There's always that possibility. If it doesn't take, we do what victors have always done with the losers. We enslave them. We make them work to build the very thing they were fighting against."

". . . And if they won't work?"

"Then we eliminate them."

"Eliminate?"

Amash looked at him. "Yes. Eliminate."

Jack thought for a moment, then said, "I think I can talk sense into Tara."

Amash looked at Jack and smiled. "It's not Tara I want. It's Taylor."

"Tara is the key to getting Taylor."

"You may be right," Amash said. "But perhaps it would be best to have them both." He turned to the soldier next to the pilot. "Are the troops ready?"

"Yes, Sovereign."

"Good." He looked back at Jack. "Let's go get the other one."

PART THREE

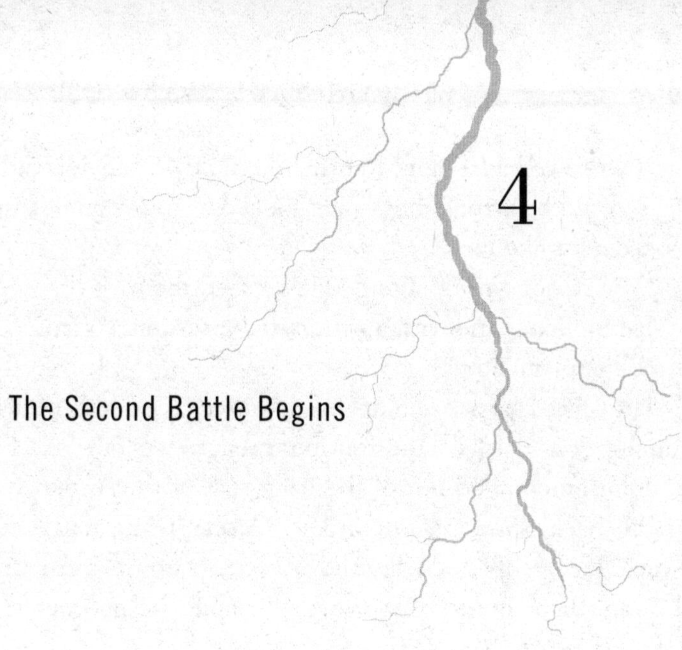

4

The Second Battle Begins

The ambient thrum of the jungle was suddenly interrupted by the chopping blades of the approaching helicopters.

I looked over at Johnson. "Do you hear that?"

He nodded.

"Is it him?" Jacinta asked. "Is it Jack?"

We looked up to see three helicopters as they came into view above us. They were moving slowly, as if looking for a place to land. Or watching us.

"Ian," I shouted to the other van. "Can you see who's in those?"

"I'll try," he said.

"Tell me they're tourists," Taylor said softly.

"We're never that lucky," I said.

"Chasqui," Ian said, walking to us. "Uniforms look like the Chasqui dudes we just took down."

"I wish we had Tanner to bring them down," Taylor said.

"I could be wrong, but"—Ian looked at me—"one of the soldiers looked a lot like Jack. . . ."

"You're not wrong," I said. "He's joined them."

Ian looked at me with a confused expression. "What?"

"I'll explain later."

Ian turned back around, then shouted, "Ground soldiers, they're coming. Four trucks about four hundred meters out."

Johnson climbed out of the front seat of the second van and ran to the back, shouting out orders. "Alpha Team, battle formations. Now!" He grabbed a rifle and a box of ammo from the back of the van, then shouted, "We've got to hold the perimeter. Bentrude, secure the gate."

Cibor and Bentrude sprang from their seats with their rifles. Bentrude ran alone to secure the gate.

"Everyone out of the vans!" I shouted. "Hurry."

As Nichelle, Tessa, Quentin, and Zeus scrambled out of their vehicles, Ian shouted, "Incoming!"

Just as Bentrude reached the gate, a grenade struck a concrete pilaster about ten meters from him, blowing a hole in the concrete and knocking down the fence. Through the smoke we could see Bentrude lying on the ground, the fence on top of him. The air was filled with the sound of gunfire.

"Bentrude's down," Johnson shouted.

"I got him," Cibor shouted, running to him even with bullets flying all around him. He knelt down next to him and put his ear against his chest.

"How bad is it?" I asked Ian.

"He's got heavy shrapnel," Ian said. "He's bleeding internally, but his heart's still beating."

Johnson turned to Jacinta. "He's bleeding. Can you help him?"

Jacinta had been a volunteer nurse at a jungle clinic before becoming a veterinarian.

"I'll try. My medical bag is in the house." She ran to the house.

Johnson shouted, "Cibor, get him inside."

With bullets still whistling around him, Cibor began dragging Bentrude away from the gate.

"The trucks are still coming," Ian shouted. "They have grenade launchers."

"Quentin, Zeus," I shouted. "You've got to stop those trucks!"

"More grenades coming," Ian shouted.

Zeus shot so much electricity from his hands, it looked like lightning. The grenades blew up outside the fence.

"That was powerful," I said.

"I helped," Tessa said.

"Hit the trucks," I shouted to Zeus.

"There's too much smoke. I can't see them."

"About two hundred meters out," Ian shouted. "Far right side of the road."

Zeus shot again, the sound of his electricity crackling like ice on a hot grill.

"Hit," Ian shouted. "You stopped the lead truck. It's smoking. They're piling out of the other trucks. They're armed."

"How many men?" Johnson shouted.

"Thirty or more."

One of the helicopters moved directly above us, the sound pounding down on us with a dull throb.

"They're directing the attack from above. Can you bring down that helicopter?" Johnson asked Quentin.

"It's too far. That's Tanner's work."

"Who's Tanner?"

"Tell you later," he said, turning to Zeus. "Can you get it?"

"I'll try."

"No," I said. "Jack's in there."

"We'll take our chances," Johnson said.

"We're not killing one of our friends."

"If he's with them, he's not your friend," Johnson snapped back.

"We're not doing it," I said to Zeus. I knew I was openly challenging Johnson's authority, but I didn't care.

Johnson hesitated a moment, then said angrily, "Friend or not, we've got to get it out of here." He raised his rifle and started firing off rounds at the helicopter. It immediately veered off to the side, disappearing behind the forest's canopy.

Another grenade hit the first van, the one the Electroclan had been in, blowing it up. A black plume of smoke rose from its wreckage.

Nichelle and Tessa ran from it and hid behind the perimeter wall.

"Hiding behind that wall won't help with the grenades," Johnson shouted. "They blow shrapnel backward."

"We need Cassy," I said.

"She's still in the second van helping unload the ammunition," Taylor said.

As if in response to Taylor's words, a grenade hit the front of the second van. The van's engine compartment burst into flames.

"Cassy!" Taylor shouted.

Johnson grabbed a fire extinguisher from the front of his van. Then a second grenade hit the other van, knocking it over onto its side and blocking the sliding door exit with Cassy inside.

"Cassy!" Jax shouted. He ran to the van's back doors and tried to open them but couldn't. "They're locked! Where are the keys?"

"They're in the ignition!" Cibor shouted back.

The front of the van was now fully engulfed in flames, which were spreading back. Jax ran to the middle of the van and, using the butt of his rifle, broke out the window. He was about to climb up when McKenna ran up next to him. "Help me up!" she shouted.

"It's going to blow."

"Just do it!"

He lifted McKenna up onto the burning vehicle, and she let herself down through the side window. Just seconds after she was inside, the flames reached the gas tank, and there was a massive explosion. Flames blew out all the windows.

"No!" Taylor screamed.

"McKenna!" Ostin shouted, running to the burning vehicle.

Johnson shoved the fire extinguisher into the van's window. The extinguisher's clouds of phosphate blew out of the van's openings.

In spite of the bullets flying around us, we were all fixated on the smoking wreck, wondering if we'd just lost two of our friends. Then Cassy's head—slumped forward and white with the extinguisher's powder—rose up through the window.

"Someone help me!" McKenna shouted from inside the van. She was pushing Cassy up through the window. Jax shouted, "Michael, cover us."

I ran to the other side of the van and pulsed, making the bullets bounce off me while Jax climbed on top of the smoking vehicle. He pulled Cassy out the broken window and handed her down to Johnson. Johnson laid Cassy on the ground as Jax pulled McKenna from the wreckage, then jumped down himself, bullets ricocheting off me and the metal around them.

I ran back around the van to find McKenna and the others gathered around Cassy's body. Smoke rose from her clothing, and her face and hair were singed and smudged with ash.

Jax grabbed her wrist to check her pulse. "She's alive."

"The blast knocked us pretty hard," McKenna said. "It knocked her out."

Jax looked up at her. "Why weren't you burned up in the fire?"

"I am the fire," McKenna said.

Cassy began to groan. Her eyelids fluttered and opened. "McKenna?"

"I'm here," McKenna said.

"I'm here too," Jax said.

"Let's get her inside," I said. "If we can."

The whistling of bullets around us had only increased. It felt like we were in a hailstorm. Except it wasn't ice flying around us; it was lead.

The Chasqui had taken position at the perimeter of the yard. They kept trying to come over the fence but were either picked off by Cibor, Jaime, and Johnson or knocked back by Zeus.

After another vault of grenades, heavy machine gun fire peppered the yard, splintering and ripping apart just about everything in its way. A wood power pole suddenly fell, tearing its wires from the house. One of the live wires danced on the ground, spraying the yard with orange-gold sparks. The lights of the compound went dark.

The firing abruptly stopped. A heavily accented voice boomed from a PA system like the voice of God.

"Electroclan, you have lost. Give us the girl Taylor, and we will let you live. If you refuse, we will kill all of you and take Taylor. Your survival is your decision. You have one minute to decide."

"Not happening," I shouted back.

Taylor looked over at me, her face strained with fear.

Johnson said to Jax, "Get Cassy into the house with Jacinta; then get back out here. They're tearing us apart."

"Yes, sir," Jax said.

"I'll cover you," I said. "Let's go."

Jax took Cassy in his arms and ran toward the house with Taylor, McKenna, and me following after, as the battle raged on behind us. I wondered just how much longer we could hold them off.

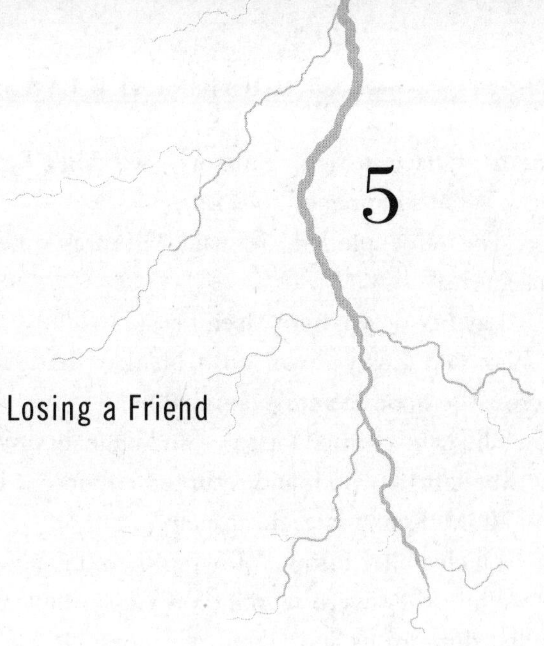

5

Losing a Friend

"What's their obsession with me?" Taylor asked as we reached the house.

"They want a prophetess."

"I'm not a prophetess. I have nightmares."

"Nightmares that come true," I said.

The house's power was out, leaving the room dim and lit only by the ambient light coming in through the mosquito-netted windows. It was still light enough to see the pain on Jacinta's face as she looked up at us. She was sitting alone on a chair outside the home's only bedroom. Her hands and blouse were covered with blood, and her face was streaked with tears.

"We lost him," she said.

Jax blinked. "Bentrude?"

She nodded, wiping her tears with her forearm. McKenna walked over and put her arms around Jacinta. They both cried. After a moment, Jacinta said, "I'm sorry, we don't have time for this right now. What's happened to Cassy?"

"The van exploded," Jax said. "She was knocked unconscious. She has burns."

"Lay her down, here," Jacinta said.

Jax laid Cassy down on a blanket that Jacinta had spread out across the floor. Jacinta examined her.

"She needs some aloe salve and bandages. Watch her, please."

She left the room and returned a moment later with a small first aid kit. McKenna said, "I can help."

"I'll clean her burns. You wrap them in gauze."

While they were working on Cassy, Taylor said to me, "They've killed three of us and taken two more. Now Cassy's hurt. They just wanted me. I could have stopped all this."

"What do you want me to do?" I asked. "Surrender you to them?"

"Do the math, Michael," Taylor said. "I'm not worth five people. Or more. They're not going to stop until they have me."

"They're not going to get you," I said. "This is no time to be a martyr."

"This is exactly the time to be a martyr."

"What are you saying?"

Taylor didn't answer. We just looked into each other's eyes. I was afraid of what she was thinking. "We'll talk later," I said. "Don't do anything stupid."

"I won't. I promise."

Jaime ran into the room. "Michael, Jax. We need you *now*."

"What about the prisoners in the cage?" I asked. "If the Chasqui free them, they'll double their forces."

"I'll cover them," Jaime said.

"I'll help," Taylor said.

"I will too," I said.

"No," Jaime said. "Johnson said he needs you and Jax up front. We're barely holding them out."

"He's right," Jax said. "You're of more use up front. We've got this."

"We'll help," Ostin said.

I said to Jaime, "Keep her safe."

"I will. I promise."

I looked at Taylor. "I'll be back."

She looked at me with a peculiar expression, clasping my cheeks with her hands and looking directly into my eyes. "I love you. Remember that. More than anything." She kissed me, then said, "Hurry. Before it's too late."

My heart ached as I left her and ran back to the battle.

6

We're All Dead Men

By the time I got back out to the front gate, the assault had intensified. Zeus was firing from both hands, knocking back men who were charging the yard, while Jax and Johnson were firing nonstop toward the gate, trying to keep the advancing soldiers from entering.

Ian waved me over to the wall that he, Cristiano, and Johnson were pinned behind. Cibor, Quentin, Tessa, and Nichelle were across from us, firing from behind the smoldering wreckage of the second van. I ran over to Johnson and Ian, bullets bouncing off the bubble I'd created.

"Wish we all could do that," Ian said. "We could use the lightning god about now."

"I could too," I said.

Cristiano looked pale. "If they catch me, I'm a dead man."

"We all are," Johnson said. He turned to me. "There's too many of them. We need Cassy back in action."

Suddenly Ian grabbed his eyes. "I can't see. . . ."

Across from us Quentin shouted, "RESATs!"

I felt the familiar twinge of pain, as piercing to the nerves as a dental drill. Except for Nichelle and me, the rest of the electrics fell to the ground. The RESAT had never worked on Nichelle, since she basically was a RESAT herself, and after being struck by lightning in Hades, I had grown past its power, though it still weakened me.

"We're screwed," Zeus said, grimacing with pain.

I looked around the yard at the advancing soldiers. "Not yet."

PART FOUR

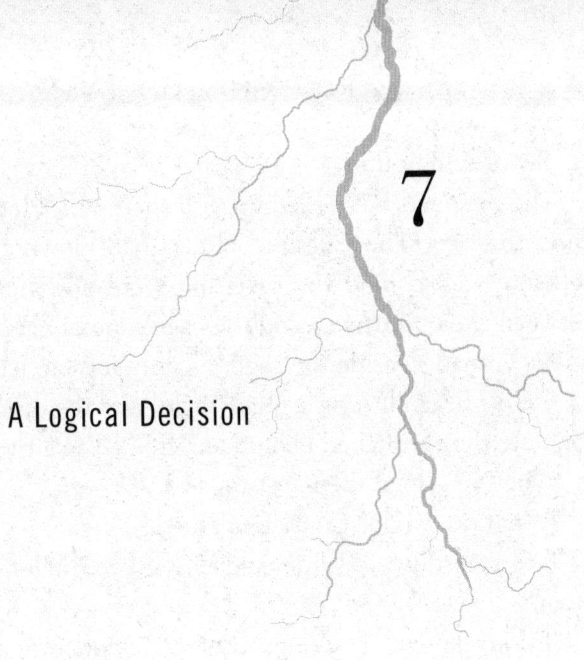

7

A Logical Decision

"Do you still have the keys to the cage?" Taylor asked Jaime.

"Yes."

"Give them to me."

He looked at her quizzically. "Why?"

"In case I need to get closer to reboot them."

Jaime wasn't sure about her reasoning but gave them to her anyway. Then he, McKenna, Ostin, and Taylor crawled along the low concrete wall that ran opposite the path that fronted the puma and jaguar cages, where the Chasqui prisoners were being held.

"Do you feel that?" McKenna asked.

"RESATs," Taylor said.

They were far enough away to not be crippled by it but close enough to feel its sting.

"If they bring them closer, we're through," McKenna said.

Taylor said nothing.

The prisoners were riled up, and there was a lot of shouting going on in the cage. The Chasqui soldiers had blown a small hole in the concrete wall behind the cage and were now occupying the space between the outer fence and the cage's metal bars. They had thrown smoke grenades inside the cage to conceal their actions.

Bullets began hitting around Taylor and the others, pinging off the concrete they crouched behind and filling the air with dust and rock.

"They've armed them," Ostin said.

"What do we do?" McKenna asked.

"We stay down," Jaime said. He asked Taylor, "Can you reboot them?"

"I don't know. They're pretty far." Taylor turned back toward the wall. "I need to see them to reboot them."

"If you stand up, they'll shoot you," McKenna said.

"Everyone, stay down," Jaime shouted. "Just stay down." He lifted his gun above the wall and began firing toward the back of the cage.

There was another loud explosion. When the smoke cleared, there was a two-meter hole in the cage, the bars blown forward and curled.

The prisoners scrambled to escape. Jaime lifted his rifle again to shoot, but the concrete wall his group was hiding behind was immediately riddled with intense machine gun fire, showering them with pieces and dust of concrete. Jaime ducked back down, his arm covering his eyes. Blood ran down his temple to his jaw.

"Were you shot?" McKenna asked.

"I was just hit by concrete," he said. "I can't see."

"They've just doubled their forces," Ostin said.

"We can't let them get around us," Jaime said, his hands over his eyes, "or they'll flank us."

"How do we stop them?" McKenna asked. "There's way too many of them."

"There's more of them up front," Ostin said.

Taylor could see the fear on McKenna's and Ostin's faces, while Jaime was trying to clear the concrete dust and blood from his face.

There was no way they could repel an attack of that magnitude.

A few feet behind her was a branch. She grabbed it, pulled off the bandanna she had around her neck, and waved it above the wall. To her relief, no one shot at it.

Ostin looked over at her. "What are you doing?"

"I'm giving them what they want." Taylor took a deep breath, then shouted, *"Don't shoot! Alto. Alto."* She slowly stood up, her hands lifted above her head.

"Get down," Jaime said. "They'll shoot you."

"I'm Taylor," she shouted. "I'm Taylor. I'm the one you came for. If you shoot me, your boss will punish you."

"Get down," Jaime shouted again. "They don't speak English."

Taylor looked down. "Then you'd better talk to them, Jaime. Tell them I'm the prophetess, before one of them shoots me. . . ."

Jaime looked at her with fear.

"Now!" she shouted. "Or we'll all die!"

Jaime shouted out in Spanish, "Stop shooting! This is the prophetess, the one the sovereign is looking for! Stop shooting."

The firing stopped.

"I'm coming to you," Taylor shouted, climbing over the low wall.

"No," Jaime said.

"Stop!" McKenna said.

"It's too late for that," she said. Taylor took the cage keys out of her pocket as she walked toward the cage, unlocked the lock, and then stepped inside. She tossed the keys to the ground; then, with her hands up, she walked to the back of the cage, with at least a dozen rifles pointing at her.

"Come and get me."

PART FIVE

8

Someone's Missing

Around the front of the zoo, the battle intensified as the rest of the Electroclan writhed on the ground, doubled over and groaning with pain. The RESAT broadcaster the Chasqui had brought was more powerful than anything I'd experienced, and even my power was weakened. Johnson and his Alpha Team looked confused. They had never seen the effect of the RESAT before. To them it was like a high-pitched whistle that a dog can hear but no one else.

Alpha Team did their best to keep the Chasqui soldiers from advancing through the gate, but it was like trying to plug a dozen holes in a boat with ten fingers. We were sinking.

Surrender wasn't an option. Our only hope was to try to escape into the jungle. That's when I heard the crisp crackling of arcing electricity. I looked over at the fallen power pole. The electric lines that came from it were flailing around like fish out of water. Pulsing with all I could to repel the bullets, I made a run for it. I jumped and grabbed the loose wire. It gave me an instant jolt.

I immediately felt energy burst within me. Electricity arced between my fingers, and my skin began to turn whitish blue. It wasn't the same as being struck by lightning, nothing close to it, but it had more than offset the effect of the RESAT.

I looked around the yard at the dozens of Chasqui soldiers that had their guns pointed at me. I reached my hand out and pulsed, knocking them all back. Then, when I felt I'd absorbed enough, I started running toward the front gate and the soldiers around it. Some of them started shooting at me; then, seeing that their bullets did nothing, they turned and ran.

I grabbed the zoo's metal fence and pulsed powerfully. About a half dozen men shouted out in agony as they dropped to the ground. Then I walked out onto the road, pulsing and throwing electric balls while they emptied their weapons at me. Their bullets made a crisp ping as they hit the electric bubble I had created around myself.

Ten yards from the gate there were two men standing behind a washing-machine-sized apparatus. I had never seen the machine before, but I could guess what it was: an oversized version of the RESAT. I threw an electric ball at it, four of them, but that did nothing other than scare off the men, who looked surprised that their machine wasn't working against me.

Even with the electricity I held, I could feel the machine's power grow as I got closer. I grabbed a handle on the machine and pulsed, and the lights on it went out. A small puff of smoke rose from the machine. I kicked it over. Almost immediately lightning bolts filled the air as Zeus began firing again at the few Chasqui who hadn't fallen back.

About a quarter mile down the dirt road a helicopter dropped below the forest canopy. There was excited chatter on the radio devices left on the bodies of the dead around me. I couldn't understand what they were saying, but from what I was seeing, it looked like a call to retreat. The firing had stopped, and the Chasqui soldiers were running to the two trucks that still remained.

Ian, Johnson, Cibor, and Jax continued firing at the fleeing soldiers as my friends made their way to my side. In the distance a helicopter rose.

When we came back together, Jax said, "We did it. We scared them off."

I shook my head. "Something's not right. Why did they give up so quickly?"

"Michael's right," Ian said. "They're not running from us. They're leaving because they got what they came for."

I looked at him. "What do you mean?" Then I saw Jaime, Ostin, and McKenna walking toward us, and it struck me.

Taylor wasn't with them.

PART SIX

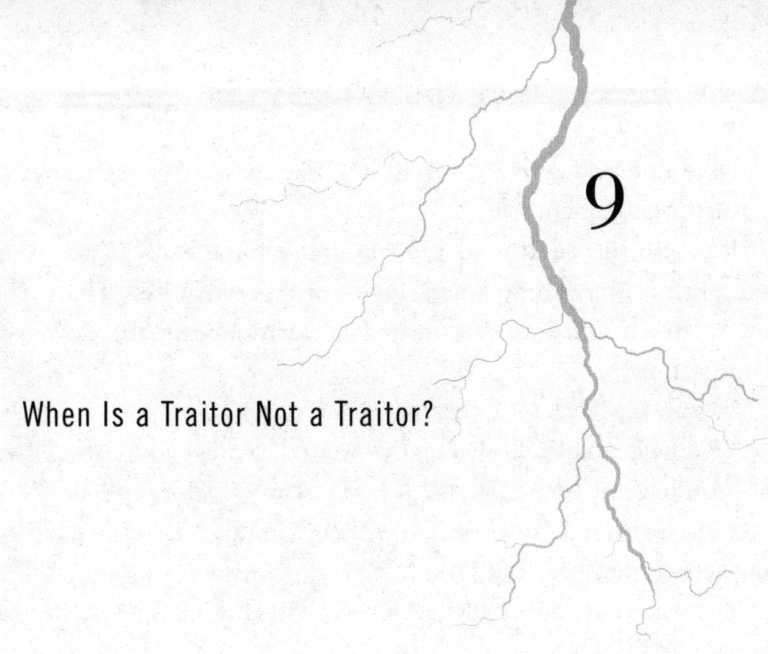

9

When Is a Traitor Not a Traitor?

Debris from the helicopter's wash nearly blinded the guards as they rushed Taylor onto Amash's waiting helicopter. There was a guard holding each of her arms, and they had handled her roughly since they'd seized her inside the cage.

"Stop pushing me," she said, though she doubted they understood her, or cared, for that matter.

The guard sitting inside the helicopter's door pushed her into a seat, strapped her down, then made a hand signal to the pilot, who turned to Amash.

"Listo?"

"Take us up," Amash said without even looking at his prisoner.

The helicopter's rotor sped up, and the craft lurched slightly forward before ascending back into the sky. Only after they had cleared the trees did Amash turn back.

"The one and only Taylor Ridley. Welcome. You recognize our mutual friend, of course."

Jack also turned around. He was dressed in a black Chasqui uniform, just as she had dreamed. Taylor just glared at him. He reached out to touch her, but she pushed back into her seat. "Keep your hands off me."

"Whatever," Jack said, turning back around.

"You have no idea how long I've waited to meet you," Amash said.

"You have no idea how much I don't care," Taylor replied.

Amash grinned. "Insolent. I like that." He nodded to the guard sitting across from her. "Put it on her."

The soldier held out a RESAT vest. "Put this on," he said in heavily accented English.

"I'd rather not."

"It's not a request," Amash said. "You're a powerful Glow. It's better to be safe than dead."

"Why would I hurt you? I surrendered to you."

"And the reason you surrendered is still a mystery. Maybe even to yourself. Perhaps you have a death wish and plan to crash our helicopter."

"I don't have that ability. Or a death wish."

"I know exactly what you can do, Taylor. And crashing this helicopter is something you could do if you put your mind to it. Definitely something you could do." He looked at her. "We're in a little bit of a hurry. I'll tell you what, put the vest on, and I won't turn it on unless you give me a reason to."

"It's just for our protection," Jack said.

She reached out her arms. "Whatever," she said, mimicking what he'd said earlier.

The guard slid the vest around her, then strapped it on, the locks clicking loudly as they fastened into place. An amber LED on the chest started flashing.

"You said you wouldn't turn it on," Taylor said.

"You'd know if it was on," Amash said. "It's just warming up in case we need it."

The helicopter was still hovering over the zoo, and Amash looked down at the battle below. Taylor looked out too. She could see Michael fighting his way past the gate.

"Looks like they might prevail after all," Amash said. "Maybe you surrendered too soon."

"Would that have gotten my sister back?"

"I think not."

"Then I didn't."

"You made the right decision," Jack said. "You'll see."

Taylor said to Amash, "Would you tell this traitor to mind his own business?"

"You are his business," Amash said. "You're all of our business. And, like they say, one man's traitor is another man's hero. Jesus and George Washington were considered traitors in their time, but that's not how history remembers them."

"You're comparing Jack to Jesus and George Washington?"

Amash grinned. "I'm demonstrating to you that if the cause is right, so is the action. No matter where you come from."

"You sound like Hatch."

"Now you're being ridiculous."

The helicopter sped east over the outskirts of Puerto Maldonado toward the river.

"Where are you taking me?"

"To your sister. That's what you wanted, isn't it?"

"And you'll let her go."

"I never said I'd let her go."

"That's not the deal. Jack said you'd trade."

Amash cautiously fingered the button on the RESAT's remote. "There was no deal between you and me. We never agreed to anything. Especially since you decided to come in on your own."

Taylor began shaking. "You liar!"

"I didn't lie. You know, we never intended to kidnap your sister. Our associates didn't know there were two of you. You might say that Tara was just in the wrong place at the wrong time. But I've always said, if life gives you a lemon . . . crush it.

"Had we gotten this right, many lives would have been spared." He looked into Taylor's angry eyes. "Don't worry. Your sister is being treated well. Just as Jack is. Just as you will be. You'll see, this is all just a big misunderstanding. So relax and enjoy the ride. You have nothing to worry about."

Said the spider to the fly, Taylor thought. She turned and looked out the window at the expanse of jungle below, a seemingly endless carpet of green occasionally parted by the snaking Amazon River. She knew Michael would come after her. That was the one flaw in her plan. He would definitely come. And Amash, Jack, and the Chasqui would be waiting.

She had thought that she was selflessly sacrificing herself for the good of all, making the noble choice. But what if Michael did the same thing? Not if. There was no question he would come after her. What if something happened to him? Her eyes suddenly welled up. She wondered if she'd just made the biggest mistake of her life.

PART SEVEN

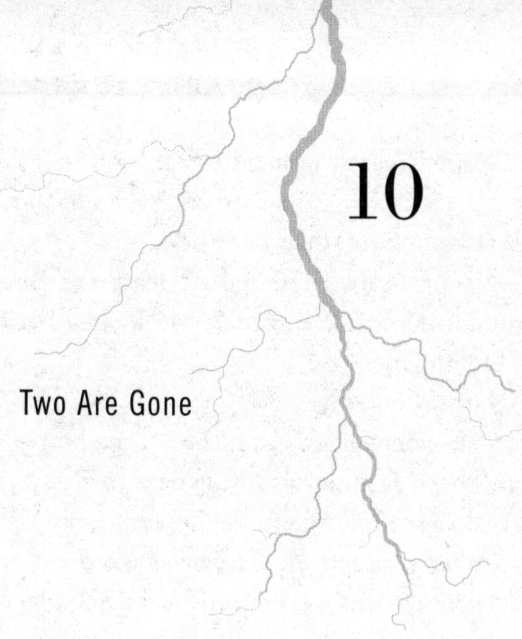

10

Two Are Gone

"Where's Taylor?" I shouted, afraid that I already knew the answer.

"They have her," Jaime said.

"How did that happen?" I said angrily. "You promised you'd protect her!"

"Michael, I would have given my life to protect her. She didn't give me the chance. She surrendered to them. She thought it was the only way to save her sister . . . and the rest of us."

"This just keeps getting worse." I turned to Cristiano. "I'm going after her. You're coming with me. I'll need your help to find her."

"Yes, sir."

"I'll go with you," Ian said. "You'll need me."

"And us," Zeus said. "You've got the Electroclan."

"What about Arequipa?" Nichelle said. "We can't just let all those people die."

"Alpha Team can handle that," Johnson said. "We'll scout out the best place to blow the road and take out those trucks. No one is better at demolition than Bentrude."

No one said anything. At least not out loud. Johnson looked around. "How is Bentrude?" He looked back at me. "What are you not telling me?"

I just shook my head.

"No," Johnson said as he ran to the house. I went after him. When I got there, Jacinta was sitting next to Cassy. Both women looked surprised to see Johnson in the house.

"Where's Bentrude?" Johnson asked.

Jacinta's eyes welled with tears. She glanced over at me but said nothing.

"Where's Bentrude?" Johnson asked more forcefully.

Jacinta wiped her eyes, then pointed toward the darkened bedroom. I followed behind Johnson as he went inside. He let out a loud groan. "No, buddy. No, no."

My heart ached at what I saw—Bentrude's lifeless body on the bed. The sheet beneath him was soaked with blood.

Johnson sat down on the bed next to his friend. He lowered his head into his hands and wept. I stood there watching him, not sure if I should leave him alone in his grief. His body was shaking, and his cheeks were wet with tears streaming down them. After several minutes I walked over next to him and put my hand on his shoulder. "I'm so sorry."

He wiped his eyes with his sleeve. "I'm a failure."

"Not true," I said.

He looked up angrily. "Let's call this what it is, Michael. I let them down. I led them down here to save Jack, and I failed, losing three of my men on the way. And now Taylor's gone too. My command has been a disaster since I got here." He looked at me. "I failed them. I failed all of you. I'm not fit for command."

I looked at him, then Bentrude, then sat down on the bed next to Johnson.

"We're still here, aren't we? We're still alive. They should have run us over. Instead, we repelled two attacks."

"*You* held them off."

"We couldn't have done it alone. And you had nothing to do with Taylor leaving."

He turned toward me. "I had everything to do with her leaving. If I hadn't lost those men, she wouldn't have felt the need to surrender. She thought she was saving us."

"They took her sister," I said. "With or without us, she would have gone. I know her. And I know how she feels. I felt the same way when the Elgen took my mother."

"You know they'll never trade Tara for Taylor," Johnson said. "They'll keep both of them. For control."

"Just like the Elgen," I said.

After a moment he looked back up at me. "What are you going to do?"

"I'm going to save them. And you're going to save thousands of lives in Arequipa. So let's get going."

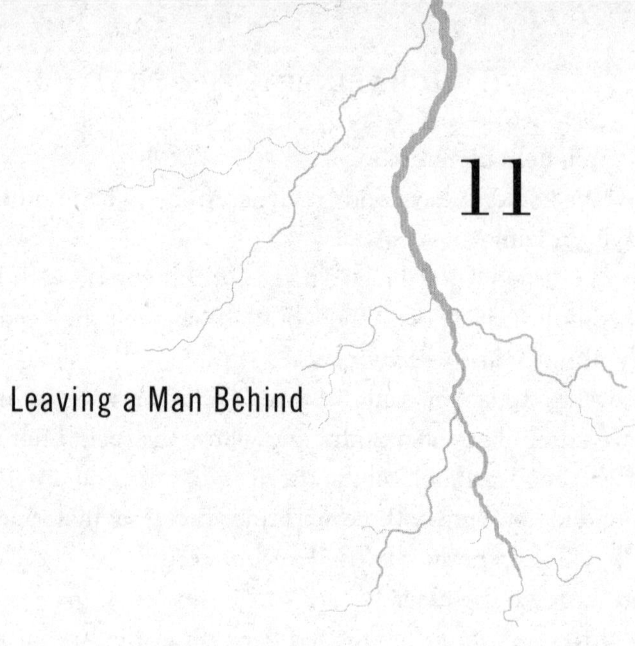

11

Leaving a Man Behind

Ian kept watch while we all gathered again in the house. Cassy was conscious but still seemed a little out of it. She was leaning against Jax, who had his arm wrapped around her protectively.

"Are you okay?" I asked.

"Physically," she said softly. "You?"

I just shook my head. "No."

Cassy took my hand. "I'm sorry. We'll get her back."

After a moment Nichelle said, "What are we going to do with . . . ?" She tilted her head toward the bedroom.

"We could leave him there and burn the house down," Jacinta said. "Like the Amazon warrior."

Johnson thought a moment, then said, "No, we'll give him a proper Ranger's burial."

"Do we have time?" Jacinta asked.

"We'll make time. Do you know a good place?"

Jacinta nodded. "There is a beautiful place behind the bird cages. It is cradled in the roots of a kapok tree, where the sun first hits the zoo. I often go there to meditate."

"Show me."

We followed Jacinta outside to the spot. The little cove was as beautiful as Jacinta said, lush and green with the massive, tall roots of a kapok tree framing the area. There was a cushion between one of the roots where Jacinta sat to meditate, and the roots that surrounded her were covered with wax and a few unspent candles.

"This is where I come to be close to God," she said. "It is where I feel him most close."

Johnson dug his heel into the spongy soil, then said, "This will do. Thank you." He took a deep breath. "We'll need some shovels."

"We'll get them," Cibor said. He turned to Ostin and me. "Help me, guys."

We followed Cibor to the warehouse, where we found three shovels and a pick. When we returned, Johnson took the pick from me and began fiercely tearing into the ground. Then Cibor, Zeus, and Jax took the shovels and started to dig. It took less than an hour to dig the grave, their work spurred on by their intense emotion.

Bentrude's body had been wrapped in a bedsheet, and Johnson and Jax went back for it. They carried it out of the house and over to the grave site. Cibor got back down into the hole, took Bentrude into his arms, and gently laid him down in the moist dirt. I helped him out of the grave.

My heart felt as heavy as ever as I remembered the losses we'd suffered since this had all begun. Today felt most like Wade again, alone, deep in the jungle. For a moment we just stood there; then Johnson spoke.

"It seems like a hundred years ago when I first met Bentrude. After spending just a week in training with him at Fort Bragg, I remember thinking, 'This is a man I want at my side in a firefight.' He was smart, skilled, and maybe the most courageous man I've ever known. I wasn't wrong about him. Through time, he became a brother to me." Johnson sniffed. "It's been said, 'Courage is a contradiction in terms. It means a strong desire to live taking the form of a readiness to die.'"

Johnson wiped his eyes. "Bentrude knew how to live. He was the first to jump off a cliff to see if the water was deep enough or let you shoot a beer can off his shoulder. You would never know that Bentrude felt fear. But he did. Just like the rest of us. I knew this from the few times he confided in me. But, unlike the rest of us, he never let it hold him back from doing what he needed to do. Not once. He said his fear was his best friend. It made him smarter and sharper. What he left off is that it also made him brave. Because you can't be brave without fear.

"The cowards who did this are going to pay for what they've done to my friend." He exhaled loudly, then looked around at us. "Would anyone else like to say anything?"

"There's just too much to say," Jax said softly. He was holding hands with Cassy, and she squeezed his tighter. "Just way too much."

Cibor nodded slowly. "Bent was always the first in action and the last to leave. I think I felt like he was my guardian angel." He wiped his eyes. "I'm going to miss him."

I picked a bird-of-paradise flower from a nearby bush and threw it into the grave. "God bless you, man."

Johnson looked around the group one more time, then said, "All right. Let's do this."

Johnson, Jax, and Cibor took up their shovels and began filling in the hole. After they were done, Jacinta and Johnson placed a concrete statue of a kneeling woman on top of the grave.

Johnson stared at the statue for a moment, then said, "Let's go before we have to dig any more."

"Where are we going?" Cassy asked.

"Michael has Taylor to save. And we have a city."

PART EIGHT

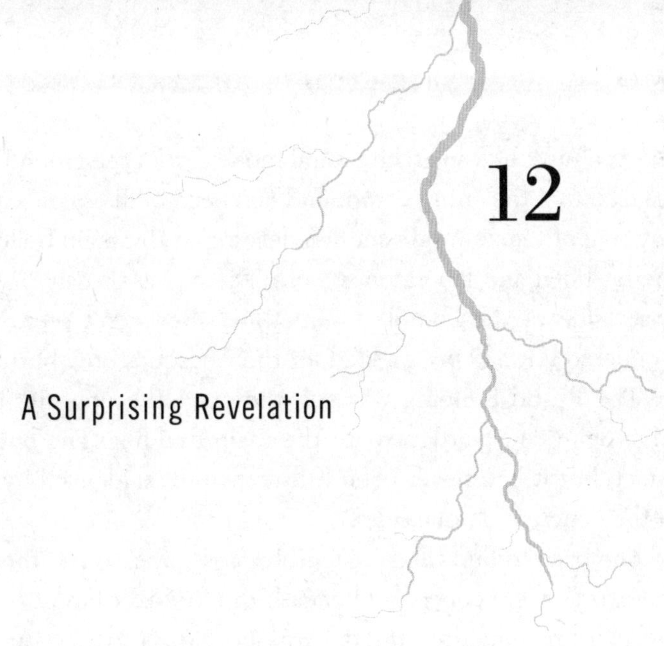

12

A Surprising Revelation

Taylor stared out the helicopter's side window as the dense Amazon forest gave way to the sprawling compound that had once been the Elgen's first Starxource plant. The Elgen had cleared hundreds of acres of forest for grazing, but the jungle now, with the cattle mostly gone, had already started to reclaim the land. There were still some cattle below, but now the beef was used more for feeding soldiers than rats.

Taylor was exhausted but too frightened to sleep or even close her eyes. Several times she caught Jack looking back at her, but she wouldn't meet his gaze. Seeing him in the Chasqui suit was a bad dream come true.

The helicopter hovered for a few minutes over the former Starxource plant while the soldiers and crew below frantically prepared for their sovereign's return.

Taylor thought it was oddly interesting seeing the compound from above, almost like an architectural model. From the ground, she hadn't realized that the entire compound had been built as concentric circles, one ring of fences inside another, leading to the main building, where the rat bowl and laboratories were. There was also an airstrip on the north side of the complex, something she hadn't seen before. She wondered if it had been added for the Chasqui's drug business.

The Re-Ed building was still there, on the opposite side of the large open courtyard, next to the main building. The bowl was still intact, but it had never been fully repaired, evidenced by the cracks in the concrete on one side.

She tried to find the Weekend Express pipes, but if they were still there, they were concealed beneath the forest's canopy.

As if reading her mind, Amash said, "I trust you recall the Weekend Express?"

Taylor looked at him. "You knew about it?"

"Of course I knew about it. I sanctioned it. It was a way to reward the faithful and root out the unfaithful."

"It's where guards deserted the Elgen," Taylor said.

"It's where they *tried* to desert. We always hunted them down. We kept it because it helped us root out the unfaithful.

"It might surprise you that Hatch never knew about the pipes. There was actually a lot Hatch didn't know about. But the tunnels have been sealed off. We welded the outside shut. A few men tried to escape, but we just locked them inside. It was like burying them alive. Horrible way to go. You can see on the metal lid where they tried to claw their way back in. Now the thing smells of death and decaying bodies. It's a deterrent."

"Death usually is an effective deterrent," Taylor said.

"Not as effective as you would think, but still useful."

"Are there still rats?" Taylor asked.

"Yes. Of course. Not nearly as many as before; we don't need them as we did. But we keep enough to generate our own power. It's either that or solar out here. Rats are more dependable than the sun. Rain or shine they produce the juice." He smiled as if he was pleased with himself.

To the east of the compound, on a loading dock on the murky brown river, there was a row of large trucks loading cargo containers onto a barge. There were at least fifty men, many of them wearing white lab coats, surrounding the containers.

Taylor had almost said something snarky about the bats but had wisely stopped herself. Amash still hadn't said anything about the bats, which likely meant he was keeping it secret, which also meant that he didn't know they knew about the bats or the Chasqui's plan to burn Arequipa to the ground. One slip of her tongue might have changed the Chasqui's plans entirely.

"What are you shipping?" Taylor asked innocently.

Amash looked at her with a peculiar gaze, then said, "The usual contraband. Fentanyl and cocaine . . . mostly." He suddenly smiled. "Fentanyl *is* the future. In the drug world it started as an additive. Dealers used to cut it in with heroin since it was more potent and cheaper than heroin, but it wasn't long before the junkies preferred the additive to the drug. It's cheap and easy to produce, and it's fifty to a hundred times more potent than morphine. Of course, that makes it dangerous. Just two milligrams can be fatal. To put that into perspective, a grain of salt is about sixty-five milligrams. So a speck of fentanyl the size of one-thirtieth of a grain of salt is enough to overdose on.

"Almost twice as many Americans died of fentanyl overdose last year than died in the Vietnam War. That must make you very proud to be an American."

"That must make you very proud to be a mass murderer."

Amash snapped back, "We haven't murdered anyone. Handing someone a knife isn't the same as stabbing them with it. If they choose to use it, that's on them." He looked down below. "That one forty-foot container can hold enough fentanyl to kill every man, woman, and child in the world. Of course, that's not our objective; you can't make money off dead people. A dead slave is of no use at all." He suddenly grinned. "I suppose that's not entirely true."

Taylor wasn't sure who was worse, Hatch or Amash.

When the other two helicopters had caught up, the lead copter began to descend slowly until it set down on the helipad near the compound's center.

For Taylor, being on the ground was like stepping back into a nightmare.

As the helicopter rotors slowed, a group of soldiers, each with one hand on their hat, the other on their weapon, ran up to the front of the helicopter and stood at attention.

When Amash stepped out, the soldiers saluted him. He casually saluted back, then walked forward, leaning in to say something to the first soldier. After he passed, the soldier went to the helicopter's side door and, with the aid of another soldier, helped Taylor out, taking her by the arm.

"You come with me," the soldier said.

"Do I have a choice?" she asked sardonically.

"No!" he barked back. "You have no choice!"

Jack stepped out of the copter behind her, and a row of guards fell in behind them. The entourage followed Amash up to two large steel doors that automatically opened at their approach. They walked inside onto a concrete floor that had been painted glossy white.

Everything was white—the floor, walls, doors and frames, even the hinges and doorknobs—giving the place an unusually sterile and austere feeling. A soft, squishing noise was piped over the sound system. It was the only sound other than their footsteps on the concrete floor. She knew that Jack was walking right behind her, so she never turned back.

They passed several white-coated scientists on their way down the brightly lit corridor.

"We have more scientists here now than soldiers," Amash said proudly. "We consider that progress. Of course, one scientist can kill more people than a million soldiers."

"What part of that do you consider progress?" Taylor asked.

Amash just smiled and kept walking.

After a few more minutes, Taylor asked, "Where are you taking me?"

"I've told you. To see your sister." He stopped and turned to look at her. "That's what you wanted, isn't it?"

"Yes."

"All right, then. Be patient and respectful. You're a guest here."

I'm a prisoner here, she thought.

They walked through a second set of doors, past a guard standing at attention. "Déjà vu," Taylor said to herself. She remembered these halls too well. They were the same halls where Hatch had released the rats and Zeus had almost sacrificed his life to protect the rest of the Electroclan, suffering terrible burns in the process.

The thought of that made her nauseous. The trauma she had faced back then, combined with Jack's current betrayal, was too much. She suddenly turned back and shoved Jack against the wall. "How could you betray us?! After all we've been through."

I'm not a traitor. We're going to rescue Tara, then get out of here. It's the only way I could think of.

Taylor looked at him with surprise. Jack's lips hadn't moved. He was thinking this.

The Chasqui guards pulled Taylor from him as the familiar screech of a RESAT dropped Taylor to her knees.

"Don't touch him," a guard said.

"It's okay, you can turn it off," Jack said. "She's just angry and scared." He crouched down next to Taylor, who was still doubled over on the floor. He spoke loudly enough for all to hear. "You've done the right thing by coming here. Once you understand the Chasqui vision for the world, you'll join us. Happily." Jack glanced back at Amash, who was gazing at him intensely.

Taylor climbed back to her feet. "I'll never join you."

Amash smiled confidently. "We'll see, dear girl. . . . We'll see."

The entourage continued on down the corridor.

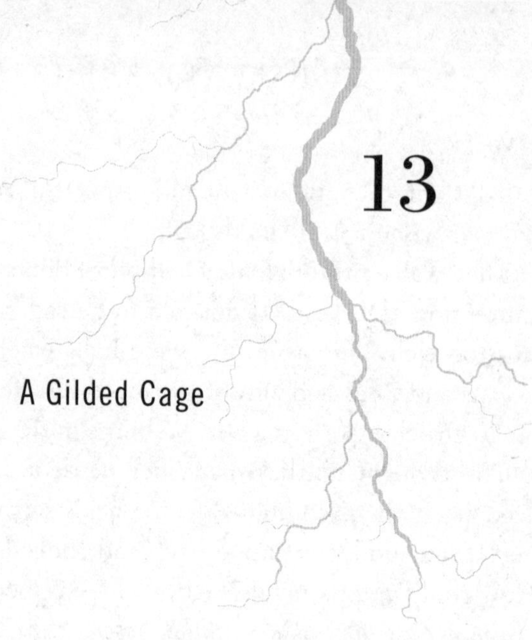

13

A Gilded Cage

About sixty feet from where Taylor had attacked Jack, they stopped in front of another door. One of the guards opened it, exposing a spacious apartment-like room.

Amash said to Taylor, "This will be your room. I trust you will find it comfortable."

"You said I was going to see my sister."

"And you will. She'll be at dinner. I wanted to give both of you a little time to tidy up. This is a celebration; it should be handled appropriately."

"A celebration for who?"

"For *whom*. For you, of course."

"Do I look like I'm celebrating?"

"No, but you should be."

"You just took me prisoner."

"You keep forgetting that you came to us. And you're not a

prisoner. If you were a prisoner, you'd be in a battery-charged cage with the RESAT on full, instead of this comfortable suite with luxurious amenities. But that's beside the point. Babies cry when they're born, but that doesn't make it any less of a time for celebration.

"Figuratively speaking, you are a baby. The true world is as unknown to you as to a newborn in a crib. If you knew the truth about this world we inhabit, we wouldn't have had to chase you down. You would have come to us willingly. As Jack said correctly, you would have joined us . . . happily."

"I wouldn't count on that."

"But I do, Taylor. And mark my words, someday you and I will laugh at this very conversation."

"That's not going to happen."

"Well, as they say, you don't know what you don't know." He looked at Jack. "Isn't that right, Jack?"

"Absolutely, Sovereign."

"From Jack's mouth to God's ear. And by 'God' I mean me." He smiled. "Dinner will be ready in two hours, so for now you have time to get a little rest. There are fresh clothes in the closet and refreshments in the refrigerator. If there is anything we can do to make your stay more comfortable, by all means, let us know. I have a concierge assigned to you."

"Concierge? You mean a guard?"

"Your room is equipped with an intercom system; all you need to do is speak."

"And you've bugged me."

"We are at your service," he said. "Now get some rest. You must be exhausted after this morning's ordeal." He held up his finger to stop her from speaking. "This morning's *battle*."

Taylor furtively glanced over at Jack. They had brief eye contact before everyone walked out of her room, the door locking behind them. She took a deep breath, then looked around the room. She honestly couldn't say it was bad in there. It was a lot better than the other cells she had been kept in. She shook her head at her thoughts. *I've become a connoisseur of Elgen prison cells,* she thought. From the look of things, Amash and the Chasqui had a different mindset than Hatch and the Elgen. This room had been "humanized." It had still-life and landscape paintings on the walls, and even the bed had a luxurious floral duvet and decorative pillows.

On the nightstand next to the bed there was a fragrant and exotic bouquet of flowers in an etched crystal vase. It was pretty—not just the flowers, which were impressive enough, but the vase itself.

"At least he has more class than Hatch," she said, momentarily forgetting that she was being listened to. The RESAT wasn't on, for which she was especially grateful. Her mother once asked her what a RESAT felt like. Taylor's best explanation was, "Do you have metal fillings in your teeth?"

Her mother said, "Yes."

Taylor said, "Then you know what it feels like to chew aluminum foil."

Her mother winced. "That's horrible."

"Exactly," Taylor said. "Now imagine that your whole body was your mouth."

Her mother didn't know what to say to that. Finally she said, "I'm sorry that you know what that feels like."

Alone in the room, Taylor realized how lonely she was. Mostly, how much she missed Michael. She hoped that he wasn't too angry at her, but then, maybe if he was angry enough, he wouldn't risk his life by coming after her.

She also wished that she had talked to her mother before surrendering herself. But what would she have said? "Hey, Mom, I'm going to surrender myself to the people who kidnapped Tara. Have a good day." That wouldn't have gone well. It was just better that she didn't know.

Taylor sat down on the bed. There was a thick book on the nightstand next to it. *Atlas Shrugged.* She opened to the first page.

Who is John Galt?

Great first line, she thought. She set the book back down. She decided to test Amash's offer and see how closely she really was being monitored.

"I wish I had some ice cream," she said softly. Then she lay down on her bed. Less than ten minutes later there was a short buzz; then her door opened. In the doorway stood a beautiful young Peruvian woman wearing an apron. She carried a silver platter with a crystal bowl filled with various ice creams.

"Ms. Ridley, I thought you might enjoy some ice cream," she said in nearly perfect English. "It is actually gelato: raspberry, stracciatella, mango, and lemon. This little pitcher has hot fudge if you like. The lemon is very tart. It's my personal favorite." She walked over to the counter and set down the tray. "I'll leave it right here."

"Thank you," Taylor said.

"My pleasure."

As the girl turned to go, Taylor asked, "How long have you worked here?"

The girl looked at her for a moment, then said, "It's been my pleasure. I hope you do not spoil your appetite; the sovereign has planned a very special dinner for you and your friends."

"Thank you," Taylor said. She reached out her hand. The girl hesitated, then took Taylor's hand. It was as Taylor had expected: the girl was terrified. "Take care," Taylor said.

"My pleasure," she said again, then hurried out of the room. The door shut behind her.

Taylor lifted the bowl and took a bite of the lemon gelato. It was as good as any gelato she'd had in Italy. *I guess he meant it,* she thought. *I wonder what would happen if I asked for a pony.*

There was one frightening question that had secreted itself in the darkest corners of her mind. Was this the first day of the rest of her life in captivity?

She ate about half the gelato, then lay back on the bed. *Will I ever see Michael again?* She hoped he'd understand. He had to, didn't he? Hadn't he done the same thing in trying to save her and his mother?

Her exhaustion from emotion and lack of sleep caught up with her, and she dozed off. She woke to an announcement over her room's intercom.

"Sorry to disturb you, Ms. Ridley, but dinner will be served in one hour in case you would like to freshen up. There are fresh clothing and undergarments in the closet. In fifty minutes, someone will be at your door to escort you to the dining room. Is there anything else I can do for you?"

"No. Thank you."

"My pleasure."

It was strange how differently things were handled than the Elgen way, which was pretty much all pain, coercion, and fear. Of course, Hatch had tried to seduce her with charm, too, when he'd sent her out shopping in Beverly Hills.

She walked over to the closet and looked inside. There were two dresses. One was a simple black cocktail dress. She looked at its label. Christian Dior.

Of course, she thought. *Wonder how much that cost.*

The other dress was just as beautiful—a leopard print on a silk fabric. Dolce & Gabbana. She took it out of the closet and held it up. She knew that it must have cost several thousand dollars. She hadn't worn anything that nice for a long time.

The dress was her size. *How did they know what size I wear?* Of course, they could have gotten her measurements from Tara, but how did they get a dress like this, deep in the jungle? It occurred to her that they had been preparing for her capture for some time. That only made her more anxious. Had she played right into their plans?

She pushed the thought from her mind. *You're going to see Tara*, she told herself. *Time to get ready.* She walked into the bathroom. It was larger than she'd expected and, like the main room, nicer. It had a heated stone-tile floor with a large glass shower. It felt like it had been weeks since she'd showered. She turned on the water, and the glass around the shower immediately steamed up. She glanced up at the camera in the corner of the room. The blinking red light on the camera confirmed that it was live. She wondered how many men were watching her. She shook her head. *Whatever.*

She took off all her clothes and put them into a clothes hamper. (Did they have laundry service?) Then, for a moment, she just looked at herself in the bathroom mirror. Her body was covered with bruises and cuts, some from that morning. They fit with the scars she carried from much older injuries. Somewhere, during the battles with the Elgen, she had stopped counting wounds.

She sighed. *Elgen.* It was a word that had started to vanish into the past. Now here she was, back at the first Starxource plant again.

She reached in to test the water's temperature, then stepped into the shower. The warm water felt luxurious. There were expensive body gels and shampoos, something she'd expect from a Four Seasons resort hotel, not a jungle cell.

She rubbed her body with a shower oil that smelled rich, like almond oil. Then she let the water run through her hair as dirt pooled in the bottom of the shower, then dissipated. Despite the circumstances, she felt like herself again.

The shower felt so nice that she wished she had more time. Still, she was eager to see Tara, so she got out of the shower, drying herself off with a thick, plush towel—another luxury one only thinks of when one has been away from civilization for a while.

She brushed her hair, then went out to the closet. There were all kinds of lotions and expensive perfumes, including one she had heard of but never tried, Roja Haute Luxe, considered one of the finest perfumes money could buy. Tara had shown it to her back at a Neiman Marcus in Phoenix. The small purple-gem-capped bottle had been selling for $3,500, almost as much as two ounces of gold. She unscrewed its cap and smelled it, then dabbed some onto her throat and behind her ears, then a little more onto the insides of her wrists and the backs of her knees. The perfume had a light floral fragrance.

"There's at least fifty dollars' worth," she said softly. "I hope tonight's worth it."

She decided on the leopard print and slid the dress on, admiring the way it looked in the full-length, gold-trimmed mirror that was in the corner of the room.

She looked back through the drawers. There were different kinds of stockings and pantyhose, which she ignored, but the shoes thrilled her. There were three different kinds, one a bright red pair of stiletto heels, the others simply black. She sat down on her bed and put on a simple low-heeled pair of patent-leather pumps.

She was looking at herself in the mirror when there was a buzz at the door.

"Come in," she said.

The door opened. A man wearing a dress uniform stood in the doorway. She was surprised to see the guard all dressed up.

"Are you ready, señorita?"

"Yes." She walked to the door.

"You look lovely this evening."

"Thank you."

As she walked out into the hallway, she saw there were actually two guards—the one in formal attire at her side, the other in the regular Chasqui guard uniform, which was identical to the traditional Elgen uniform except for a purple belt and the Chasqui patch.

They walked about fifty yards through two separate doorways, then took a turn into a part of the compound where she had never been. The entrance to the room was decorated with gilded-framed paintings and tapestries on the wall, thick carpets, and chandeliers. She guessed that the room had been built for entertaining dignitaries.

Two soldiers opened the intricately carved wood doors to a luxurious candlelit dining room.

"Taylor!"

Taylor turned around. Tara was running up behind her, also dressed in a gown. The two sisters embraced.

"Are you okay?" Taylor asked.

"I am now," she said. She leaned back. "How did they capture you?"

"They didn't. I surrendered. For you."

Tears welled up in Tara's eyes. "You shouldn't have done that."

"Of course I should. How have they been treating you?"

Amash had warned Tara that he would turn on the RESAT and torture both her and Taylor if she said, or even implied, anything negative at all.

"It's been . . . fine."

"The rooms are a lot nicer than the ones Hatch kept us in."

Tara just forced a smile. Since her arrival she'd been kept in a RESAT vest in a bat- and guano-filled cave. She wondered why Taylor hadn't seen that when they'd touched.

Amash walked up to them, his eyes darting back and forth between them.

"Ladies, you look lovely this evening. It's good to see the two of you together again."

"It's good to be together," Taylor said.

"Thank you," Tara said, doing her best to conceal her contempt for him.

"You're welcome," Amash said. "I'm sure you're both hungry. We have an amazing celebratory meal planned for this evening—a seventeen-course meal, in fact."

Despite her pain, Tara's mouth watered. She had been fed almost nothing during her confinement.

"Come in, please. Let's dine."

The twins followed him into the dining room. The room was similar to Hatch's dining room in Tuvalu, with stained wood paneling and brass and crystal chandeliers. The table was long and spread with a cream-colored linen cloth, and set with fine blue-and-white Delft porcelain and polished sterling silverware. Such fineness seemed out of place in the jungle. But even in the remote wilderness, Hatch had always found a way to surround himself with the luxuries of life. Always.

Amash walked to the front of the room. In addition to the waiters and guards, Jack and two other men were standing behind the table. One was in a military dress uniform; the other wore a white floor-length robe with a white cap.

Amash tapped a spoon against a wineglass to get everyone's attention. "Welcome, my friends. I'm pleased that you've joined me this evening, especially our newest guest, Miss Taylor Ridley." He turned to the men next to him. "Be assured, gentlemen, you are not seeing double; these beautiful young ladies are twins."

All the men, except for Jack, laughed.

"Now for the seating arrangements." He turned to the women. "I'm sure you have much to catch up on, so I'll let you two sit next to each other in those two seats," he said, pointing. "Jack, you sit right there, across from Taylor."

"Yes, sir." Jack sat down, looking into Taylor's eyes as he did. Tara wouldn't look at him, afraid that she might reveal her true feelings.

"Introductions are in order. To my right is Maxwell Neilsen. He is the chief of guards."

"PizzaMax," Taylor whispered to Tara. Tara giggled.

Amash's brow furrowed. "Excuse me?"

"Nothing," Taylor said. "Sorry."

"To my left is Dr. Raman, our head scientist."

The doctor bowed slightly. "It is my pleasure," he said with a heavy accent.

"Everyone, please sit." After everyone had taken their seats, Amash continued. "Now on to our present business. To begin, our wines today, compliments of the former Dr. C. J. Hatch, are a Mouton Rothschild 1955, acquired, no doubt, at auction. Someone described its flavor as a celestial blend of mint, leather, and lead pencil, which I recognize is, at the least, a very ironic description.

"For a white wine we have a 2009 Domaine de la Romanee-Conti Montrachet Grand Cru—a satiny citrus-and-honey-noted chardonnay. Dr. Hatch acquired an entire case of this delightful wine at twenty-five hundred dollars a bottle, which might sound a bit excessive but was a shrewd investment, as they are now valued at four times that amount. There were many things about the former leader to dislike, but his expertise in selecting spirits was not one of them."

At that, he gave a subtle command, and servers holding bottles of wine made their way around the table.

"I'll have the red," Taylor said, holding out her glass.

Tara said, "Me too."

"Too fruity for me," Jack said. "I'll have the white."

"Maybe you should try something yellow," Tara said, biting back her anger. She furtively glanced over at Amash, afraid that he might have heard her, but he appeared distracted, comparing wines with the scientist.

As Jack took a sip of wine, he slipped off a shoe, reached his foot across the table, and touched Taylor on her calf. Taylor continued to act like she was in conversation with Tara as Jack thought to her.

This is the plan. When I spill my wine, reboot everyone in the room; then have Tara make herself look like Amash and make Amash look like her. Scratch your nose if you understand.

Taylor casually reached up and scratched her nose. Then she added into her conversation, "Tara, be ready."

Good luck, Jack thought, then slipped his shoe back on.

A couple of minutes later a man wearing a chef's smock and hat walked into the room and whispered into Amash's ear. Amash nodded, then said, "*Gracias.*" Then, as the chef walked back to the kitchen, Amash again tapped his spoon against his glass.

"The chef's assistant has just informed me that dinner is ready. But, before we eat, let me offer a little explanation about our meal today.

"Our chef has joined us from the famous restaurant Central in Miraflores, Lima. I'm not boasting when I say it is considered the best restaurant in South America, and one of the top Michelin restaurants in the world. Or maybe I am boasting, but I'm not exaggerating. Either way, you are in for a real treat.

"I'm not exaggerating either when I say this is a seventeen-course meal. Yes, it might sound a bit excessive, but today is a special day after all, the reuniting of sisters in a cause we love more than we can say.

"We'll begin our culinary adventure with scallops and pepino melon, with Charapita pepper. This will be followed by sea bass and clams on quinoa leaf, squash and shrimp, and then duck and squid. I guarantee you have never had the pleasure of such a culinary adventure before.

"I know you have a bit of a sweet tooth, Taylor. So, for you, we have four kinds of dessert, including a cacao mousse, a sort of clay in coca leaves in shaved-ice jelly, and, the most interesting of the *dolce* offerings, huamp gel, which are small, translucent balls of algae.

"So, before we begin, let us raise our glasses to our newest compatriot, Taylor Ridley." He raised his glass. Everyone in the room raised their glasses.

Amash looked into Taylor's eyes. "To Taylor."

"To Taylor," the group echoed, clinking each other's glasses.

"Did they do this for you too?" Taylor asked Tara.

Tara just bit down and forced a pained smile.

As everyone sipped their wine, the servers streamed into the room.

"So it begins. *Buon appetito*," Amash said, setting down his glass.

The meals were served on platters as unique as the entrées themselves—wood and stone bowls and plates woven from palm leaves.

By the seventh course, Amash was in a jovial mood and invited the four guards to imbibe in a glass of wine. As soon as they started drinking, Jack reached for a plate, purposely knocking over his wineglass. Everyone looked over at him.

"What a waste," Jack said. "That's like two hundred dollars of wine."

Taylor took her cue and rebooted everyone in the room except Tara and Jack. While everyone was in a state of confusion, Taylor turned to Tara and said, "Stand up and make yourself look like Amash, and make him look like you."

Taylor rebooted the room again as Tara did as Taylor had said. She stood up, holding out her chest like the sovereign. Taylor saw them change images.

"Now tell the guards to handcuff her and cover her mouth," Taylor said.

"Guards, handcuff her," Tara shouted. "Cover her mouth."

The guards, still disoriented from Taylor's rebooting, looked back and forth at each other, not sure how their sovereign had so quickly changed places. One of the guards asked Tara, "Should we turn on the RESAT, sir?"

"No. Just handcuff her. Then we'll take her back to her cell."

Amash, who now looked like Tara, shouted angrily, "You won't get away with this."

"I got this," Jack said. He grabbed Amash and threw him to the ground, then pressed his knee into Amash's chest. "I got her," Jack shouted to the guards. "Bring me some cuffs. Hurry!"

"Help him," Tara shouted.

The chief guard grabbed Amash as two of the other guards scrambled over to help.

"Give me your gun!" Jack said to the chief.

He was about to hand it over when Amash shouted, *"Coventry!"*

The room froze. Suddenly Taylor and Tara both screamed out, then dropped to the ground as intense broadcasted waves of RESAT filled the room.

Amash regained his form as Tara fell over, unconscious. The startled guards standing above him moved their guns from Amash to Jack.

"Get him off me!" Amash shouted.

The guards pulled Jack off Amash, then pinned him to the ground. Amash rolled to his side, then stood. He looked down at Jack and said, "Beat him and cuff him."

All four of the guards fell onto Jack with their batons until he was unconscious and their batons were dripping with Jack's blood.

Amash walked over to Taylor. "This is how you repay me for my kindness? And you thought you could get away with that." He turned to Tara. "And if you think you suffered before, you're going to learn a whole new meaning of the word."

Tara was still unconscious, but her body was heaving from the intensity of the RESAT. Taylor began vomiting, then fell to her side, her body convulsing wildly. "You're going to kill us," she screamed. "It's too much."

Amash grinned. "You might be right," he said as he watched the two women in their torturous flails. "But it's fun to watch." It was almost a minute later when he said calmly, "Turn the RESAT to five."

Tara's and Taylor's bodies immediately stopped jerking. Taylor passed out.

"Cuff them," Amash said to Maxwell. "Leave the RESAT as is."

"Yes, sir. Where would you like them held?"

"Drag them to the corner for now. I'd like to finish my meal."

"Yes, sir."

When Taylor finally came to, she was drenched in sweat and lying on her stomach, her hands cuffed behind her back. There was a guard standing directly above her, a boot on either side of her head. Painfully, she turned her head toward Tara, who was about ten feet away and in the same predicament.

She forced out two words. "What happened?"

"Silence," Amash shouted. "You failed. Now don't disturb my meal."

Amash and Dr. Raman went back to eating as if nothing had happened. Maxwell was no longer at the table. He was furious that they had tricked and shamed him on his watch, which he was taking out on Jack with his truncheon.

Dr. Raman looked over at Taylor and said, "That is a rather remarkable power she has. Making people look like someone else."

"It's actually the other one," Amash said. "It's Tara."

"How can you tell the difference between the two?"

"All things being equal, they're identical. But a week in the caves has its effects." He wiped his mouth with his napkin. "So, the power to make people appear as someone else was something the Elgen taught her back in the early days of the Elgen Academy. The people don't actually change form, of course. She changes the mind's image of them. Dr. Hatch had the idea of replacing the president of the United States with himself. It was a bold plan. I personally think that the idea still has merit."

"What power does the other sister have?" Dr. Raman asked.

"That confusion you felt just before everything went down, that was her. She has the ability to reboot minds."

"Reboot?"

"It's basically a hardwired scramble of the cerebellum. Like restarting a computer."

He slowly nodded. "Interesting."

"She has that as well as the gift we are most interested in."

"What is that?"

"She has the ability to see the future."

"If she can see the future, why did she make such a foolish attempt?"

Amash grinned. "A fair question. From what we understand, it doesn't work quite that way. Her gift isn't specific. She has prophetic dreams. We've known for some time that she had this power, but until now we've never had the opportunity to help her develop it."

"You think she will cooperate?"

Amash looked at Taylor, who had opened her eyes. "That depends on how much she likes her sister. So far she has shown great loyalty to her. She even surrendered herself for her. I don't think she has much desire to watch her sister slowly and painfully die or to be the cause of her death."

"How about this one?" Maxwell asked, pushing Jack with his foot. "What do we do with traitors?"

Jack was conscious again and in severe pain from his beating. A hematoma had already developed over his eye. Like the women, he was on his stomach, handcuffed, with a guard standing over him. His hair was red with blood.

"What won't we do?" Amash said. "Such a tragic disappointment. I admit he fooled me. I honestly didn't think he was that clever." He smiled darkly. "The recreation for tonight has changed to something a little more entertaining. After dessert, we'll take him out and shoot him."

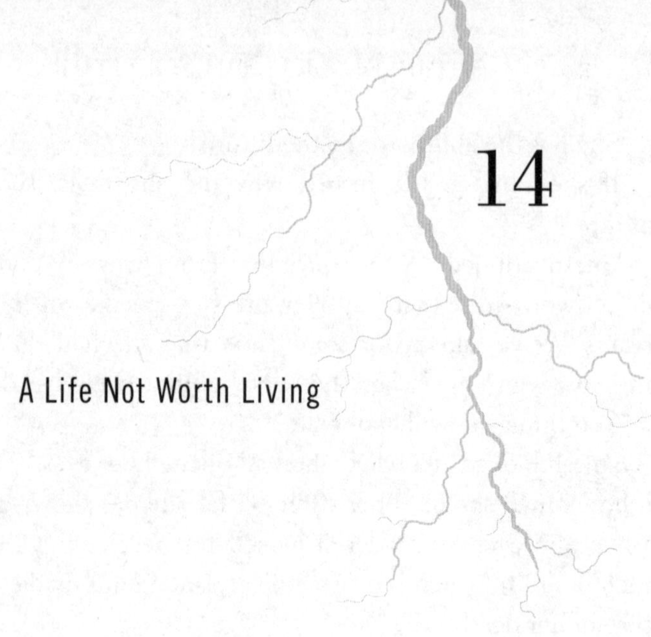

14

A Life Not Worth Living

"No," Taylor said. "Please, don't. I'll do whatever you say."

"Of course you'll do whatever I say anyway. I don't need this traitor around to assure that." He moved closer to her. "Why would you think I would care about what you want? The Chasqui have a strict code of rules we live by, which is how we've survived for centuries. Betrayal is punished by death. No exceptions."

"He has to be a Chasqui to betray the Chasqui, doesn't he? I mean, I fought you, but you didn't say that I betrayed you."

Amash looked at her with an amused expression. "Go on."

"There must be some kind of oath to be a Chasqui."

"Of course."

"Did Jack take the Chasqui oath?"

An amused smile crossed Amash's lips. "I heard that you were clever." He squatted down next to her. "So, Ms. Ridley, what do you think we should do with your friend? Because truthfully, as a prisoner of ours, he may desire death over the existence that you're choosing for him.

"Or am I correct in assuming that you want to keep him around until your friends liberate him? Because, if so, I assure you, that's not going to happen. You see, we've choreographed this entire mission of yours. We are well aware of your 'Alpha Team'—at least what's left of them. We could have taken them out at any time. Our plan was that they would deliver you to us, and, just as we planned, they have.

"So, you see, we've been miles ahead of you the whole time. As you fight for your friend's future, you should bear in mind that Jack's existence won't be pleasant, and, ultimately, he'll be begging for death."

Taylor looked at him, fighting the tears that wanted to fall. Still, Amash read the pain in her eyes. "Reality can be painful, I know. But truth is truth. I just thought you should know that everything has gone according to our plan."

"You underestimate us," Taylor said, trying her best to sound confident. "Just like Hatch did. Look what happened to him."

A wry grin crossed Amash's lips. "That's the spirit, my girl. I would expect nothing less from you. Unfortunately, it's that blind faith in your compadres that will be your undoing. And, make no mistake, Hatch was a fool."

"Hatch was smarter than you."

"Says the writhing girl on the floor," Amash said. He lightly sighed. "But enough for now. I will, for the time being, let your friend live, if only to amuse myself with his suffering. But no promises. I'll probably change my mind tomorrow.

"When the drug lord Pablo Escobar was betrayed, he'd chain the offender to a tree on his mile-long driveway, so those driving in would see his victims in various stages of suffering and death. It sent an indelible message to those who did business with him. Lead or silver was always the choice. You could profit off your association or suffer.

"Of course he'll try to escape—we expect that—but we have a

simple solution for that. For you we have RESAT vests that fire on full if you leave the premises. Obviously, that won't work on him. But we wouldn't want him to feel left out." He turned to look at Jack. "For you, dear boy, we'll wire you with an explosive vest. You'll appreciate it. It's lined with C4. If you leave the facility, it blows up. If you try to take it off, it blows up." His voice lowered. "If you displease me in any way, it blows up.

"Actually, I should say 'blows *in*.' Just in case you decide to play the martyr and try to take out a few guards with you, it doesn't work that way. All the shrapnel blows inward, shredding you and leaving your surroundings untouched." Amash turned back. "You see, Taylor, we really have thought of everything. To defeat your enemy, you must be your enemy, at least get into his mind." He took a deep breath as he looked at Jack. "It may sound cruel, but the vest's a blessing, really. When Jack finally decides that he can't take it anymore, and he will, he can just do himself in." He turned back to Taylor. "What do you think of your idea now?"

"I think you talk too much."

Amash laughed, then turned to the guards. "Take her away. Put the girls in RESAT vests set at five and put them in separate bat cells."

"What's a bat cell?" Taylor asked.

"Ask your sister. She knows all about your new accommodations."

He glanced down once more at Jack. "What a pitiful wretch you turned out to be." He turned and walked out of the room.

PART NINE

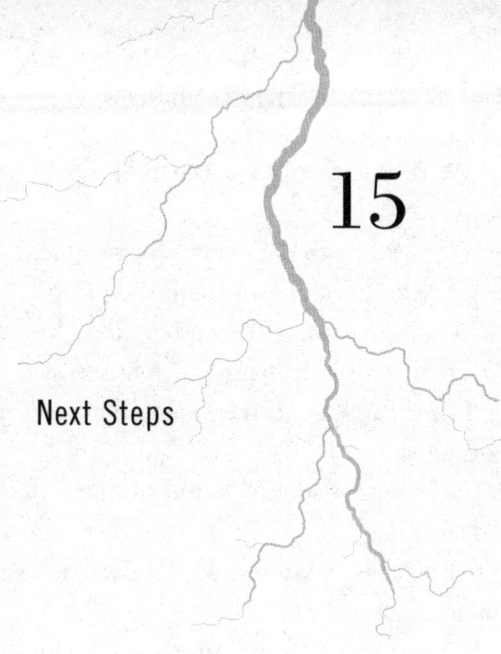

15

Next Steps

I was about to walk out of the house when Ostin and McKenna approached me. "I don't know what to say, Michael," McKenna said. "I feel like I let you down. I'm so sorry."

"It's not your fault," I said. "And I'm going to get her back."

"We're going to help you," Ostin chimed in. "We were just talking to Cristiano. He says he can lead us to the cave."

"You think she's being held at the cave and not the plant?"

"Cristiano does," Ostin said. "His reasoning makes sense. He says the cave has more jail cells, and it's better protected than the plant. But we can put the RADDs up once we're close to make sure."

"We left the RADDs back at the compound," I said. "I don't know if it's safe to go back. Let's go see what Johnson is planning."

We walked out of the house. Johnson was on the porch talking with Cibor and Jacinta. They looked over at us as we approached.

"We're going to need the RADDs," I said. "They're still at the compound."

"We need to go back there for supplies," Johnson said. "Hopefully, the Chasqui haven't ransacked the place."

"What if it's a trap?" Jacinta asked. "And they're waiting for us."

"Then we'll keep fighting," Johnson said. "But I doubt it. They got what they came for. If they wanted us all dead, they would have kept fighting us."

His answer made my stomach hurt. All they'd wanted was Taylor. And they had her.

Cibor said, "My question is, how do we get there? Walk? They've blown up all our vans."

"I have an old tour bus parked behind the warehouse," Jacinta said. "I haven't driven it in a while, but I am pretty sure we can get it running."

"My father was an auto mechanic in Kraków," Cibor said. "He taught me everything he knows. I can get it running. Take me to it."

All of us walked around to the back of the warehouse. The bus was so covered by fallen and decaying palm leaves, climbing vines, and moss that the bus looked like it had been camouflaged.

"When was the last time anyone drove this beast?" Johnson asked Jacinta.

"Maybe four years."

"The battery will be shot," Cibor said. "Do you have another?"

Jacinta shook her head. "No."

"We'll find one," he said. "We've got enough vehicles around here. One of the batteries must have survived."

The bus was a fourteen-seat tour bus that Jacinta had stopped using years before, so she'd just parked it behind the warehouse. Jax and Cassy repaired the bus's two flat tires while the rest of us cleared the vines and leaves from its roof, which were wet and decaying and nearly six inches thick.

Cibor and Johnson pulled the bus's door open; then Jacinta went inside and tried to start it. As Cibor had guessed, the bus's battery was dead.

Johnson asked Ian and Quentin to check all the vehicles for a working battery.

"On it," Ian said. "C'mon, Q."

"While they're looking, I can help," I said to Cibor. "I used to jump-start my mom's car."

"I didn't think of that," Cibor said. "It can't hurt."

I walked over to the front of the bus, where Cibor had lifted the hood, and grabbed the battery's terminals. "Tell me when."

"Turn the ignition," Cibor said to Jacinta, who was in the driver's seat.

"Okay."

He turned to me. "Now."

I pulsed. The bus's starter motor clicked, then jerked forward as if breaking free from ice. It slowly began to crank.

"Stop," Cibor said. He fussed around the engine again, then said, "Okay, try again."

I pulsed while Cibor continued working on the engine, until it suddenly fired up to life, shuddering like a woken beast.

"Let it run awhile," Cibor shouted to Jacinta over the roar of the motor. She gave him a thumbs-up.

About ten minutes later Ian and Zeus returned. They were each carrying a car battery.

"Looks like you started without us," Ian said.

"I was their battery," I said. "We'll still need one of those."

"One of these should work," Ian said. "I couldn't see any internal damage."

Cibor replaced the battery, then had Jacinta start the bus again. The bus rattled and smoked but started. Cibor slammed the hood shut, then took over driving for Jacinta. He revved the bus's engine for a few minutes, then drove the bus back out to the front of the zoo.

Out in the open, we could better see the bus. It was covered with amateurish hand paintings of jaguars, toucans, sloths, and tapirs, along with the words:

PUERTO'S WORLD-FAMOUS RESCUE ZOO

I suppose the "world-famous" was a bit of hyperbole, but I got it. As everyone was dispersing to go to the bus, Johnson said, "Michael, can we talk?"

"Yeah."

I followed him behind one of the cages, where we were alone.

"What's up?" I asked.

"I just wanted to thank you for what you said this morning. I needed that more than I realized."

"You're welcome. Even warriors need support."

"Especially from another warrior. Good luck getting Taylor."

"Thanks. Good luck on your mission. It's somewhat bizarre to think that all those people don't even know that their lives depend on someone they don't know and will never thank."

"If we do it right," Johnson said, "they won't even know they've been saved. Just like you and the Electroclan bringing down the Elgen."

"I wonder how many times throughout history that has happened."

"Probably more than we can imagine." Johnson smiled. "You're a good man, Vey."

"So are you." We shook.

"We'd better get going," Johnson said.

"Think the bus will make it?"

He grinned. "If it's anything like its owner, nothing will stop it."

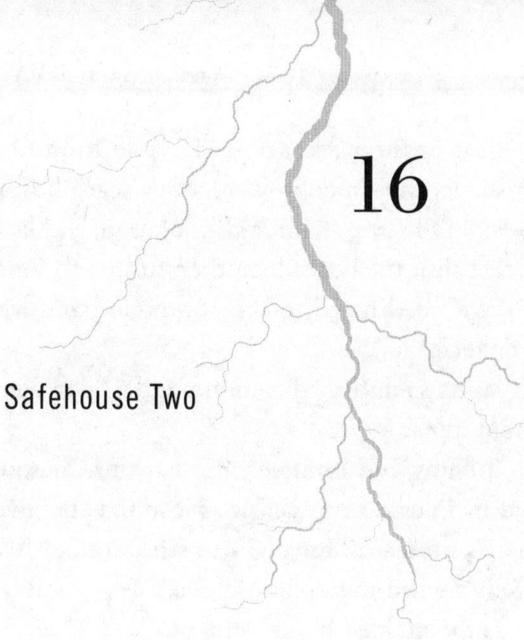

16

Safehouse Two

We gathered what was left of our things—which wasn't much, since most of our possessions had been blown up or burned up in the vans—then got on board the old bus. It smelled of mold and rot and diesel fuel. I was hurting more than I let on. What Johnson had said earlier was true. We'd lost too many. It wasn't his fault, but I understood why he felt it was. I felt that way after we lost Wade.

I'd thought that after the Elgen were gone, my life would be easy. But life never is easy. And trouble just seemed to hunt us, like a predator, patiently waiting in the shadows for the right moment to drag us back to its lair. That's what it felt like.

The question that haunted me was, what would the Chasqui do with Taylor? Her question to me was a valid one. Why were they so obsessed with her? And what did they plan to do with her gift, as if it were separate from her? It wasn't.

I sat in the back, across the aisle from Ostin and McKenna. Ian, Cristiano, and Quentin were a few seats in front of us. Cassy sat next to Jax in the front with Jaime, Johnson, and Jacinta. Cibor was driving.

He shut the bus's door, then turned to Johnson. "Where to, sir?"

"We need to go to the compound and load up on supplies and ordnance."

Jaime said, "But the compound's been compromised. They know about it."

"I know. But I'm guessing that the Chasqui used every man they had in Puerto to attack us. Now that they've got what they want, there's no reason for them to stick around. We'll pull everything we need, then go to safe house two."

Jaime nodded his agreement.

"Let's go, Cibor."

The transmission's gears ground loudly as Cibor shoved the bus into drive. The beast rattled and groaned, then lurched forward. The bus's shocks were stiff or gone, and we felt every bump as we drove over the fallen front gates and down the dirt lane. We passed the three burned-out trucks of the first Chasqui wave, then the lead truck of the second—the one that Zeus had hit with lightning. It was still burning.

Jacinta quietly looked out her window. I couldn't imagine what was going through her mind, leaving everything she had built behind. Earlier that morning, I had noticed her brushing back tears as she released her animals. I wondered where she would end up. The truth is, I don't think she even cared anymore. I suppose I fought the same emotions. In some ways our current situation felt more hopeless than it had with the Elgen, even on Hades, when I climbed the radio tower to sacrifice myself. Maybe it's because it wasn't me who was gone now. Or maybe, back then, we were just so filled with adrenaline that we couldn't worry. Or maybe—the worst of all possibilities—deep inside I worried that my luck had finally run out.

After we left the zoo, Quentin came back and sat down in the seat next to me. He said, "Hey, buddy, I don't really know what to say, other than I'm sorry."

"That's all you need to say."

"It's not your fault, you know."

This statement bothered me. "Why did you say that?"

"You seem angry."

"I am angry."

"Of course you are. You have a good reason. I was just worried about who you're really angry at. The Chasqui? Taylor? Yourself?"

"I don't know. All of the above."

"Save it for the Chasqui. What Taylor did was brave. And noble. At least let her have that."

"What does that mean?"

He took a deep breath. "Look. It's not like I'm some expert on love. But sometimes the truest love isn't shown in what we give. It's shown in what we give up. She loves you. She loves Tara. She did what she thought was best for the two of you, not her. Giving herself up to the Chasqui wasn't for her. She must have been terrified. But she did it anyway."

"She could have talked to me about it."

"Really?"

I exhaled slowly. "No. I guess not."

"Be strong, brother. You're a hero, and we're still counting on you. We're going to get her back. And Tara *and* Jack."

I shook my head. Jack was a whole different story. After all we'd been through, how could he betray us like that?

"I don't know if Jack will come back, even if he has the chance."

"I think there's more to Jack's story than we know. You know him. What does Jack value most of all?"

"Courage."

"Even more than courage."

"Loyalty."

"Exactly. It's his defining virtue. Don't forget that." He slapped me on the knee. "Remember, I'm with you until the end, brother." He went back to his seat.

It took about a half hour for us to reach the compound. Not much was said on the way. We were anxious as we approached, but

Ian kept a lookout for anything suspicious, and there was nothing. Like Johnson thought, the Chasqui had gotten what they wanted and disappeared back into the forest, vanishing like a raindrop in the Amazon River.

Johnson said, "We're going to grab some munitions and MREs, then head off to safe house two. Keep things fast and stay alert. Ian, if you'll keep an eye on things."

"Both of them, Chief."

Once the outside gate had closed behind us, Johnson got out and opened the warehouse door, and Cibor drove inside.

"Michael, could your guys give us a hand?"

"Whatever you need."

We went to their storage and brought out several boxes marked C4 EXPLOSIVES.

"Don't drop those," Johnson said.

I almost laughed. "I figured as much."

We then moved everything inside, filling the bus aisle with the supplies.

Johnson and Jax dropped a box of paper into a metal drum outside the overhead door, then set the box on fire. We momentarily stopped what we were doing to watch.

"What's that?" Cassy asked Jax.

"It's called a destructor kit," Jax said, stepping back from the drum. "It's designed for the destruction of confidential materials. You'll want to step back."

The fire quickly grew hotter until the black smoke turned white; then flames began shooting upward more than twenty feet. The barrel itself turned bright red.

"To be exact, it's an E12 destructor kit from the Army Chemical Corps," Ostin said. "It consists of a hundred pounds of nitrate, one package of igniter compound, two fire starters, and a wire screen and connectors to a basic steel drum."

"He really does know everything," Jax said.

"It was unnecessary, though."

"Why do you say that?"

"You could have just asked McKenna to burn everything. She's hotter than nitrate. Nitrate burns at seventeen hundred degrees Celsius. That's a little over nineteen hundred kelvins. McKenna can do three thousand kelvins."

"Your girlfriend burns hotter than nitrate?" Cibor asked.

"Yes."

Cibor smiled. "You have a hot girlfriend."

"Tell me something I don't know."

"I don't know if that's possible. But I'll give you some advice."

"What's that?"

"Don't ever get her mad at you."

We were in and out of the compound in less than thirty minutes. The barrels were still burning when we left, but everything inside them was already destroyed. There was another van in the garage, but we decided to abandon it and stay together on the bus. According to Jaime, there were more vehicles at the next safe house.

Safe house two was about sixteen miles away from the compound. Like everyone else, I was exhausted, but I couldn't sleep on the bus. There was just too much weighing on my mind.

"How soon can we start upriver?" I asked Jaime.

"You're the boss, so whenever you say. To me, it would make more sense to go in the morning."

"Why?"

"Tourists don't go into the Amazon at night."

"I'm not a tourist."

"No, but we want the Chasqui to think you are. At night, you'll look suspicious to the Chasqui who patrol the river." He looked at me. "Besides, you need sleep."

"I don't need sleep."

"Everyone needs sleep. You are upset and filled with adrenaline right now, but your body will eventually come down. How many hours of sleep did you get last night?"

"Two, maybe."

"Exactly. You have a long hike through the jungle, then who

knows what you'll face. You will need rest. Sometimes emotion writes checks the body cannot cash."

"You're right," I said. "I'll try."

A large fence surrounded the property, and we were stopped at the outer gate by an armed sentry in a guard booth. He didn't speak English, so Jaime got out of the bus and spoke to him. Then he got back into the bus, the gate rose, and we drove up to the hacienda.

Unlike the Alpha Team's compound, safe house two was an actual house, and a beautiful one at that. At one time it had been the homestead of a wealthy rancher, and it still functioned as a ranch, though with carefully screened employees. It was perfect for a safe house since it was surrounded by hundreds of cleared acres and no neighbors. Like the Starxource plant.

"This is nice," Tessa said. "How long have you owned this?"

"About six years ago the man who owned it moved to Lima to work for the president," Johnson said. "We're safe here, at least for a while. I suggest we get some rest, then make our plans."

He turned to me. "Michael, I know you're eager to go after Taylor, but a few hours won't make much of a difference for them, and it will for you. We study sleep deprivation in Special Forces, and a thirty-minute nap significantly improves performance."

"They call it the combat nap," Ostin said. "It improves performance by thirty-four percent and alertness by one hundred percent."

"Thank you for that . . . ," Johnson said. I think he was still getting used to Ostin's addendums. "I recommend that we go inside, eat lunch, then rest for an hour. Then we'll meet and go over our plans."

I nodded. "That works."

We left our things on the bus and went inside. Jaime had called ahead, and the hacienda staff had already prepared lunch for us. Ceviche, roast beef sandwiches, rocoto relleno (stuffed spicy peppers), and a garden salad. We had various juices, including a drink called chicha morada, made from purple corn, cinnamon, cloves, apple chunks, and pineapple peels.

I was hungrier than I'd realized, and I ate until I was full. Then I found one of the empty rooms and lay down to rest for a few minutes. When I woke, it was dark outside. I looked around the room. I was alone. I got up and walked out. I could smell meat on the grill. There was a chef and two other Peruvian women in the kitchen cooking, but I couldn't see any of our people. I walked to the back of the house to a glass sliding door. Jax, Cassy, Johnson, and Jacinta were outside on the back patio talking. They stopped as I walked outside.

"Hey, sleepyhead," Cassy said. "We weren't sure you were going to wake up."

"Why didn't you wake me?" I asked.

"You needed the sleep," Johnson said.

"Sit down, Michael," Jax said. "Have a drink with us."

I sat down. "What are you drinking?"

"I'm having a pisco sour," Jax said, lifting his glass. "After a day like today, I needed it."

"Michael doesn't drink," Tessa said. "I'm having a coca tea."

"I'll have some tea," I said.

"I'll pour you some." Cassy poured hot water from a thermos into a coffee cup. "Would you like some *azúcar*?"

"Yes, please."

She dropped a sugar cube into the cup, stirred it, then brought it over to me. "Here you are."

"Thank you." I took a sip of the tea. It had been a while since I'd had it, but it tasted like I remembered, which was basically like alfalfa soaked in tepid water.

"That is what we drink for altitude sickness," Jacinta said.

Johnson set down his glass. "Jaime has things set up. Your team will leave for town at six a.m. It will take about thirty-five minutes to reach the boat. It's a tourist boat, so you'll want to look as touristy as possible."

"How do you look touristy?" Cassy asked, smirking.

"You know, T-shirts with llamas on them, high black socks with shorts."

"I'm not wearing high black socks with shorts," she said. "Or the llama shirt. Sounds like a fashion nightmare."

"What were you talking about before I interrupted?" I asked.

"We *were* talking about the Chasqui's plan to burn down Arequipa," Johnson said.

Jacinta said, "The Chasqui's plan is not much different from the Allies' firebombing of Dresden or Tokyo in World War II."

Johnson bristled at the comparison. "Except that *those* countries had started a conflict that killed millions of people."

"That is true," she said.

"Just like the Chasqui. Peace doesn't serve aggressors." Johnson glanced down at his watch. "It's about time for dinner. We'll meet after dinner to plan."

The hacienda's chef had prepared a big meal for us, consisting of lomo saltado, a beef stir-fry made from the ranch's own beef; a juane—a mix of rice, olives, meat, eggs, and spices wrapped in *bijao* leaves; and aguadito de pollo, a traditional chicken soup.

Such an extravagant supper made me feel like we were having our last meal. Still, it was a rare moment of relaxation, and as I watched everyone laugh and talk, a disturbing thought crossed my mind: *Which one of us won't make it back?* I pushed the thought from my mind. Maybe none of them. Maybe just me.

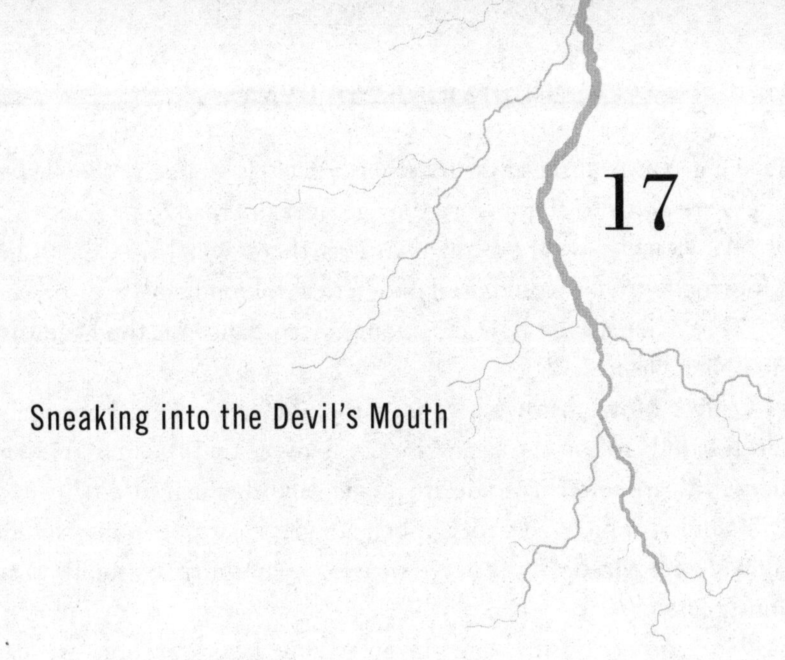

17

Sneaking into the Devil's Mouth

After dinner we cleared away the dishes, then gathered around the table to make our plans. Johnson stood at the front of the room.

"It's late," he said. "But not too late. Michael's team will be leaving early, so we'll keep this as brief as possible." He looked at me. "We've got two missions ahead of us. Michael, which would you like to begin with?"

"Let's start with saving Arequipa," I said.

Before Johnson could speak, Ostin said, "I've been thinking about the Arequipa mission. We don't have to blow the road. Or the trucks."

"You have a better idea?" Johnson said.

"Yes," he said. "Blowing up the road would be like broadcasting to the world where we are. Also, I'm assuming it will take more than one truck to transport all those bats, so unless those trucks are traveling dangerously close together, which is unlikely, the slower trucks are going to stop before they go over the road."

"We don't know how many trucks there will be," Cibor said. "How many trucks would it take to haul a million bats?"

"That's like asking how many angels can dance on the head of a pin," Nichelle said.

Ostin's brow furrowed. "That's nothing like asking how many angels can dance on the head of a pin. How is that possibly relevant unless you are referring to destroying angels, in which case—"

I think Nichelle sensed a much longer answer coming, so she quickly apologized. "I'm sorry for saying something so stupid. Continue, please."

"No worries," Ostin said. "In answering Jax's question, we can logically assume that the Chasqui will want to use as few trucks as possible, since the larger the convoy, the more attention they'll acquire and the greater chance of mechanical difficulties.

"To transport the bats, they will likely use a standard forty-foot Conex shipping container, the kind used on shipping barges around the world. The container is forty feet by eight feet by eight feet, which gives it a cubic area of two thousand five hundred and sixty feet. Technically, that could, in fact, hold a million bats. But the overall cubic area is largely irrelevant since the bats wouldn't survive being stuffed into a container like potato chips, so we can safely assume that the bats will only occupy a set surface space, which would be three hundred twenty square feet per ceiling. Bat researchers figure bat populations by estimating the amount of cave ceiling covered and multiplying it by approximately two hundred fifty bats per square foot. So, a single container could hold about eighty thousand bats. At that number it would take about twelve and a half containers to carry a million bats."

"Truly you have a dizzying intellect," Jax joked.

"Wait until I get going," Ostin replied. "As I said, that is too large a convoy to avoid attention. So, if the Chasqui are smart, and they are, they would construct multiple layers of frames within each container, the same way that beekeepers stack frames in a beehive.

"As far as the bats, I would think that the Chasqui would use the *Tadarida brasiliensis*, the Brazilian free-tailed bat, because of its speed, availability, and size. They are only nine centimeters long, about three and a half inches, which means they can enter spaces in structures smaller than a dime. This means they can inhabit spaces much smaller than, say, your more common Megachiroptera, or fruit bat, which is almost three times larger, with a wingspan as wide as forty-two inches. Because the size of the spark required to start a fire is almost irrelevant, the free-tailed bat would be a much more efficient delivery method of an incendiary device. . . ."

"He's speaking English, right?" Cibor asked Johnson.

"Yes, just a little different version than most people do."

"I suspect, to properly protect the bats, the Chasqui scientists would space each frame about twenty to twenty-four inches apart, which is the standard of most bat houses. . . ."

"Bat houses?" Quentin said. "What's a bat house?"

"You've heard of birdhouses?" Ostin asked.

"Yes."

"Same thing, except for bats. As I was saying, twenty to twenty-four inches apart is the standard height distance, which means an eight-foot cargo container would give them approximately four frames, or five surfaces counting the ceiling. That means each container would hold close to four hundred thousand bats. If Cristiano is right and they're shooting for a million bats, then they could haul all the bats in just three trucks."

Everyone looked at Ostin with wonder.

"He really is brilliant," Jax said.

"You'll get used to it," Cassy said.

"How does he know all these things?" Jacinta asked.

"He reads," I said. "And he never forgets anything."

"Anything?"

"Anything. I once asked him if anyone had ever escaped from Alcatraz prison. He said, 'Yes' and asked if I wanted to know their names."

"Three trucks . . . ," Johnson said, steering us back on track.

"Yes, three trucks," Ostin said. "That's what I think they'll be running."

"And you don't think we should just blow them up?"

Ostin shook his head. "I think not. There's a better way."

After such an impressive display of intellect, I don't think anyone wanted to disagree with him.

"What's your idea?" Johnson asked.

"The road from Puerto Maldonado to Arequipa is roughly five hundred and fifteen miles, most of which is a winding mountain highway. It has a change of elevation of almost seven thousand feet. Our best course of action would be to find a tight corner of road—best case a hairpin turn on a slope with a steep drop-off. Then, as the trucks get close to the turn, Cassy freezes them. They can't take their foot off the gas, they can't turn, and they can't hit their brakes. So they just drive right off the side of a mountain, taking their bats with them. It looks like human error, and no innocent people get killed driving off a road that no longer exists because we blew it up."

"That is a brilliant plan," Johnson said.

"So we'll take Cassy with us," Jax said.

I could see he was all for that. Cassy too, as she was smiling.

"And Tessa for the added distance," Ostin said. "I'd take Quentin too. As backup. If something goes wrong, he can, at least, shut down the trucks. Then you could still blow them as a last resort."

"We could hit them with rocket launchers," Cibor said.

Johnson thought for a moment, then said, "We'll still need advance warning to know when they're coming."

"I can go downriver with Michael," Jaime said. "Maybe to Jacinta's friend's lodge. When I see the containers go by, I'll radio you. Then I'll head back to Puerto and keep an eye on the port and the progress of the Chasqui's loading of the cargo containers. I'll just keep a few miles ahead of them the whole way."

"That's a solid plan," Johnson said. "That's what we'll do." He turned to me. "Now let's talk about your mission. Where do you think they'll take her, the Starxource plant or the cave?"

"Cristiano thinks the cave," I said.

Cristiano said, "Not many people know where the cave is, and it is easier to defend than the Starxource plant."

"I was afraid of that," Johnson said, shaking his head. "I hate cave and tunnel warfare. I had my fill of it in Afghanistan. We definitely have the easier of the two missions."

"Nothing's easy about any of this," I said. "And you have a hundred thousand lives to save."

Johnson exhaled slowly. "The closer you get to the Chasqui, the more eyes there will be on the river. How will you get to the cave without being seen?"

"I have a friend in Puerto with a tourist boat," Jaime said. "He takes groups up the river every day, so the Chasqui won't suspect him unless you get too close to their interests. You will have to hike the last three or four miles in through the jungle."

"The Chasqui have sentinels all along the river, and they have installed many more cameras as well," Cristiano said. "The closer we get, the more surveillance they have."

"More than the Elgen?"

"Yes," he said. "Much more. But I know a safe path through the jungle that leads to the caves. It is used by a native tribe. The Chasqui don't know about it."

"The Amacarra?" Ostin asked.

"Yes. You know of them?"

Ostin nodded. "We've had dealings with them."

"The Chasqui's cave was once a sacred place for them. It was where they buried their chiefs for many centuries. They tried to reclaim the caves, but many of them were killed by the Chasqui. The Amacarra hated the Elgen, but they consider the Chasqui living demons."

"I know the Amacarra," I said. "They helped me escape the Elgen. That's where I met Tessa. She was practically part of their tribe."

Tessa smiled. "The Amacarra are my friends. I even know a little bit of their language. And you're right, they hated the Elgen."

"We should take Tessa with us," Cristiano said. "In case we run into them."

"No," I said. "Alpha Team will need her more than we will." I turned to Cristiano. "Earlier you said 'caves.' Is there more than one cave?"

"It is really a network of caves. Before the Chasqui came, there were two different caves, which they tunneled through and connected, making a larger cave. There are more than two miles of explored tunnels, but it is even bigger than that. Some of the tunnels go deeper into the earth and have never been explored."

"What's in the caves?" McKenna asked.

"They've turned the caves into a fortress. Amash started building it after the Electroclan destroyed the Starxource plant and he started selling drugs. He wanted a safe place he could hide in case the Peruvian government or American DEA ever came after them. Or Hatch and the Elgen. General Hatch never knew about the caves. The caves are well hidden and easy to defend. They are also safe from bombing from the air. It was very smart of them to use the caves."

"Cave warfare has been around for centuries," Johnson said. "Just like the Chasqui. During the Vietnam War, North Vietnamese soldiers took shelter in Phong Nha-Ke Bang, one of the most expansive cave systems in the world. It had more than sixty miles of limestone caves. In places it's as wide as a football field and twice as high. It had ventilation, lighting, and even a hospital."

Of course Ostin chipped in with his knowledge. "Also, in Afghanistan, bin Laden's Tora Bora cave complex protected him from aerial bombings. It was a safe place for them to store arms and munitions. Since the Chasqui originated in the Middle East, I would expect that they took a page from bin Laden's playbook and built something even more secure."

"I wish Gunnar was here," Johnson said. "He was part of the Delta Force team that took Tora Bora during the Afghan War."

"They took a lot of casualties," Ostin said.

Johnson frowned. "Many."

"That's not an option," I said. "Can you draw out what the cave looks like?" I asked Cristiano.

"Yes. Do you have paper?"

"Just a moment," Jaime said. "I will get some."

Jaime went to the pantry, where he tore off a meter-long section of white butcher paper. Then he brought it back to the dining room. He handed Cristiano a pencil. "You can draw the cave with this."

Cristiano stood as he drew out a map of the cave system. His drawing reminded me a little of the Lichtenberg figures on my arms—the fernlike scars I got in Mexico. The cave spread out in smaller and smaller tunnels, trailing off into what might have been miles of small capillaries. After ten minutes or so he stood back from his drawing. "I'm sure I missed a few of the smaller tunnels, but I think that's about right."

"How do you know the cave so well?" Jax asked.

"One of my assignments was to give tours of the caves to the new guards, so I got to know them very well. In my free time, I explored a lot. After the Chasqui killed my friends, I started looking for a way to escape. I found a way out no one knew about."

Cristiano touched his pencil to two different points on his map. "These are the two entrances to the cave." He touched the pencil to the point farthest south. "This is the main entrance. It is the most heavily guarded. This big cavern here is where they built their dining room and lounge area. And this is where the beds are."

"Hmmm," Ostin said. "I've seen this drawing somewhere before." He suddenly grinned. "I know. Your cave resembles the human digestive system."

"You are right," Cristiano said. "I thought the same thing. I was a pre-med major at ASU."

Ostin ran his finger down the map. "The main entrance, here, is the mouth, the tunnel is the esophagus, which leads into the stomach. Over here, this cavern, is the liver. This section is the pancreas, leading to the small intestine."

"This is getting weird," Nichelle said.

"The liver is where the sovereign lives," Cristiano said. "It is next to the treasure vault. They just call his room 'the palace.' The stomach is, coincidentally, the cafeteria and meeting room. The pancreas is the guards' quarters and gym. This section right here . . ."

"The duodenum," Ostin said.

"Yes, the duodenum is where they store their weapons and bombs."

"Where do they keep prisoners?" I asked.

"Over here, what would be the ascending colon," Cristiano said.

"Fitting," Nichelle said.

"Yes. The south end. You enter through the guards' barracks. There's also a rarely used entrance in the back tunnel near the control center. You get there through the storage and utility rooms."

"What do they keep in their storage?" I asked.

"Everything. Food, uniforms, alcohol. It is next to the utility room, where the electricity and ventilation come in.

"Down this tunnel is the main control center. It is where the cameras and locks and ventilation are controlled. They can see any part of the cave from the control center."

"How many Chasqui are there in the cave?" I asked.

"Most of the Chasqui live in the old Starxource plant, but the cave can house more than fifty soldiers." He bent back over his drawing. "This section here is their medical center."

"The spleen," Ostin said.

"They have a medical center?" Tessa asked.

"Do not let the stone walls deceive you. The Chasqui's cave is a very luxurious place. In places it is like a palace for the kings of old. The walls of the sovereign's room are covered with real gold, so the walls shimmer. I was allowed to see it once, only because I was carrying things to the room. That is where they built the vault."

"What's in the vault?" Nichelle asked.

"It is filled with gold and precious gems."

"Like the *Joule*," I said.

"Yes, many jewels."

"Michael meant the *Joule*," Ostin corrected. "It was one of Hatch's ships, named after the scientist, James Prescott Joule, an English physicist who—"

I raised my hand to stop him. "How much gold is in the vault?"

"I have never been inside the vault, but a guard secretly told me there was more than twenty tons of gold bullion."

"Whoa," Ostin said. "Twenty tons? That would be more than a billion dollars."

"They've got their own private Fort Knox," Johnson said. "No wonder they keep it secret."

"It is one of the methods they use to launder their money. They buy gold from the Amazonian miners, especially the illegal miners. It is a symbiotic relationship. The miners want currency, especially Euros and American dollars, and the Chasqui are trying to trade off their currency.

"There is also expensive art inside. There are important paintings bought on the black market. I have seen them. The cave has special ventilation just for the paintings."

"What paintings?" Ostin asked.

"Do you know art?" Cristiano asked.

"He knows everything," McKenna said.

"They have a painting called *The Storm on the Sea of Galilee*—"

"By Rembrandt," Ostin said. "It was stolen in 1990 as part of a half-billion-dollar heist. I would die to see that."

"I hope not," I said.

"What makes it special," Ostin said, "besides being a Rembrandt, is that there are fourteen people in the boat, and since Jesus and his disciples only add up to thirteen, it is believed that Rembrandt painted himself in the boat as a self-portrait."

"There are other paintings," Cristiano said. "There is a Renoir of a woman. She is leaning like this. . . ." He leaned against the table with his elbow.

"Madeleine Leaning on Her Elbow with Flowers in Her Hair," Ostin said.

"Renoir was an incredibly talented painter," Tessa said, "but not so clever with naming his masterpieces."

"He was pragmatic," Ostin said.

"And there is a Picasso called . . . I believe, *The Pigeon*."

"Le Pigeon aux Petits Pois," Ostin said. "That painting is valued at

more than twenty-eight million dollars. But it was believed to have been discarded and destroyed."

"Who would destroy a Picasso?" Cassy asked.

"There are those who don't value valuable things," Tessa said.

"That is too true," Jacinta said.

"'Valuable' is objective," Ostin said. "A cell phone is of no use to the Amacarra, while a blow dart is of no use to a downtown businessman."

"It could be," Nichelle interjected.

"Tessa is right," Cristiano said. "There are things of great value that the Chasqui do not value."

"Other than the sanctity of life and human rights," I said, "what do you mean?"

"When the Chasqui were first excavating the cave, in addition to the Amacarra's sacred burial mounds, they also came across bones and cave drawings that were many thousands of years old. Early evidence of primitive man. They took them to Amash to see what he wanted them to do with them. He told them to throw them away like they were trash."

Ian shook his head. "Those things are priceless."

"Pearls among swine," Johnson said.

"The Chasqui *are* swine," Jacinta said. "Though that is an insult to the pigs."

"How did they even find these caves?" Nichelle asked.

"There are hundreds of unexplored caves in the Amazon," Jacinta said. "It is only recently that anyone has taken an interest in them. Unfortunately, most of those people are with mining companies and are destroying the caves to mine their rich deposits of iron ore. The Chasqui cave is farther south than most and has fewer tourists and industry. That is one of the reasons why Hatch chose this location for the Starxource plant."

"The tribes have known about this cave system for hundreds of years," Cristiano said. "They call it *la boca del diabolo*—the devil's mouth."

"I thought you said it was sacred to them," Nichelle said.

"Yes, it is. I do not understand their culture."

"It's not so hard to understand," Ostin said. "The Amacarra don't believe good is the opposite of evil. They believe good and evil are part of the same wheel—one can't exist without the other."

"Like the Chinese yin and yang," Cassy said.

"We're getting off track," Johnson said. "You were telling us how they found the cave. Please continue."

"Yes. The Chasqui scientist found the cave by accident. They were tracking the bats they were studying, and the bats led them to the cave. They found more than a million bats inside."

"That's where they found the bats they electrified," I said.

"Some of them," Cristiano said. "There are many, many caves in the Amazon."

"What is the cave's infrastructure like?" Ostin asked.

"Infrastructure?"

"I mean how they run the place. Lighting, plumbing, cooling, electrical, things like that."

"Oh, yes," Cristiano said. "They have all those things. There are natural springs of fresh water, which they collect and pump. The electric wires and pipes are attached to the walls in conduits."

"If we could take out their power, we could move through the dark. Where does their power come from?"

"There is a power line running all the way from the Starxource plant. When the Chasqui started building inside the cave, they ran wires from the plant for power. Then they dug a four-mile trench and buried the wires."

"Then anyone could follow the trench to the cave," Jax said.

"You cannot see it anymore. The jungle reclaims its own quickly. After just one rainy season, you could not see the trench anymore. Now it has been years, so it is completely invisible and covered with plants and leaves."

"I could see it," Ian said.

"So could I," I said. "I mean, I could feel it." When I was nine years old, I noticed that I could feel where the electric lines in our home's walls were.

Cristiano looked back down at the map. "There are electric lights throughout the entire cave, like in a mining shaft." He touched his finger to the map. "Right here is where the electricity goes into the cave. From here it goes into a large battery room, so if the power is shut off, they still have more than a month of electricity."

"That's smart," Ostin said. "Auxiliary power."

"So there *will* be light," I said. I turned to Cristiano. "How do we get into the cave?"

"Trying to get in by any of the entrances would be too dangerous," Cristiano said. "They are well guarded, with many cameras and guards. You cannot get within a hundred meters without being seen. If we got in through the main gate, there are two other gates behind it that automatically close. They would shut up like a turtle in its shell, then alert the guards at the plant to come to their aid. They can hide in there for a very long time."

"So what do we do?" McKenna asked.

"There is another way," Cristiano said. "Like I said, there are many, many smaller tunnels in the cave. Too many for them to care about. This small tunnel right here is partially filled with water. At its end is a deep cave pool. The pool has an underground opening. You can swim underneath and come up into another cavern where water comes in through a hole from the outside. If we widen the hole, we could get in and swim to the tunnel."

"That counts me out," Zeus said.

"Sorry," Nichelle said.

"The Chasqui don't know about this tunnel?" I asked.

"They know about the tunnel, but it is one of many, and they do not use it. Like I said, it is mostly filled with water. I think I am the only one who has been to its end."

"If the tunnel is filled with water, how do we get through it?" McKenna asked.

"There is space."

"It has an air bell," Ostin said.

"What's an air bell?" Tessa asked.

"It's an air space in a flooded tunnel between the water and the ceiling," Ostin said.

"Yes, that is what it is," Cristiano said. "You have to crawl through it. It is flooded with water, with only one foot between the water and the ceiling. That is why no one besides me has gone down it."

"How did you find it?" Johnson asked.

"Like I said, I was curious and wanted to see where the tunnel went. I followed it down to the pool. It was my private pool since no one else ever went there. I was diving in the pool when I found the hole in the cave wall about six feet below the surface. I swam through it and came up in a cavern with air and a small beam of light. I could hear water falling. Near the top there was an opening where the water was coming in from the outside."

"How big is the opening?" I asked.

"Maybe this big," he said, holding his hands about eighteen inches apart. "Not big enough for us to climb through. But the rock is soft, so it would not be hard to break through it."

"Are there any other ways in besides that?" Zeus asked.

Cristiano shook his head. "I do not think so. There is a ventilation shaft. It might be wide enough to crawl through."

"Where is that?"

"I think it is up around this area, but it has a very thick metal cage around it and cameras. It also has motion detection devices all around it. We could not get within one hundred meters of it without them knowing we were there. We had a sloth come near it once, and they shot it within a few minutes."

"They shot a sloth?" McKenna asked.

"They shot it and ate it."

McKenna looked horrified. "That is so cruel. Sloths are kind animals. They don't hurt anyone."

"You can eat sloth?" Nichelle asked.

Cristiano nodded. "It is not good."

"Then you've eaten it," Nichelle said.

"Yes. Once is enough."

"I hate you," McKenna said.

"Did you know that a sloth can hold its breath underwater longer than a dolphin can?" Ostin said.

"I don't want to talk about sloths anymore," McKenna said.

Nichelle shook her head. "Enough about the sloths. Why don't we just put poison gas through the vents? That would take care of them."

"With Taylor and Tara in there?" Ostin asked.

"Sorry," Nichelle said. "Forgot about that. Bad idea."

"I think entering through the water tunnel is our best option," Ostin said. "Except for Zeus."

"I think you're right," I said. I turned to Zeus. "You might have to sit this one out, amigo."

"Not happening. If I have to wait outside in the jungle, I'll do it. You don't know when you'll need an extra lightning bolt."

"We'll need someone to watch the entrance," Ostin said.

"I'll do that," Zeus said.

"Next question," I said to Cristiano. "Once we're inside, how do we get them out of the jail? How do they lock the cells? Electric, or old-fashioned lock and key?"

"They have locks in the doors. Like in jails."

"I could melt through them," McKenna said.

"Easily," Ostin said. "Carbon steel melts at twenty-six hundred to twenty-eight hundred degrees Fahrenheit. McKenna can go almost double that. But she'll need water."

"To put out the fire?" Johnson asked.

"No, for her. Fire dehydrates her."

"What if they're broadcasting RESATs, like they did at the zoo?"

I turned to Cristiano. "What do you know about their RESATs?"

"I know nothing. It is not something they used when I was with them."

"We need to expect that they'll be using them," I said. "The RADDs will tell us."

"What if they don't have the RESATs on?" Quentin asked.

"If Tara and Taylor are there, they'll need them on." I exhaled slowly. "A lot of moving parts."

"You're going to be making this up as you go," Johnson said.

"That's the story of my life," I said.

"As soon as they know we are there," Cristiano said, "they will call the guards at the Starxource plant to come join the fight."

"How many guards do they have at the plant?" Cibor asked.

"Hundreds. It would be best not to fight with them."

"Yes," I said. "Let's not do that."

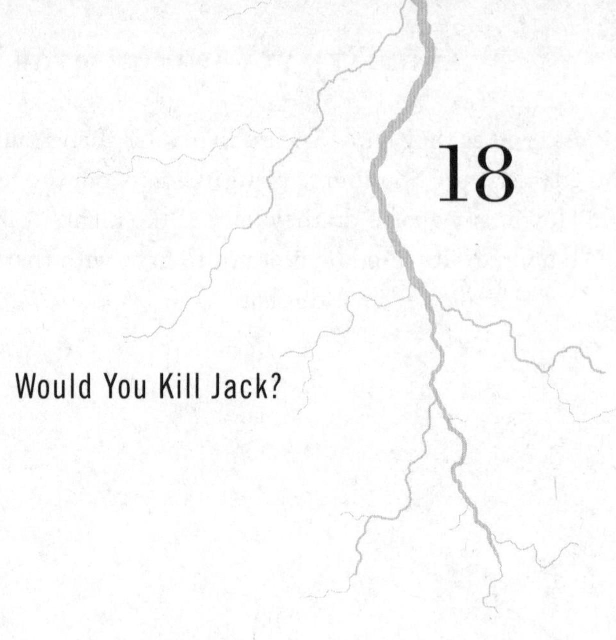

18

Would You Kill Jack?

"What do the guards do during the day?" I asked. "Are they inside or out?"

"Both. They have patrols in the jungle. Inside the cave the off-duty guards are in their barracks or the dining room. The on-duty guards are stationed at the outer doors, guarding the sovereign's room or the jail."

"What about at night?"

"It is the same, but with fewer guards. At nighttime it is difficult for them to monitor the jungle. There are many distractions since there are thousands of jungle animals and they all hunt at night. The guards are now so used to their motion detectors being set off by animals that they usually just turn them off. It happens many times every hour."

"That's good for us," I said.

"No one has ever attempted to attack them, so they are quite . . . what is the word . . . when you are lazy about something?"

"Apathetic," Nichelle said.

"Yes," Cristiano said. "That word. Apathetic."

"That will change," I said. "Like Ostin said, they will be expecting us."

"Why will they be expecting us?" Cristiano asked.

"They know we are loyal. We don't leave our friends behind."

Cristiano frowned. "Then your loyalty is your weakness."

"Our loyalty is why we're strong," I said.

"I have a question," Ostin said. "After we drop Jaime off at the lodge, where will the rest of us start hiking?"

"We should hike in the last four miles before the cave," Cristiano said. "After that there are too many cameras and guards on the river."

"How far would that be from the lodge?" Ostin asked.

"I don't know. There are many lodges on the river. Which lodge is it?"

"Makisapa Lodge," Jacinta said. "I believe it is the farthest lodge downriver."

"Is it the lodge with the yellow flags with the picture of the Nazca makisapa monkey?"

"That is the one."

"I have passed it many times. It is maybe seven miles from the cave."

"Then we will go past the lodge about three miles. That will put us four miles out," Ostin said.

"Four miles, then two miles," Cristiano said.

"What do you mean?" Nichelle asked. "You just said it's four miles."

"The cave is four miles down the river from the lodge, but the cave is two miles from the river."

"That's going to be thick jungle. How far is your trail from the river?"

"About a mile and a half. It will be thick jungle, but our speed will pick up once we reach the trail."

"So we'll be hiking about six miles in all, a mile and a half of it through heavy jungle." I turned to Jaime. "How far is it to the lodge? In hours?"

"It is almost six hours."

"Six hours, plus another hour to our drop-off point. Then around three hours hiking."

Cristiano nodded.

"That's ten hours. If we leave the dock in Puerto at seven in the morning, we'll arrive at the cave around five in the afternoon."

"That will give us one hour before the sun sets," Ostin said.

"Which means we'll be hiking out in the dark." I remembered all too well the nightmare of the last time I fled the Elgen through the jungle. "How do we get back to Puerto?"

Jacinta said, "There is a helicopter pad at my friend's lodge. If you can get to the lodge, we can pick you up there. It is that or taking a boat. But I think the river will be too dangerous."

"The river is too dangerous," Cristiano said. "The Chasqui have armed speedboats and many sentries. We would never make it back to Puerto on the river."

"That means we will be hiking back through the jungle at night, about twelve miles."

"I'm afraid so."

"How far does the Amacarra trail go west?"

"Maybe ten miles. The last few miles will be thick jungle."

"You'll need GPS," Johnson said. "It's impossible not to get lost in the jungle. It's like a house of mirrors."

"If we're being chased, that may work for us as well as against us," I said. I turned to Jacinta. "What is your friend's name?"

"Lars. Lars Forsberg."

"He's not Peruvian?"

"No. He's Swedish. But he's been in the jungle for more than twenty years, so he might as well be Peruvian."

"We can trust him?" I asked.

"I would trust him with my life."

"Would you trust him with *our* lives?" Zeus asked.

Jacinta looked like she might be offended. "Do you think I would send you if I didn't?"

"He didn't mean anything by that," Johnson said. "So, Michael, your team will radio us when you're clear. We'll arrange for the helicopter."

"What if you're not done with your mission?" I asked.

"If we don't answer, you might have to hide out at the lodge for a little while," Johnson said. "Remember, Jaime will be there. We'll be in contact with him, so he'll know what's going on." He looked around. "Anything else?"

Cristiano raised his hand. "I ask one thing. If we are captured, you will kill me immediately."

"No one is killing you," I said. "Why would you say that?"

"Sovereign Amash will most definitely kill me. There is nothing the sovereign hates more than traitors. He will kill me, but only after he makes an example of me. He will make me suffer so terribly that his men will never think of betraying him." He looked around at all of us. "I will go with you, and I will risk my life for you, but I will not let the sovereign humiliate and torture me and kill me like he did my friends."

We were all quiet for a moment. Then Johnson said, "We have cyanide capsules. I'll give you one. If it comes to that, you can do it yourself."

Cristiano nodded. "Okay. . . ." The room fell into silence.

Finally I said, "We should pack."

"Let's get to it," Johnson said.

We walked out to the garage. Jaime unlocked a double-bolted door at the back of the garage. Cibor turned on the lights, and we followed him inside. The room was a huge gun locker. There were all sorts of weapons—rifles, pistols, shotguns, and machine guns. On one side were boxes of land mines, grenades, and C4 explosives.

Our team consisted of seven of us—me, Ian, Ostin, McKenna, Cristiano, Zeus, and Nichelle.

Cibor gave us backpacks made of durable green-and-brown camouflage fabric. We also picked through a bin of camouflage clothing.

"We will need machetes," Cristiano said. "The jungle is heavy."

"How many?" Jaime asked.

"Two will be enough."

Jaime handed two green-handled machetes to Cristiano.

"Gracias," he said.

Cibor and Jaime oversaw the packing of the rest of the munitions, while I filled one of the packs with energy bars and water. The water made the pack too heavy.

"Is the water in the cave clean?" I asked.

"I have drunk the water," Cristiano said. "I did not get sick."

"Then we'll just bring two bottles each," I said. "Three for McKenna."

"That will only last us one day," Zeus said.

"If we're not out of there in a day, we'll have much bigger problems than thirst," I said.

As Cibor and Ostin were going through each pack, Johnson put his hand on my shoulder.

"Hey, Michael, do you have a second?"

"Of course."

"Let's go back inside."

I followed him back into the house to a vacant bedroom. Johnson's expression was grave.

"I have a difficult but vital question for you. If faced with the opportunity, would you kill Jack?"

I didn't answer but just looked into his eyes.

He lightly exhaled. "That's what I was afraid of. You're not sure. In times of violence, hesitancy is the surest way to get yourself killed. You need to make that decision now, before you're faced with that reality. You wouldn't bring down the copter with him on it, so I'm thinking you won't."

"If Jack fights us, we'll fight back."

Johnson's expression remained grim. "That's not good enough. That means you're giving him the chance to strike first. That might be all the time he needs to kill you."

I took a deep breath. "This is a demon's decision."

"It may be, but it's yours to make. Let me make it easier for you. As you said earlier, you are loyal. To a fault. But, like Cristiano said, it can be a weakness. In this case, it's also what is causing you to question what you should do with Jack. If it comes down to a choice between the Chasqui and Ostin, or Taylor, who would you choose?"

"I'd choose the latter."

"Of course you would. That's why you need to make that decision now. When you see Jack, you must strike first."

"I'm not going to kill Jack without giving him a chance to come back."

"That's your call. Just remember that you're risking your life and your friends' lives. That's the reality of war—kill or be killed." He looked at me for a moment, then said, "I don't want to see Jack die either. I came down here to *save* him. But he's made a choice, so now you have to as well." He breathed out heavily. "It's not fair, but it's what it is. Just think about it."

"I will."

"I know you'll do the right thing." He slapped me on the arm. "Let's finish packing."

We walked back out to the garage. We had filled the packs about as full as we could when Johnson said, "Michael, don't forget this."

He handed me a GPS tracker. "You're going to need this. The jungle is as dangerous as the Chasqui."

"I'll give it to Ostin," I said. "He can be our navigator."

"And don't forget this." He brought out the black case my father had sent with us. The RADD. "Did your father show you how it works?"

"No."

"I can show you." Johnson opened the case, revealing the drone and several remotes.

"Hey, Ostin," I shouted. "Come here."

He walked over. "What's up?"

"Johnson's going to show us how the RADD works."

"It looks simple."

"Everything looks simple to you," I said.

"It's pretty basic," Johnson said. "Have you ever flown a drone?"

"We both have," I said.

"Good." He took one of the remotes from the box. "So what's

different about these controls is this meter right here." He held out a small black control that looked like a calculator with multiple screens. "When the drone detects a RESAT, you'll hear a series of three short beeps. Then this blue diode here will light and stay on as long as the RESAT waves are detected.

"This first number reads how far away you are from the originating signal, no matter what power the RESAT is set to."

"That's in meters?" Ostin asked.

Johnson nodded. "It reads in meters." He pointed to a round screen below, which looked like a radar screen. "This screen will show the distance and relation of the signal to the drone."

"Just like a radar," I said.

"Exactly like a radar. This second number is the level the RESAT is set at. This third number is your drone's distance from the controller. Remember, the drone is measuring the signal's distance from itself, so if the RESAT is a half mile away from the drone, and the drone is two miles from you, you'll need to combine those distances."

"How far away can it pick up a signal?" I asked.

"Up to a mile away. But the problem you're facing is the cave. It's going to obstruct the intensity of the waves."

"How much?" Ostin asked.

"We don't know, since the depth of the cave and the thickness of the cave walls vary. But remember, the main purpose of the RADD is to locate your friends. Where there are RESATs, there will be electrics."

"What's the flying range on the drone?" Ostin asked.

"Six miles."

Johnson looked over at our backpacks on the ground. "Looks like they're done here. You'd better get some rest. Morning will be here soon enough."

As we walked back into the house, Cassy walked up to me. "Michael, could I talk to you for a minute?"

This was beginning to be a thing. "Of course."

"In private?"

"Sure."

She took my hand and led me into one of the empty rooms. She shut the door behind us.

"What's up?" I asked.

"Before you left, I just wanted to tell you to be careful."

"Thank you. You be careful too."

"Our situation isn't as dangerous as yours. You're going into the mouth of the devil. Literally." She just looked into my eyes for a moment; then she leaned in and kissed me.

"Cassy . . ."

"I know. I'm sorry. I just figured it would be better to ask forgiveness than permission. I've just always wanted to do that. I want you to save Taylor. But . . ."

"But what?"

She hesitated for a moment, then said, "If something happens to one of us, I don't want to regret not ever doing that."

"I'm coming back. With Taylor."

"I hope so," she said.

"What about Jax?"

"Jax is a good man. But I'm still just getting to know him. You and me . . . we have history, you know?"

I nodded. "I know."

"Good luck, Michael." She started to turn to leave, then stopped. "And thank you for not getting mad at me for doing that. And please don't tell Taylor. She already doesn't trust me."

"You know she can read minds."

"Oh. I didn't think about that." She suddenly grinned. "Then don't think about it." She winked at me, then walked back to her room.

19

Splitting Up

Everyone got up the next morning before the sun. Again, I didn't sleep well. Considering what was ahead, I guess that's not surprising. It wasn't the first time I wondered if it would be the last day of my life. I know that sounds dramatic, but death is pretty dramatic. And then there was the nightmare I had. It was about as pleasant as one of Taylor's. I dreamed of Taylor and Tara in cages while Jack was hitting the bars with a sparking cattle prod and laughing. I got so fired up that my electricity burned the sheet I was on.

I pulled on my pants, then woke up Ostin, who, I swear, can sleep through anything. He was talking in his sleep about something I couldn't understand, which wasn't a whole lot different from when he was awake.

The ranch staff had made picarones for breakfast—a kind of Peruvian doughnut—and sliced mangoes with sweet cream. My stomach was unsettled, but I ate anyway. It was the last normal meal we would have for a while. I drank some Coke to settle my stomach, then got my backpack and carried it outside with everyone else.

Everyone met us as we gathered at the van. Cassy was holding Jax's hand. She smiled at me, but it was a sad smile.

"Do we have everyone?" I asked. "Jaime, Ian, Ostin, McKenna, Cristiano, Zeus, Nichelle. All here."

"Not everyone," Quentin said. He walked up and hugged me. "I wish I were going with you."

"Me too. But you're where you need to be."

"I know. I just hate splitting up the team."

"It won't be for long."

He nodded. "Be safe, brother."

"You too," I said. "Save Arequipa."

"You just bring everyone back."

As Quentin walked away, Tessa came up to me.

"Last night I couldn't stop thinking about the first time we met in the jungle."

I smiled. "That was a ride."

"If you see any Amacarra, tell them Hung fa says '*Ni hau.*'"

"I'll be sure to do that."

Her eyes welled up. She wiped a tear from her cheek, then said, "I told myself I wasn't going to do that."

"You've gotten sentimental on me?"

She grinned. "No. It's just allergies."

I grinned. "Right."

"I know, I just hate goodbyes . . . and I just had this feeling. . . ."

"What?"

"It's nothing," she said. "I'll tell you when we're all back." We hugged. While I was still holding her, she said into my ear, "Be safe, Michael. I don't want a world without you in it."

"I don't want a world without you in it too," I said.

As we parted, she wiped her eyes again, then stepped back. "Ciao."

"*Hasta luego*," I said. "I'll see you soon."

"Let's go, amigo," Cibor said. "We're burning daylight."

"I'm coming." I glanced over at Cassy one more time. She was looking at me. She touched two fingers to her lips. I mouthed a goodbye, then got into the van.

"Let's do this," I said.

I was lost in thought as Cibor drove us through the still-quiet country streets into Puerto. As we neared the town, Jaime gave Cibor directions to his friend's place of business.

"There is a big sign that says 'Amazing Amazon River Tours.'"

"What's your friend's name?" I asked Jaime.

"Kale," he said. "Like the leafy vegetable."

"How much does he know about us?"

"He knows that we are enemies of the Elgen. I've known Kale for many years. He's been running the river since he was a small boy. His father had one of his boats sunk by the Elgen when he went too far upriver to fish, so his hatred of them runs deep."

"That's kind of a pattern with these guys."

"They're not very good neighbors."

"How much does he know about the Chasqui?"

"To him there is little difference between the Elgen and the Chasqui. But he knows that the Chasqui are drug smugglers. He keeps his distance."

"What did you tell him about our mission?"

"He knows that he is taking me to the lodge. He has been ferrying foreigners there all week, so he has no reason to suspect anything. I told him I was bringing my American friends with me and asked him to take you a few kilometers downriver past the lodge. I told him you are from a university, and you are studying the plants and animals. As long as we do not get too close to the Starxource plant, he is fine. He will not go near the plant."

"Can you blame him?"

"No. Not at all."

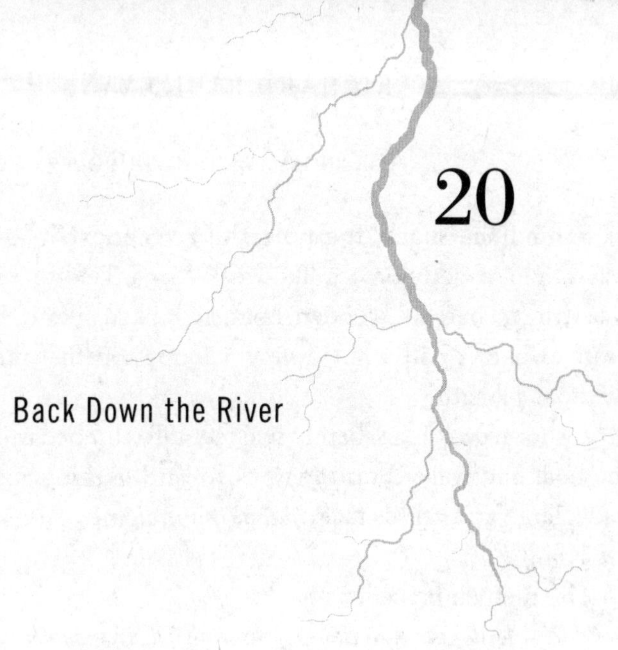

20

Back Down the River

Puerto was awakening when we arrived, the morning twilight growing in brightness before the sun's near appearance. At Jaime's direction, Cibor pulled the van up next to a white stucco wall about thirty feet from a boat dock.

We climbed out of the van, then went to the back to grab our packs. Once we had everything, I walked up to Cibor at the driver's window.

"We're ready," I said.

"All right," Cibor said. "I'll be off. *Vaya con Dios*."

"You too," I replied.

"Quede con Dios," Jaime said behind me.

Cibor saluted, then pulled off into the now heavy traffic. I wondered if I would ever see him again.

"This way," Jaime said.

We carried our packs to a thatch-roofed wooden shack with a hand-painted sign that read:

AMAZING AMAZON RIVER TOURS

Behind the shack, the powerful river moved slowly. The water was a light, muddy brown like weak cocoa. Tied to a wood-slat dock was a long, narrow wooden boat. It looked like it had seen many years of use. It had a faded vinyl canopy top that ran two-thirds of the boat's length.

A short squat man, barely five feet tall, climbed out of the back of the boat and walked up the dock toward us, his arms extended. He had a large grin on his face. *"Jaime, mi amigo."*

"Amigo!"

The men embraced.

"Ha sido demasiado tiempo, mi amigo. Otra emocionante aventura?"

"Espero que no."

"Simplemente no vayas demasiado río arriba. Cuanto tiempo estarás?"

"No lo sabemos con seguridad. Hablaremos por radio cuando podamos. Recibiste comida para el almuerzo?"

"Sí. La tengo en la caja. Y la hielera tiene bebidas."

"Gracias."

"Podemos irnos de inmediato. Haz que tus amigos pongan tus cosas en la parte trasera del bote."

"En este barco, aquí?"

"Sí."

Jaime turned back to us. "This is the boat we will be going in. Put all your things inside. We will leave shortly."

We carried our packs down the plank walkway to the dock, except for Zeus, who stayed on the road looking down at all the water. After we'd put our things in, I walked back up to the road.

"Does it still make you nervous being around the water?" I asked.

"Always," he said. "Do you remember as a kid playing that the floor was lava?"

I smiled. "Yes."

"Same thing. Except to me, it's real."

"I'll carry your pack," I said. Zeus and I got a gallon bottle filled with mango and passion fruit juice and some plastic cups from a street vendor and brought them down to the boat. We got in, then poured cups of the juice for everyone. The boat's benches ran along the sides of the boat, so we'd laid our packs in the middle.

Kale loaded another bright red jerry can of gasoline on board, then started the motor. The smell of exhaust mixed with the gasoline fumes and the fresh smells of the jungle. Kale untied the rope holding us to the dock, then revved the outboard motor, pulling us out into the northeastern flow of the river. Within minutes the city was behind us as we sailed out into the jungle.

After we were alone, Kale turned on a cassette player with Peruvian folk music. It was almost tempting to believe that we were on a leisurely river cruise. I missed having Taylor next to me.

The boat moved quickly through the wakening jungle, the brown water splashing against the side of the boat, the cool air blowing through our hair. The steady sound of the outboard motor soothed my mind. I thought of the first time I went up this river to save my mother. I had hardened since then. I suppose we all had.

PART TEN

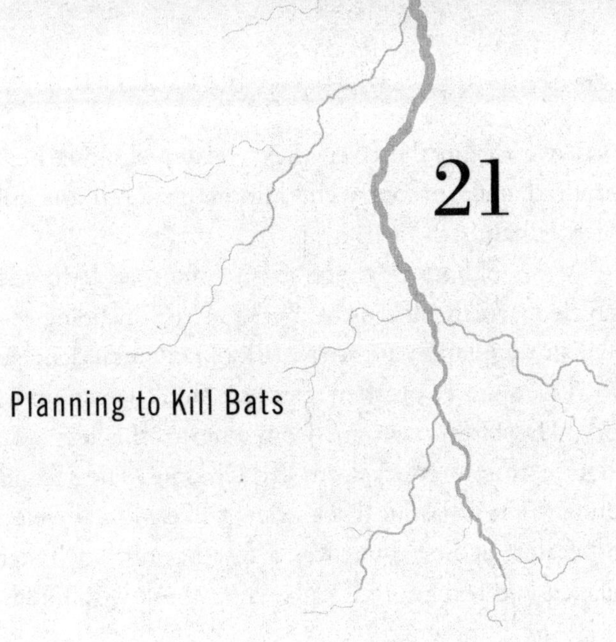

21

Planning to Kill Bats

After dropping Michael and the others off in Puerto Maldonado, Cibor returned to the hacienda to meet with Alpha Team and plan their attack on the Chasqui's cargo of electrified bats. When he arrived, Johnson, Jacinta, Tessa, Quentin, Cassy, and Jax, were sitting outside the kitchen drinking coffee. There was a large highway map of southern Peru spread out across the table.

"The mighty chauffeur returns," Johnson said as Cibor walked in.

"Thank you for that new title. Where are we?"

"Just waiting for you to get back to go over our plan. Gather in, everyone."

Everyone congregated around the table.

"This is where we are," Johnson said, drawing an *X* on the map. "From Puerto to Arequipa is roughly eight hundred thirty kilometers, that's about five hundred miles for us Americans. Once they have loaded up from the river, they will travel along highway 30C for a hundred and seventy-eight kilometers until the highway forks in Puente Inambari.

"We could attack there, except the road before the fork is more traveled, which puts us at a greater risk of being seen and puts the civilian population at greater risk of collateral damage.

"There are two other reasons I think we should attack after the fork. The farther we are from Puerto, the less we need to worry about a counterattack from the Chasqui. The second factor is more human. The Chasqui truck drivers, like most travelers, will be much more alert at first, but after a few hours they'll start getting more relaxed and less aware. That's why I think we should attack after the fork. Any comments?"

"I concur," Jax said. "We don't want to fight the Chasqui again with only half our forces. It was overwhelming last time."

"That's for sure," Quentin said. "We've got Cassy, but Tessa's and my powers aren't exactly lethal."

"Okay," Johnson said. "We're in agreement. So once the Chasqui reach Puente Inambari, they have two options. A, they continue on 30C, which would add an hour and forty minutes to their drive, or B, they take the shorter route onto highway 34B.

"I believe that's the road they'll take. If we gamble on 34B, our best chance to take them out, with the mountainous terrain and the least traffic," he said, touching his pen to the map, "is anywhere along here. It's approximately a hundred kilometers from the fork to the end of the Andes mountain range.

"Once they're out of the Andes, we'll lose the steep grade Ostin's plan requires, and we'll have to resort to grenade launchers or explosives to stop them."

"What if they do take the longer route?" Cassy asked. "Then what?"

"If they take 30C, our next opportunity to strike will be here," he said, pointing farther south on the map, at the San Antonio de Chuca district. "This will be as a last resort only. It will be a direct, out-in-the-open head-on attack with massive explosives.

"Of course, our escape will be much more difficult, and if we cripple the trucks without taking out their bats, they are still close enough to reach Arequipa."

Jax said, "Let's hope they take 34B."

"Agreed. Once we determine the best place to strike, we'll divide up into two groups. Strikeforce One—consisting of Cassy, Jax, and Tessa—will be positioned ahead of us and higher up the mountainside. If all goes well, Cassy will drop the trucks off the side of the cliff without even being seen.

"Should Strikeforce One fail in its mission, Strikeforce Two—consisting of me, Cibor, Jacinta, and Quentin—will take out the trucks with conventional munitions, blowing the road if we need to. Any questions?"

"When do we leave?" Jax asked.

"We pack up. Then once we hear from Jaime, we'll go. Strikeforce One, I recommend you get some rest. It's going to be a long night. Strikeforce Two, come with me. We'll load up the van with munitions, grenade launchers, and C4. Strikeforce One, you're dismissed."

After Strikeforce Two had completed loading the van, they retired to their individual rooms to rest and await Jaime's call.

PART ELEVEN

22

What Happened to the Lightning God?

I was about to lie down on the boat's long bench to sleep when Jaime slid up next to me.

"Michael. Can I ask you something?"

"Of course."

"They told me that in the final battle of Tuvalu, you were all-powerful. Almost like a god."

"You could say that."

"Do you still have that power?"

"If I did, I would have already brought Tara back and destroyed the Chasqui."

"Why is your power gone?"

I shook my head. "I don't know for sure. The way Ostin explains it, my body is like a capacitor. It can store electricity. In the battle of Hades, I was struck by lightning. I had so much electricity inside me that I became more energy than matter. It gave me the ability to pass through matter, even fly."

"You could fly?"

"For a while."

"That would be nice. How long did it last?"

"After I was struck by lightning, it was a couple of weeks before I could really control my body again. Just in time to help my friends defeat the Elgen.

"Even then, I had to keep my distance, since I would have occasional seizures that would pulse out enough electricity to electrocute someone.

"But I could feel myself becoming less electric every day. It was two months before I was almost back to normal. At least what was normal to me."

"Almost?"

"I still have more electricity than I had before."

Jaime nodded slowly. "That is good. You were dangerous before."

"I have to be more careful now. I can be fatal."

"I hope you don't need to be fatal today." Jaime slapped me on the leg, then went back to where he had been sitting. I lay back down and fell asleep, rocked by the boat's consistent sway.

I woke to the smell of something cooking. I sat up and yawned.

"Welcome back," Nichelle said. "You're just in time for lunch. Hot tamales."

I stretched, cracking my neck. "How did we get hot tamales on a . . ." I looked over at McKenna. "Oh. Right."

"Here's one for you," McKenna said. "Pork tamales criollos." She put it into a napkin and handed it to me. "It's a little hot."

"Thank you."

"You're welcome."

"'*Criollo*' means 'of pure Spanish descent,'" Ostin said.

"And this," Zeus said. Even though it was hot and humid, he was sporting a rain jacket. "Your favorite Peruvian drink, Inca Kola." He handed me a cold bottle.

"Thanks, bro."

After we had all eaten, I sat alone near the bow of the boat just looking out at the passing jungle. There was a consistent light spray of water, which I found refreshing in the hot jungle.

Jaime was in the back of the boat talking to Kale, while Cristiano, Zeus, and Nichelle played cards, and McKenna and Ostin were lying on the packs napping. Ian, like me, just looked out from the boat. At one point he said, "Guys, you should see this."

We all looked over the side of the boat. We couldn't see anything. "See what?" Zeus asked.

"Sorry. It's down fifteen feet. There was a pack of giant sea otters teasing an alligator."

"The big otters don't fear anything in the river," Cristiano said. "We call them '*los lobos*.' The wolves."

This only reinforced my belief that Ian saw a completely different world than the rest of us.

About two hours later Cristiano crouched down next to me. "Michael."

I turned back. "What's up?"

"Look carefully. Do you see that reflection up ahead?"

About a hundred yards in the distance I could see an occasional flash of light. "What is it?"

"It is the first Chasqui sentry. The light you see is the reflection from their camera."

I turned back. "Hey, Ian."

"Yes, sir," Ian said.

"There's something up ahead, about a hundred meters."

"I see it. There're some cameras. And a machine gun. No one is manning it."

"It is one of many," Cristiano said. "There are usually soldiers at the guns."

"There he is," Ian said. "He's watching a soccer game. He's only wearing pants."

Just then Kale said something to Cristiano in Spanish. Cristiano nodded, then turned back.

"What did he say?" I asked.

"He was pointing out the guard too. He knows where all the Chasqui sentries are on the river. He is very nervous around them."

"For good reason," I said.

"Yes. They sank his boat. This is not a place I would like to sink. There are piranha, caimans, and electric eels."

"Hardly the county swimming pool," I said. I looked back at Kale. He looked anxious. "How frequent are these lookouts?" I asked.

"The next sentry is about four kilometers downriver."

"Are there a lot of these sentries?" McKenna asked.

Cristiano nodded. "At least a dozen between Puerto and the Starxource plant. The closer we get to the plant, the closer they are to each other. They all have radios. They report to a central place at the plant."

"What about the cave?"

"The plant communicates with the cave. The cave has its own security on land. Because the plant is close to the river, it patrols the river."

As we neared the sentry, Cristiano looked more nervous. "No one look at him," he said.

Our boat passed quickly in the center of the river.

"What is he doing?" I asked Ian.

"Nothing. He went back to his game."

"You said they have cameras," I said to Cristiano.

"Yes. They monitor every boat. But there are many boats. So they look for boats that are suspicious."

"What makes a boat suspicious?"

"All men, mostly. People who don't look like tourists."

"Will they suspect us?"

"I don't think so. They will probably think this boat is going to the lodge."

"How far are we from the lodge?"

"We are close."

I took the GPS navigator from my backpack. "Ostin, take this."

"The GPS," he said. "Remember the first one they gave us? It was disguised as an iPod."

"That was a long time ago," I said. "Drop a pin at the lodge so we know how to get back."

Ostin began navigating through the device. "No problem."

About twenty minutes later Kale pointed to the south riverbank and said, "There it is."

We looked out. In the distance was a pontoon dock with two other boats, both bearing the makisapa logo. On the front corners of the dock were tall poles, each with a yellow flag imprinted with the lodge's namesake, the makisapa monkey, the design copied from the Nazca Lines. A large banner read:

BIENVENIDOS, AMIGOS OF THE AMAZON RAINFOREST

"I need to call in," Jaime said, taking out the satellite phone. "Johnson, it's Jaime. We are just arriving at the lodge. . . . Nothing. We saw no cargo containers yet. . . . I will report as soon as I do. . . . Thank you. . . . Be careful." He hung up the phone and slid it back into his pack. "They're ready to scout out the area for their mission. All according to plan."

"Of mice and men," Ostin said. "Of mice and men."

PART TWELVE

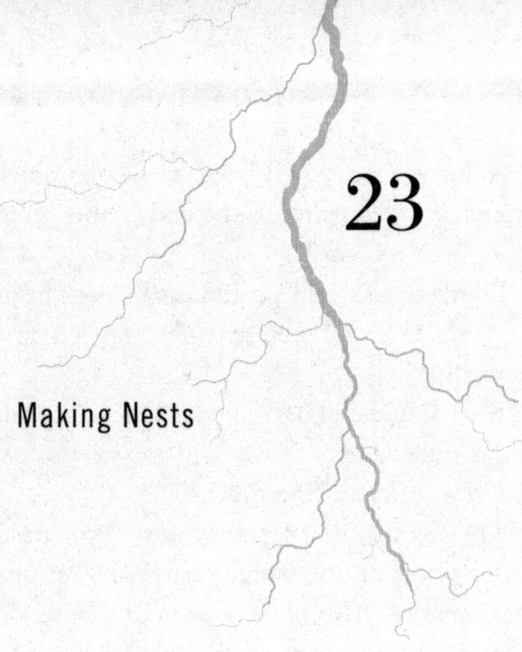

23

Making Nests

It was about three hours after Alpha Team had finished making their plans when Jaime called Johnson to let him know that they had reached the lodge. Alpha Team immediately got into their vehicles and set out to find the ideal location to take out the Chasqui convoy. They found it about three hours south of Puerto.

"This is the place," Johnson said, pulling the heavily fortified van off to the side of the road. "More than twenty miles to the nearest town, a hundred-and-eighty-degree turn with a two-hundred-foot drop-off on one side, and a long enough stretch for three trucks to be together. It's like it was custom-made for us."

Strikeforce One's Hummer pulled up behind the van. Everyone got out of the vehicles.

"What do you think?" Jax asked, walking up to Johnson.

"I think it's perfect. Let's grab some radios and scope it out.

Strikeforce One, you'll want to be stationed where you can guarantee full paralysis up to the end of the kill zone. How far can your power reach, Cassy?"

"With Tessa's help I could easily reach both sides of the kill zone."

"Perfect. So as soon as truck three is in the queue, you freeze them all."

She saluted and barked out, "Freeze the kill zone. Roger that, sir."

Jax nudged her.

Cassy grinned. "Too much?"

Johnson continued. "Jax, you set up a nest high enough that you have a visual on the whole road. We'll set up a nest around the corner. If any of them make it around the bend, Strikeforce Two takes them out, no matter what. Even if it means bringing the whole mountain down on them."

"Jacinta will be waiting in Puente Inambari, near the bridge. That's the fork between the two highways. If we guessed wrong and the Chasqui choose 30C instead of our road, we'll know immediately and we'll reroute.

"If they follow our route, Jacinta will tail them at a distance and keep us updated on their movement. If, for some reason, the last truck stops before the kill zone, she will shoot the trailer from behind with a rocket-propelled grenade."

"What vehicle will she be taking?" Jax asked.

"She'll take our van," Johnson said. He looked up at the sun. "We've got maybe five hours of sunlight. We need to stake out our positions.

"Once the containers hit Puerto Maldonado, they could be here as soon as four hours. Puerto Maldonado is about halfway between the Chasqui's headquarters and where we are, so once Jaime reports seeing the containers from the lodge, we'll have about eight hours."

"How do you want to spend tonight?" Cibor asked.

Johnson looked at his watch. "It's about four now. Even if Jaime called right now, they wouldn't be here until midnight at the earliest. Still, it could be another twenty-four hours. So let's find our positions and set up. Then we'll head back to the hacienda and wait for the call. There's no sense spending the night out in the open."

"With bugs," Tessa said. "Sleeping on dirt."

"Keep your radio on," Johnson said. "We'll meet up as soon as we're done."

Jax turned to Cassy and Tessa. "Let's go, ladies. Strikeforce One is on the move."

They went back to the Hummer for their backpacks. They needed minimal supplies—food and water, binoculars, and a radio. Jax carried two pistols and a sniper rifle.

He pointed to a place on the mountain that jutted out from the surrounding terrain. "I think that little outcrop there might give us the best protection. Let's check it out."

They strapped on their backpacks and hiked up the side of the mountain. The mountain was thick with bushes and trees, and it took them thirty minutes to reach the outcrop.

"What do you think, Cassy?"

"If I can see them, I can freeze them."

"I was hoping you'd say that."

Cassy leaned over and kissed him.

"Come on, Cass," Tessa said. "We're on official business."

"Don't be so uptight," Cassy said.

"We've got work to do."

"I think I know that. Just chill a little."

They laid a thick tarp on the ground and some camouflage netting around the back side of their nest. After they were done, Jax radioed Johnson. "Come in, Johnson. This is the death technician. We are secured and ready."

"Roger, DT. We are still thirty out."

"Roger. We'll just lounge until you call. Over."

"Over."

"Lounge?" Cassy said.

"Come here," Jax said. They began to kiss again.

Tessa groaned. "Really, guys. This is so unprofessional. I mean, get a room."

"Sorry, Tess," Jax said. "It's just been a long time."

"You don't have to stay here," Cassy said.

"I'm not. I'm going down to the Hummer."

Jax drew back from Cassy. "Here, you'd better take the keys." He tossed them to her.

Tessa picked the keys up from the ground, then worked her way back down the hill.

Johnson and his crew had set up about a hundred yards down the road after the road doglegged. They chose an assault position ninety feet above the road, close enough to engage but out of the blast radius of their explosives.

They had carried out all their weapons, C4, and detonation switches from the van. Then Jacinta and Johnson had run wire from their position under the foliage to the road, where they installed three different charges: one designed to take out the trucks, one set to create an avalanche, and a third that would take out the road completely, stopping all possible advancement.

Quentin and Cibor prepared the nest they would operate from, as well as laying out the weapons. Quentin was laying down the artillery when he asked, "Hey, Cibor. What's this thing? Its official name."

"It's a German-built Panzerfaust 3 shoulder-launched, antitank rocket-propelled grenade launcher. We just call it an RPG for short. It can penetrate more than nine hundred millimeters of tank armor, which means it can stop anything."

"Even these trucks."

Cibor nodded. "Like shooting pumpkins with a shotgun."

Quentin smiled. "And I'm carrying C4 explosives strapped to my back."

"Just don't bump them on anything."

Quentin stared at him. "What? You said they were . . ."

Cibor laughed. "I'm kidding. C4 is stable. You can shoot it with a five-hundred-fifty-six round, and it won't go off. It needs a trigger mechanism. That's what's in that other bag."

"How many will it take to blow up a truck?"

"Three to be safe. We need to make sure the bats are killed along with the trucks. It's got a blast radius of about twenty-five meters. That's why we're this far back."

"We've got serious redundancy," Quentin said.

"That we do. If Cassy fails, we've got you to stop the trucks and the RPGs to take them out. If that fails, we blow the trucks with C4. If that fails, we just take out the whole road."

"Cassy won't fail," Quentin said. "Neither will I."

"That's what I'm counting on."

Johnson and Jacinta climbed back up to their nest. "We're wired," Johnson said. "You guys done?"

"We are done, sir," Cibor said.

"All right, then." Johnson lifted his radio to his mouth. "Strikeforce One, this is Strikeforce Two, over."

"Strikeforce Two, what are our orders?"

"Let's go home and get some dinner."

"Still no word from Jaime?"

"Not yet."

"We'll meet you back at the hacienda, over."

PART THIRTEEN

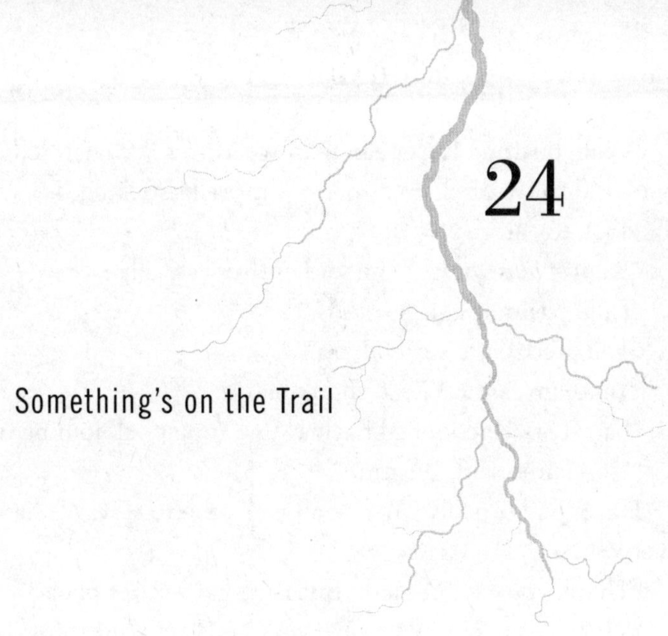

24

Something's on the Trail

We had made better time than we had planned and were nearly a half hour ahead of schedule as the boat pulled up to the Makisapa Lodge's dock. The edge of the lodge's property was lined with palms and broad-leafed banana trees. Past them we could see about a dozen thatch-roofed dwellings, all close together, encircling the main lodge.

Between us and the buildings was a cleared yard with manicured grass. There was Peruvian folk music playing over a PA system, and there were guests happily milling about. On one side of the yard four people were playing badminton.

Kale slowed the boat as he pulled up to the dock.

"Jaime, *amárralo, por favor.*"

"Muy bien," Jaime said, grabbing a yellow vinyl rope. Kale shut off the boat's motor as Jaime lashed the boat to one of the dock's wrought-iron cleats.

A tall, bearded European man wearing a Peruvian fedora and carrying a drink with a small paper umbrella sticking out walked onto the dock toward us.

"Bienvenidos, amigos," he said enthusiastically.

"Hola," Jaime said. *"Gracias."*

"You are Jacinta's friend, no?"

"Yes, I am Jaime." They shook hands.

"I am Lars." He looked back at us. "You are all joining us?"

"No," Jaime said. "Just me."

He smiled broadly. "You're all welcome to stay. We have room for everyone."

"Thank you," Jaime said. "But they have other plans."

"Well, we are happy to have you. Let's get your things." He turned and whistled. "José, come and help Mr. Jaime with his bags."

A young Peruvian boy wearing a Chicago Bulls baseball cap and basketball shorts ran up to the boat.

"I only have a pack," Jaime said.

"José, take Mr. Jaime's pack to his room in the main lodge."

Jaime handed his pack to the frowning young man, who slung it over his shoulders, then walked back toward the lodge.

"Gracias," Jaime said to the boy, then turned back to Lars. "Let me say goodbye to my friends, and I will be right with you."

Jaime walked back to the boat and crouched down next to me. "Good luck, Michael. I will be praying for your success. If you need me, you know how to reach me."

"We'll see you in a few days," I said.

"*Vaya con Dios*." He turned to Kale. "Time to go. Cristiano will know the place."

"Bueno."

Kale started the boat's motor as Jaime untied the rope from the cleat, then threw it into the boat. Kale backed us away from the dock, then pointed the boat back downriver.

"I love badminton," McKenna said. "Maybe we should stop there on the way back for a few days."

Nichelle looked at her. "You're kidding, right?"

McKenna said, "Not kidding. Just wishing."

Cristiano, Ian, and I sat near the front of the boat.

"We're about an hour from our drop-off," I said.

Cristiano nodded. "Yes."

"We'll hike to the Amacarra trail. Then we'll send up the drone."

"What if they're not there?" Ian asked.

"Then we'll hike to the plant."

"We'll be short on water."

"I know of a spring a few miles from the plant," Cristiano said.

"We'll be okay," I said. A few minutes later I asked, "Will we pass another sentry before we get off?"

"No," Cristiano said. "That would not be wise. We will get off a kilometer before the next sentry."

About twenty minutes later Cristiano pointed to a small inlet ahead of us.

"Allí," he said to Kale.

Kale steered the boat toward the shore. Once we'd left the main river, he cut back on power, and the engine putted into the small cove. Tree boughs and vines hung over the water and, in places, rubbed along the boat's canopy. Monkeys and birds screeched wildly at our intrusion.

The shore was overgrown with branches and tree roots that spilled out from the banks over the water, making it hard to access the sloped bank. After a few moments Kale said something to Cristiano, who turned to me.

"The driver wants to know if we can wade into shore."

"Zeus can't go into water," I said. "We need to get off on dry land."

"Sorry, I forgot." Cristiano turned and told Kale, who just nodded, his eyes set on the shoreline.

We putted along through the cove until we found a place where we could drive the boat into the shore. Kale said something. Then Cristiano said to us, "Hold on, everyone."

Kale revved the engine, and the bow of the boat ground ashore. After grabbing the docking rope, Cristiano and I jumped off the boat's bow onto the marshy bank. Above us a flock of brightly colored macaws took flight. Kale gunned the outboard a bit more while we pulled the boat up onto the bank.

"Much appreciated," Zeus said, stepping off the bow onto dry ground.

We took all the packs and the RADD case off the boat and drank our fill of water. Then Cristiano and I helped everyone else off the boat.

After we were all off, I waved to Kale. *"Gracias."*

"Gracias, señor."

Cristiano and I pushed the boat back out into the river. Kale fired up his outboard motor and spun the boat around. He casually waved at us, then drove off. I felt as stranded as we were.

"Let's get into our camouflage," I said.

We changed into our camouflage clothing. Then, after Ostin had set our coordinates, we followed Cristiano into the jungle.

Our path through the jungle quickly turned dark, a roof of thick branches always above our heads, leaving us in enough shadow that the faint glow of our skin could be seen. Zeus and Cristiano carried the machetes and cleared the thicker foliage, while Ostin tracked our location. I carried both my pack and the RADD case.

It took us nearly an hour before we reached the Amacarra trail, which I would have missed without Cristiano.

"This is it," he said.

"This is what?" Zeus said.

"The Amacarra trail."

"Not much of a trail," Nichelle said.

"It is narrow. The Amacarra move in a single file, so the trail remains hidden from most eyes. But, as you can see, it is cleared of all heavy branches and bushes. And there are stones in marshy places."

"Let's go," I said. We moved much faster on the trail. We had gone about a mile when we came to a place where there was a small clearing in the canopy.

"We'll rest for a minute," I said. "Let's put up the RADD."

Everyone sat down on their packs and took out their water. We were all dripping from sweat and the jungle's dense humidity. Ostin and I set up the drone while Cristiano looked on.

"I'm curious to see if it works," Ostin said.

"If they're using RESATs, it will work," I said.

"It's the thickness of the cave walls I worry about," Ostin said.

I took the drone's controls, put on the goggles, and then sent the drone straight up through the clearing above us. I could see us getting smaller as the drone climbed. I wanted to take it high enough that the Chasqui couldn't see or hear it.

"I'm headed northeast," I said.

"Just stay parallel to the river," Cristiano said.

I had only flown two miles when the remote in my hand began to beep. A blue diode flashed.

"We've got RESATs," Ostin said.

"Let's see how far." I had flown the drone another seven thousand meters when an orange light flashed quickly, went steady, and then began flashing again.

"That's the source. Go back to it."

I reversed the drone's course until the orange light was steady again.

"There," Ostin said. "That's the RESAT."

"That's the cave," Cristiano said.

Ostin looked over the coordinates, then logged it into his GPS monitor.

"It's seven kilometers."

I looked at my watch. "At this rate we'll be at the cave a half hour earlier than we planned. Which side of the cave is the water entrance?" I asked.

"It is farther south. This trail runs south of the cave, so we will be close."

I pushed the home button on the drone, and it switched to autopilot. It was only a few minutes before it was above us again and slowly descending. We put the drone back into the case. I hid the case in some bushes.

"Aren't you taking the drone?" Zeus asked.

"We don't need it anymore."

Zeus looked disappointed. "It's a nice drone."

"I'll get you one when we get back."

We had hiked another ten minutes when Ian said, "Hold up, everyone."

"What is it?" I asked.

"There's something on the trail." He turned to me. "It looks like bodies."

"Chasqui?"

"Hold on." He shook his head. "It might be. The boots look military. It's hard to see. There are at least a dozen vultures around them."

"Vultures eat people?" McKenna asked.

"Of course," Nichelle said. "We're just meat."

"The king vulture and the yellow-headed vulture are Amazon canopy dwellers," Ostin said. "And indiscriminate carrion eaters."

"I liked the way I said it better," Nichelle said.

"See if you can tell who they are," I said to Ian.

Ian just stared for a moment, then said, "There are three men. At least what is left of them. Black uniforms, utility belts. Their guns are on the ground, so they must have had them out. . . . Wait. . . . Okay, I see them." He turned to me. "Chasqui patches."

"Dead Chasqui soldiers on the secret trail." I turned to Cristiano. "I thought you said the Chasqui didn't know about this trail."

"They didn't."

"Well, they do now."

"Maybe they just found it. Maybe that is why they are dead."

"Who killed them?"

"I think the Amacarra. Or maybe the Chasqui."

"Why would the Chasqui kill their own men?"

"The Chasqui kill their own men all the time. If they were trying to desert the Chasqui, the loyal guards would hunt them down and execute them by firing squad. I have seen it many times."

"It's simple enough to tell," Ostin said. "Do you see bullet holes or darts? The blowgun darts are made of wood, with fur or feathers on the end."

Ian kept looking. "Yes. I see one. Three. Six darts."

"I told you the Amacarra do not like the Chasqui," Cristiano said.

"You're sure they're dead?" I asked Ian.

He looked at me darkly. "If not, we won't have to worry about them."

"Why is that?"

"The birds ate their eyes out."

"I'm going to be sick," McKenna said.

"Let's check them out," I said. "Keep going."

We'd hiked about two hundred more meters when we came to the flock of birds, squawking, pecking, and jostling each other for position over the dead men. It reminded me of a Black Friday sale at Walmart. They flew off at our arrival.

Cristiano walked up to one of the corpses and pushed it over with his foot. There were two darts in its back.

"I'm guessing the poison is from the poison dart frog," Ostin said.

"They are more likely to use the poison from the curare plant," Cristiano said.

"Yes, but these men are still on the trail. The curare poison from the *chondrodendron tomentosum* can take ten to fifteen minutes to kill. They would have tried to make it back to the cave."

"What's to say they're not going to shoot us right now?" Nichelle said, looking around.

"I don't see anyone around," Ian said. "But look at these foot tracks."

"One was barefoot," Ostin said. "The Chasqui had boots."

"Look how deep they are. He was running."

"So the Chasqui were chasing someone barefoot," Zeus said.

"It must have been an Amacarra native," I said.

"Whoever they were chasing couldn't have shot them in the back," Ostin said. "The guards must have run into an ambush."

"What are the Amacarra doing this close to the Chasqui?" I asked. "I thought they hated them."

"They were always keeping an eye on us," Cristiano said. "We were their unwelcome neighbor."

"How long have these bodies been here?" I asked Ostin.

Ostin looked at the corpses. Then he knelt down and dipped his finger into a black bottle-cap-sized spot of blood that had fallen onto a leaf.

"What are you doing?" McKenna asked.

"It's still tacky. We're in around eighty-seven percent humidity, so I'm guessing this happened about eight hours ago."

"Early morning," I said.

Ostin nodded. "Yes."

I turned to Cristiano. "Will the Chasqui be looking for them?"

"Yes, though probably because they thought they were deserting. If it was a morning patrol, they would have been expected back around two."

"That would be three or four hours ago," I said. "This is an opportunity we were hoping for. Those guys are about our size. We can put on their uniforms. Cristiano, put your uniform back on."

We stripped the bodies, then went through the pockets. We didn't find much—a magnetic key, some coins, and a bag of chewing tobacco.

Then Ostin, Zeus, and I dressed in the uniforms. Zeus was taller than the tallest guard, so his pants were about an inch above his ankles, but they still fit at his waist. Ostin and I were pretty close fits. We dragged the bodies off the trail, then walked back out.

"Ian, keep a watch for Chasqui patrols."

"What about the Amacarra?" Nichelle asked.

"Them too," I said.

About a hundred yards from where we found the bodies, we came to where the Chasqui had started chase. We hiked about another forty minutes, the jungle getting darker with each passing minute. Suddenly Cristiano said, "There it is up ahead. The water to the cave."

The stream of water was only a couple of feet wide. It snaked its way as a shallow creek toward some limestone jutting up from the ground, then disappeared into a crevice in the rock. As we got closer, we could hear the sound of the waterfall echoing in the cavern below.

"There is the entrance," Cristiano said.

I walked up to the crevice and put my hand over the opening. "I don't feel RESAT."

"Neither do I," Ian said.

"Can you see anything inside there?" I asked.

Ian shook his head. "Just a big pool of water."

"No crocodiles?" Nichelle asked.

"No crocodiles. The piranha must have eaten them."

"What?"

"I was joking," he said.

"The hole is bigger than it was," Cristiano said.

"There's a reason for that," Ostin said. "As the Amazon rainwater becomes higher in nitric and sulfuric acids, it reacts adversely with the limestone's calcite by dissolving it."

"In other words, acid rain is our friend," Nichelle said.

"Another six inches, and we could all fit through that hole," I said. "Who has the pickax?"

"I have it," Zeus said. He took it out of his backpack, then took a swing at the rock. The blow fractured off only a small chunk, but it was loud enough to be heard over the jungle's cacophony. He lifted the ax again.

"Hold up," I said. "That's too loud. They might hear us."

"It's better than an explosive," Zeus said.

"If you're trying to be quiet, pretty much everything's better than an explosive," I said. I turned to Ostin. "What's the melting point of limestone?"

"I should have thought of that. Limestone is a sedimentary rock. It melts into magma at 1,157 degrees to 2,192 degrees Fahrenheit." He turned to McKenna. "You could melt this."

"Okay." She knelt down next to the hole. "Where?"

"We just need to make a space big enough to crawl through," I said. "Maybe take out these two sections on the sides."

She put her hands into the water and grabbed the two surfaces. The water around her hands began to boil, then flashed to steam until a large column of it rose up to the canopy. The rock turned orange-red like lava, then sloughed off, falling into the hole. Within a couple of minutes she had melted a hole nearly two and a half feet in diameter.

"That's big enough," I said.

McKenna let out a deep breath. The water was still steaming as it cooled the rock.

"Can someone get her some water?" Ostin asked.

Nichelle took a water bottle from her pack and handed it to McKenna. McKenna downed the entire bottle. When she was done, Ostin dipped the empty bottle into the stream, then poured it over McKenna's head.

McKenna let out a loud sigh. "Thank you."

"We'll let that rock cool down a bit more," I said.

"So, if this cave is based on the human digestive system," Nichelle asked, "what part of the anatomy is this hole?"

"That would be the rectum," Ostin said.

"The what?"

"It's the butt," Zeus said.

"Great," Nichelle said. "We're climbing in through the cave's butt."

"Michael," Zeus said. "Where do you want me?"

"We need you to guard this entrance while we're in there."

"I can help," Nichelle said. "I don't know what good I'll be to you down there, but I can help Zeus keep an eye out. Magnify his lightning if needs be."

"I'll hang with Nichelle," Zeus said.

"Cool," she said.

I reached into the water. The stone was still warm but cool enough to touch. It was about a half hour before sunset, and the cavern below was pitch-black.

"Let's go, Cristiano," I said. "Show us the way."

"Sure thing, boss." Fully dressed, he sat on the rock with his feet in the hole. He started letting himself down by his arms, then dropped down into the pool. We heard a loud splash.

"How far a drop is that?" Nichelle asked.

"Around eight feet," Ian said.

"How will they get back up?"

"We're going to have to climb out," I said. I took a rope out of my pack. I wrapped it three times around the trunk of a rosewood tree, tied it with a knot, and then handed the rope to Zeus. "Throw this in after we're down."

Ostin looked down into the abyss of the cave. "I don't like jumping into something I can't see."

"I can give you some light," McKenna said. She reached her hand into the hole and lit up the cavern. We could see Cristiano below treading water.

"Come on down," he shouted, his voice echoing in the cavern. "It is not easy to swim in a Chasqui uniform and boots."

Ostin put his legs into the hole and dropped down into the water. He was followed by Ian, McKenna, then me. McKenna had illuminated the entire cavern, which was larger than it looked from above—about the size of my parents' living room at home. The water was cool and comfortable.

Zeus and Nichelle leaned over the opening and looked down at us.

"How's the rectum?" Nichelle asked.

"Wet," I said.

"I'm dropping down the packs," Zeus said.

He dropped the first pack into the water. I caught it, and it initially pulled me under. I swam back up, struggling with the weight.

"It's heavier than I thought."

"That's the pack with grenades," he said.

"I can tell," I said, struggling to stay afloat.

"Here's the second one," Zeus said. "It's water for McKenna and C4. It weighs almost as much as the first pack."

"It won't in water," Ostin said. "The water will equalize, and the C4 is foamed, so it floats."

"Whatever," Zeus said. He dropped the second pack. Ostin was right, of course. It sank into the water, then popped back up. Ostin grabbed the pack.

"Where to?" I asked Cristiano.

"The entrance is over here."

"Off to the colon," Nichelle said from above.

"Thanks, Nichelle," I said.

"I see it," Ian said. "It's about five feet down. It leads to another chamber."

"That is the way into the cave," Cristiano said. "Once you swim through it, you go up into an air pocket. The tunnel into the cave is on the opposite wall. It only has a foot of water in it. We will have to crawl through it."

"How long is the tunnel?" McKenna asked.

"About fifty yards. The last twenty feet should be dry. We must be careful once we reach the tunnel entrance," Cristiano said. "There should not be anyone there, but it is possible."

"Ian will let us know if anyone is around," I said.

We took turns swimming down through the passage, then popping up on the other side. It was nearly pitch-black. The only light came from our skin and the dim glow from the cavern we'd just come from.

Cristiano swam to the tunnel and crawled in. We followed him, single file, with Cristiano, me, and Ian in front, then Ostin and McKenna. The tunnel was about three feet in diameter with sand in the bottom, easy enough to crawl through.

McKenna kept the tunnel lit until we were all in. Then she cut her light back just enough so we could still see where we were going.

"Can they see her light?" I asked Cristiano.

"There is a bend in the tunnel near the end, so we are okay until then."

We crawled for about ten minutes more before the water receded and we came to a slight jog in the tunnel.

"Tell McKenna no light," I said to Ian. "Pass it back." A moment later the tunnel went dark. "Ian, you'll need to guide us," I said. "Come ahead of me."

Ian crawled around and ahead of me but was still behind Cristiano, who had spent enough time in the tunnel to know where he was. As we progressed, the tunnel increased in diameter until it was tall enough for us to walk, stooped at first, then completely upright.

"Watch your head," Ian warned. "There are small stalagmites."

I passed the message back.

"Tell Ian they're stalactites," Ostin said from behind me. "Stalagmites are on the ground. You'd have to be walking on your hands."

I didn't pass along his message. Before long we reached the end of the tunnel and climbed out into the larger cave.

"How do we find our way back to this tunnel?" I whispered.

"There is only one other tunnel down here," Cristiano said. "And it only goes ten meters." He reached over and touched the stone wall next to the tunnel. "I marked this one."

In the light of my own glow, I could see where he had carved a dinner-plate-sized letter C.

"Which way?" I asked Cristiano.

"Right will lead us up to the supply and utility room."

"Where does the left path go?"

"It ends after twenty meters. I went there once, and I could hear the guards in the prison, so that is what is behind the walls. Maybe McKenna could melt through them."

"They'd see us on their cameras and attack," I said. "We'll stick to the original plan. Up to the command center."

As we walked through the cave, the only sound was the squish-squash of our water-filled boots. We could see the supply room door from a distance, since light came from the space underneath it.

"Is anyone inside?" I asked Ian.

"It's vacant," he said.

I opened the door. The room was brightly lit by fluorescent lighting. It was large, filled with rows of metal shelving stacked with plastic bins. Against one wall there were two five-thousand-gallon stainless steel tanks. We could hear the constant sound of air being pushed through the vents.

"That must be the ventilation," I said to Cristiano.

Cristiano nodded. "The utility room is on the other side of the supply room. There is a large cooling unit and many filters. The electricity and air come in from the outside vents."

I stepped back out into the tunnel.

"Where is the command center?"

"It is just ahead. It is that door."

There was a single metal door about thirty feet in front of us.

"Ian, can you see what's inside?"

"Yes. There are two guards."

"Are they armed?"

"No."

"That's surprising," I said.

"Not so much. There are at least fifty armed guards in the room in front of them, so they probably don't see any threat."

We walked another twenty feet to the control room's back metal door.

I grabbed the knob and tried to turn it. "It's locked," I whispered.

"Here," Ostin said, taking from his pocket one of the magnetic keys we'd taken from the guards on the trail. "Try the key."

I held the key up to the door. The light turned red. "It's not for this."

"I could melt the lock," McKenna said.

"Or we could blow it with the C4," Ian suggested.

"I have a better idea." I knocked on the door.

Cristiano's eyes grew wide. "What are you doing?"

Suddenly the doorknob turned. Then the door opened. A large Peruvian guard stood in the entrance. From the look on his face, I doubted that this door was ever used.

"Qué desea?"

I was still holding the other side of the doorknob, and I pulsed. He yelped in pain before hitting the floor. His partner was looking at us. I pulsed again, slamming him against his console. The row of monitors above the console briefly flickered, then came back online. I stepped into the room. "Tie them up."

"With what?" Cristiano said. It was a good point. We didn't have any handcuffs, and I'd left our only rope with Zeus.

"Find something," I said.

While Ian and Cristiano dragged the man away from the console, I checked the front door of the room and locked it, then looked back at the first man I had shocked. He was still lying on his back, unconscious.

"You hit him with a lot," Ostin said.

"I think he hit his head on the wall," I said.

There were no windows in the control room, just rows of screens. It was exactly as I'd hoped. We could see everything, and no one could see us.

Cristiano and McKenna went back out to the supply room to find something to tie them up with. They returned with four rolls of duct tape. We put tape over the guards' mouths and eyes, wrapping it around their heads until they looked like mummies swaddled in silver gauze. We taped their hands behind their backs and their legs together, then dragged them to the corner of the room.

"You just knocked on the door," Ian said with a chuckle, as if he'd just gotten the joke.

"It usually works," I said. I squatted down next to the two guards, both of whom were now conscious. Then I put my hands on their shoulders. "I want you to feel something." I shocked the two men hard enough that their bodies strained at their bonds. "That was a small jolt. If you make a sound, if you try to escape, I will electrocute you. Nod if you understand."

Only one of them nodded. I put my hand on the other and was about to pulse again when Cristiano said, "I think this one does not speak English." He translated what I had said to the man, and the guard nodded emphatically.

"All right," I said. "Put tape over their ears too. I don't want them hearing anything either."

McKenna put a strip of tape over their ears, then wrapped tape around their heads a few more times.

There were three large screens above us, with nine video images on each screen. Two monitors were of night-vision cameras outside the facility. The other showed various rooms around the cave, including the barracks, where most of the guards were sitting on their cots in various stages of undress.

What I was looking for was Taylor and Tara. I was also looking for Jack, figuring he'd be in Chasqui uniform, but taller and whiter than most of them. I didn't see any of them.

"Why isn't the prison showing up on the screens?" I asked. "Ostin, can you figure out the console?"

"Simple enough. Looks like it came from RadioShack." A moment later he looked back at me. "This panel controls water pumps and sewage. The biggest panel controls all the lights around the facility. This panel controls electric locks. And this portion controls ventilation.

"And this panel with the little toggle switches controls the movements of each camera. It looks like there are fifty-four individual cameras, but we can only see twenty-seven images. But if I push this . . ."

Suddenly all the images on the monitors changed. There, on the central monitor, were Taylor and Tara. Though, from their positions I couldn't tell who was who. They were being kept in separate cells, and both were wearing RESAT vests. They were clearly in pain. Seeing it made me want to go after Amash right then.

"Are those *bats* hanging from the ceiling?" McKenna asked.

"Looks like it," I said. "Ostin, what about the controls for the RESATs?"

Ostin looked a moment, then said, "Seeing how the Electroclan had already fled the jungle when Amash started his tricks, RESATs wouldn't have been high on his list. It was probably an add-on to the system." He spun around in his chair, then said, "There they are. On the wall."

There was a series of black dials, each numbering from zero to ten. They were all set to zero except for two. One was set to four, the other six.

I turned them both off, then looked back to the screen. Even though they were both lying down, I could see their bodies relax.

There was a ring of white-coated keys hanging below the dials. I guessed they were the keys to the vests. I had learned that even when the vests were turned off, taking them off without the keys could be fatal.

As Ostin was poring over the monitor, a voice snapped over the speaker.

"Control, adjust the palace room to sixty-nine degrees, twenty-five percent humidity."

Cristiano stepped up to the speaker where the voice had come from. "Yes, Sovereign."

I looked at him. "That was Amash?"

"The sovereign himself."

On the screen, Taylor sat up in her bed. She looked confused and afraid.

"Let's go get them," I said. "Can you unlock the doors from here?"

"If I knew the room numbers," Ostin said.

"I can help," Cristiano said. He looked over the buttons. "There are two ways to get to the jail. There is a door at the back of the guards' room, and there is one through the supply room. The prison door is locked from the outside. The guards can open the door with a magnetic key."

"Not if we weld it shut," I said. "Can they get in here?"

He shook his head. "Only the guards for the control room have the key. They trade it off at each shift. That is the protocol."

"That's good for us," I said. "McKenna, while I free the girls, I want you to weld the guardroom door shut. Ian, stay with her, so you can warn her if some guards come."

"Yes, sir."

"Cristiano, you and Ostin keep this room. We'll be right back. Hopefully."

McKenna, Ian, and I walked back out the door we'd come in, then less than ten meters down the opposite side of the supply tunnel to another thick metal door. There was a sign on it that read CÁRCEL. As we approached, I could hear the door click unlocked.

"Ostin found the lock," I said.

We stepped into the prison. The lights inside flickered and buzzed, though I think it might have been designed that way for effect.

"There's your door," I said to Ian and McKenna, pointing to the door leading to the guards' barracks. While they went to weld the door shut, I walked down to the cells.

There were at least six cells, and the locks on all the doors clicked simultaneously.

Good job, Ostin, I thought, giving a thumbs-up to the camera. Taylor was in the second cell, lying on the cot. There were hundreds of bats hanging above her.

As I opened the cell door, several of the bats flew toward me. I shocked them out of the air like a bug zapper. Taylor looked up at the sound.

"Michael?" Her voice was hoarse. She weakly brushed her matted hair out of her face. "Is it really . . . Is this a trick?"

I put my finger over my lips to quiet her, then said softly, "Let's get you out of here." I threw my arms around her. She was trembling.

"I'm so sorry I did this. I thought I could save Tara."

"You did."

I put the key into her RESAT vest and unlocked it, threw it to the floor, and then helped her stand up. Her legs were wobbly, and she could barely make it to the cell door. Once we were outside, I said, "Lean against the bars for a minute. I'll get Tara."

Tara was in the last cell of the tunnel. She was lying on her cot, staring at the door, her eyes glazed. There were piles of white bat guano all over her clothing and body. She didn't move, even when I opened her cell door and walked in next to her. For a moment I feared she was dead.

"Tara?"

She didn't move for almost a minute. Then she slowly blinked and looked at me. Her face was nearly purple, and her eyes were glassy. I guessed that her RESAT was the one set to six.

"What have they done to you?"

She didn't speak. She looked almost catatonic.

"Come on, I'll help you."

When I put my hands on her to lift her, she let out a short squeal: "RESAT!"

"It's okay, we've shut it off. Here." I took out the keys. I unlocked her vest and took it off, then threw it into the corner of the room.

"Come on, we need to go."

"Abigail," she said softly. That's when I knew just how bad a shape she was in. It's like they had broken her.

"Abi's not with us."

"Abi . . ."

"I'll carry you." I lifted her to her feet, then put her over my shoulder. I couldn't believe how little she weighed. The last time I'd seen her was in Boise. I didn't know if they were starving her or if she'd been unable to eat with the RESAT set so high, but she'd lost at least twenty pounds.

I carried her out to Taylor and put my arm around Taylor so she could lean against me. Then the three of us started back to the tunnel.

"We've got a problem, Michael," Ian shouted to me. "There are guards coming, and McKenna's not done."

Despite the approaching guards, McKenna couldn't hold back her emotion when she saw the girls. "Taylor? Tara? You're really here."

"McKenna," I shouted. "Heat the doorknob."

"Sorry." She turned back. Her hand turned bright red.

There was a shout of pain from the other side of the door.

"Ian, come get the girls. I'll help McKenna."

He ran over and took Tara from me, then reached out to Taylor.

"I can walk," Taylor said, steadying herself against the cave wall. "Just take care of Tara."

"Keep welding," I said to McKenna. I put my hand against the door and pulsed as hard as I could. There was another shout of pain. It only took another thirty seconds before the door was glowing red and the lock was fused.

"All right," I said. "Let's get out of here."

McKenna and I ran back out the first door we'd come in through. I pushed it shut.

"Do you want me to seal this one too?" McKenna asked.

"Yes. I'll get you some water."

"I'll get some," Ostin said, his head sticking out of the control room.

"Give it to Tara first," McKenna said.

Ian sat Tara down on the ground, then sat down next to her, pulling her hair back from her face.

"You're going to be okay," he said.

She still didn't respond.

Ostin came out of the control room with water bottles that must have belonged to the Chasqui. He handed one to Ian, then gave the second to McKenna. Ian lifted the back of Tara's head and helped her drink.

Ostin gave the third bottle to Taylor. She immediately guzzled the whole of it. When it was gone, she said, "Could I have some more?"

"All you want." I went into the control room, found more bottles, and brought three back. I gave one to Taylor, one to Ian, and then the other to Ostin for McKenna, who was still welding the door.

Taylor finished the second bottle, then breathed out heavily. "Thank you."

"How long has it been since you had something to drink?" I asked.

"I don't know. There's no time down here. No night or day. No clocks. Just pain."

"No one will ever hurt you again," I said.

"It was my fault."

She tossed the empty water bottle to the ground. "I shouldn't have surrendered."

"We still haven't found Jack," Ostin said.

"Taylor, where's Jack?" I asked.

"Jack," she said softly. She looked at me. "We need to save him."

"He's not Chasqui?"

She shook her head. "He tried to help us escape. Amash ordered him killed."

I was both relieved and frightened at the same time. "Where is he?"

"I don't know. He didn't come with us. I think he's still at the plant. That's where they took us. That's where our plan failed."

"Are you sure he's alive?"

A tear rolled down her cheek. "No."

I wiped her tear with my thumb. "If he's alive, we'll save him."

Cristiano looked scared. "We can't go to the plant. There are hundreds of guards at the plant. We could never get in."

"We did it before," Ostin said, joining the conversation.

"They will be looking for us. It will be a . . . death trap."

"Unless they're *not* there . . . ," Ostin said.

I turned to him. "You've got a plan?"

He nodded. "Where is the cave's ventilation system?" he asked Cristiano.

"It is at the end of the supply room in the utility room. We passed it on the way here."

"What's in the supply room?"

"A lot of things. Food. Water. Uniforms. Boots. Some of the weapons. But we are not safe there. There are two entrances to the utility room. There is one from the guards' barracks, and there is an outside entrance near the ventilation."

"All the better," Ostin said. "This is my plan. We fill the cave with smoke so they either have to evacuate the cave or die of smoke inhalation. After they're out, we'll lock all the doors. To get back in, they'll have to fight their way in, which means they'll call for reinforcements."

"How do you know they'll do that?" Ian asked.

"Because it's their only way back in. While they're doing that, we go back out the way we came, hike to the Starxource plant, and rescue Jack. It's the ultimate distraction."

"How do we fill the cave with smoke without killing ourselves?" Ian asked.

"There aren't any ventilation shafts back here; they are all in the rooms. The airflow will carry the smoke to the front."

"And the control room," Cristiano said.

"We'll close off the vents with the duct tape."

"That might work," Cristiano said.

"It *will* work," Ostin said.

"How do we get Tara out?" Ian asked.

"We'll have to carry her," I said. "But we've got to move now. Those welds aren't going to hold all night."

"I'll need everyone's help with the fire," Ostin said.

"Let's go," I said.

We went back down the tunnel to the supply room—the place I'd stopped on our way in. The room was about seventy feet long, with rows of metal shelving, filled with plastic bins. Ostin picked up a shovel as he walked by one of the shelves.

"The utility room is through that door," Ian said.

About ten yards from us was a metal door near the back with the word UTILIDAD.

"Is there anyone in there?" I asked.

"It's clear."

We walked inside. The room was loud with the hum of belts and electric motors and moving air. To the left of us there were several large propane tanks connected to water heaters. They were next to a bright red door.

"That must be the barracks door," I said. "Ian, is there anyone trying to get in?"

"No. Looks like they're all going to sleep."

"Good. McKenna, we need you to weld the barrack door shut while we start the fire. If anyone comes, fry them."

"Okay."

Directly ahead of us, on the ceiling of the cave, we could see the outside entrance, a hinged metal hatch that opened to the room, aligned with metal rungs bolted to the wall to climb down on. The hatch was next to where a large air duct came in from the outside, then dropped to the ground, where it fed through an air-conditioning and a humidifying unit, then back up through more metal ductwork to the stone ceiling and through a hole cut through the stone wall.

"I think I got it," Ostin said. He inserted the point of the shovel between two of the metal pieces and pried a metal panel off the last filter. We could hear the apparatus sucking air into the vent.

"This is the place," Ostin said. "This will feed whatever we give it into the main ductwork." He looked up. "Gather anything that will burn. Rubber and plastic are good. Any kind of accelerant will help."

The three of us went back out to the supply room. We gathered up anything that had wood or paper. There were several wooden pieces of furniture and a large wooden chest.

"The plastic bins," I said. "They'll burn, right?"

"Like torches," Ostin said. "Let's get them all."

I began tipping all the bins over.

"Guys, I struck gold," Ian said. "You wanted an accelerant. These barrels are full of rum."

Ostin came over to inspect the barrels. "No surprise, the way the Elgen used to drink. They're all overproof. One hundred fifty proof, seventy-five percent alcohol. These puncheons will burn like kerosene."

We rolled six barrels over to the filters, then covered the barrels with the furniture and plastic bins.

"See if you can find an ax," Ostin said. "We need to break holes in the barrels. We don't want them to explode."

"Why not?" Ian asked.

"It could put out the fire."

"Here's one," Ian said. He started smashing the rum barrel lids like an old-time Prohibition agent.

Ostin and I tipped one of the barrels into the wooden chest, filling it with rum. We then threw rubber boots into the chest, which created a thick black smoke. After we finished, our pile of flammables was more than eight feet high. It looked like a funeral pyre.

"Now we just need a fuse," Ostin said.

"On it," Ian said. He started tying Chasqui uniforms together into a long rope.

"Those uniforms won't burn well," I said.

"They will after we soak them in rum."

"Smart." I began helping him tie the uniforms together. We then dunked our "fuse" into the chest until they were drenched with rum, then laid them on the ground all the way to the door to the supply room.

"Will those propane tanks blow?" Ian asked.

"Most likely," Ostin said. "If the flame gets to them."

"Let's increase those odds," I said. I laid the pack with all the grenades next to it.

"There's a man trying to come in through the door," Ian said. "Probably a rum run."

"McKenna!" I shouted. "We need you to light the fuse." I waved everyone else over. "Everyone into the tunnel. This thing is going to blow."

Once we were back out in the tunnel, McKenna flamed up her hand and touched it to our makeshift fuse. The pale blue alcohol flame moved quickly down the uniforms toward our pyre. When it hit the barrels, flames blew upward to the top of the cavern, illuminating the entire utility room. We could feel the initial blast of heat from where we stood.

"We'd better shut the door," Ian said. "Before we get smoked out."

We closed the door, then ran back to the control room. Cristiano had taped up all the room's vents, though the smell of smoke had already permeated the room. Cristiano and Taylor had brought Tara inside, and she was sitting on the ground, her eyes closed. Taylor and Cristiano had been watching the monitors. They could see some of the men still trying to get into the prison.

"Your weld is holding," Taylor said to McKenna.

"I do my best," she said.

One of the screens showed the utility room. Our fire was burning wildly, and the top half of the room was already filled with smoke. One of the barrels had tipped over and spread the fire toward the barrack door and the propane tanks.

"We made a good fire," Ostin said.

"Boys and matches," Taylor said, which made me happy. She was sounding like herself.

"For the record, McKenna started it," I said back.

The smoke in the room swirled around as it was sucked into a vortex near the center of the room, where Ostin had opened the ductwork.

"It's working," I said.

"I turned the cave ventilation system on full," Cristiano said.

"Now let's shut out all the lights," I said.

"This switch right here," Ostin said.

The entire place went dark. McKenna lit up so we could see. Even in the dark caverns, we could see on the monitors black smoke pouring into each of the rooms. Most of the guards had been sleeping, so the thick smoke caused intense confusion and fear. Chaos broke out, with men screaming and shouting.

I asked Taylor, "How is Tara?"

"She's coherent."

"Can she walk?"

"No. If she'd been on that RESAT much longer, her heart would have stopped." Her eyes welled up. "She would have died."

"Amash should pay for this."

Almost as if we'd summoned him, Amash's voice came over the intercom. "Control, what is happening? There is smoke coming out of my air vent."

Cristiano answered, "There is a confirmed fire in the utility room, Sovereign. We are fighting it. You should evacuate immediately."

"Why haven't you activated the suppression system?"

"We have, sir," Cristiano said.

"Then where are the—"

Cristiano shut down the PA. "I hate his voice."

"There's the switch for the alarm system," Ostin said. He pulled the switch, and a warning siren squealed throughout the cave, adding to the chaos.

The guards, in various stages of dress, some holding clothing or pillows over their faces, rushed toward the front exit. Within minutes a large group of them had gathered. Ostin said, "There's a control to a remote machine gun. Should I fire on them?" His hands were on the remote.

"Let them all get out," I said. "But if you get a shot at Amash, take it."

Eventually the screens displaying the inside of the cave were completely black with smoke. The cameras on the outside showed the men congregating near the front exit, likely awaiting their orders.

"I don't think they know that we did this," Ian said.

"You're probably right," I said. "Only a few of them knew the door to the prison was locked."

"The doors lock automatically when there is a fire," Cristiano said.

"And they felt the doorknob was hot," Ian said. "They probably thought the room was on fire."

"I think they are all out of the cave now," Cristiano said. "No one has come out for a while."

"I didn't see Amash come out," Taylor said.

"If they're not already out, they're not breathing," Ostin said.

"I don't see anyone left in the cave," Ian said.

"Okay, lock the doors," I said. "Let's seal this place up."

"On it."

"Cristiano, do a broad sweep with the guns. Time to let them know we're in here."

On one of the monitors, we could see men scattering or falling as dirt and foliage flew up around them.

"Now they know we're here."

"There," Cristiano said, pointing at the monitor. "That's Amash. He's the one on the radio. I didn't see him go out."

"Can you hit him?"

"No. He knows where to stand."

I groaned. "Of course he does. He's no doubt calling for reinforcements. Let's get out of here."

"What about Tara?" Taylor asked.

"We'll have to carry her," I said. "Cristiano, give me a hand."

"How are we going to get her through the tunnel?" he asked.

"We'll figure it out when we get there."

Cristiano and I put Tara's arms around our shoulders, then lifted her. We walked out of the control room back into the tunnel. Smoke had seeped out from under the supply room door into the tunnel but not so much as to stop us.

"McKenna, you'd better light the way," I said.

The tunnel lit up. As we ran past the supply room, we could hear explosions.

"I think that would be ammunition," Cristiano said.

"The entire supply room is on fire," Ian said. "We did a better job than we planned on."

"Keep moving," I said.

We made our way back to the small exit tunnel.

"Ian, you go first," I said. "Cristiano and I will bring up the rear with Tara."

Together we carried Tara as far down the escape tunnel as we could, until we could no longer stand and had to kneel in the water.

"What do we do now?" Cristiano asked.

"I'm . . . sorry," Tara said weakly, uttering her first words.

"We've got you," I said. I got down onto my stomach. "Do you think you can hold on to my back?"

"I'll try."

"Cristiano, help her."

Cristiano helped position Tara's body on my back, with her arms draped over my shoulders. I crawled on my elbows and knees until the end of the tunnel, when I had to crawl on my stomach, barely holding my head above the water. By the time we reached the first cavern, I was exhausted. My elbows and knees felt raw. When we got to the edge of the pool, Ian swam over to me. "Michael, let me help you."

"It's going to take both of us to swim with her." I asked Tara, "Can you hold your breath?"

"I think so."

"We've got to go underwater for just a few seconds. It's the only way out of here." I said to Ian, "When we get to the other side, we'll tie the rope around her and pull her up."

"How can I help?" Ostin asked.

"Swim behind her and help us lift her up after we go through the opening."

"Got it."

Ian and I each took one of Tara's arms and swam with her to the opposite side of the cavern. McKenna was in the water next to us, lighting the place.

"McKenna, when I tell you, go through so we can see the opening."

She nodded.

I looked at Tara. "Are you ready for this?"

She nodded. "Yes."

"You can do it," Taylor said.

"I'm going to count to three, then say 'dive.' At three, take a deep breath, then hold it until we come up on the other side. You're sure you can do this?"

She nodded.

I looked at Ian. "You ready?"

"I'm ready."

"McKenna, go ahead."

McKenna dove down and swam through the opening in the rock wall. Even with McKenna's light gone, I could see Tara's face from the glow of her skin. "Ian, watch her head on the rocks." He nodded. "One, two, three." Tara took in a deep breath. "Dive."

Ian and I dove under, pulling Tara down with us. It wasn't easy swimming with just one hand and pulling her, but we kicked hard, taking her through the entrance and then up as quickly as possible. Ostin swam up behind her. He had both hands on her waist, and he helped us bring her up. When we broke the surface, Tara gasped for air.

"Good job," I said. "Good job."

She rubbed the water from her eyes. "Thank you."

Taylor came up behind us, followed by Cristiano. We were treading water with our legs, and I was just about spent. "Let's get her to the rope," I said. "I've got to rest."

"Michael, I got her," Ostin said, grabbing on to the rope and reaching out. He pulled Tara up next to him. Taylor swam over to help.

"We'll get you out of here," I said. I looked up at the opening. "Zeus," I shouted.

There was no response.

"Zeus! Nichelle!"

Still nothing.

"Where are they?" I asked.

"They're not up there," Ian said. "No one is up there."

"No one? Are there Chasqui?"

"Not that I can see."

"What if the Chasqui got them?" Cristiano asked.

Taylor turned to me. "What if they're waiting for us?"

"If they wanted to trap us, why would they leave the rope?" Ostin said.

"There's no one up there," Ian repeated.

"How far can you see?" Cristiano asked.

"Far enough."

"This just keeps getting better," I said. "I'm going up."

I worked my way around Tara, then, scissoring my legs around the rope, shimmied back up, my legs and arms burning with each pull. At the narrow stone opening on top, I stuck my head out and looked around, then grasped the rock and lifted myself up until I was sitting on the rim of the rock crevice, then pushed myself out.

For a moment I just lay on my back to catch my breath. Then I leaned up on my elbows and looked around. There was no trace of them. I couldn't believe we'd lost Zeus and Nichelle—we'd rescued two people just to lose two more.

Ian came up the rope after me. I took his hand and helped him out. He was also winded.

"Still nothing," he said from his knees. He sat on the ground next to me.

"Why would they leave?"

"They'd only leave if they had to."

"That's not comforting."

I turned back to see Cristiano climbing up through the hole. "They have tied the rope around the weak girl," he said. "So we can pull her up."

"Her name is Tara," I said. I got up and walked over to the hole. Looking down into the cavern, I shouted, "Is she ready?"

"I tied a bowline around her," Ostin shouted. "Pull her up."

The three of us pulled Tara up, slowing when she got near the top so she wouldn't bump her head. I grabbed her arms and pulled her out, then laid her down across the ground. I untied the knot, then threw the rope back down the hole. Ostin tied the knot for the other two women, and we pulled them up. He insisted on climbing up himself.

After everyone was up, we just sat on the ground, resting.

"Any clue where Zeus and Nichelle went?" Ostin asked.

"Your guess is as good as mine," Ian said.

"I never guess," Ostin said.

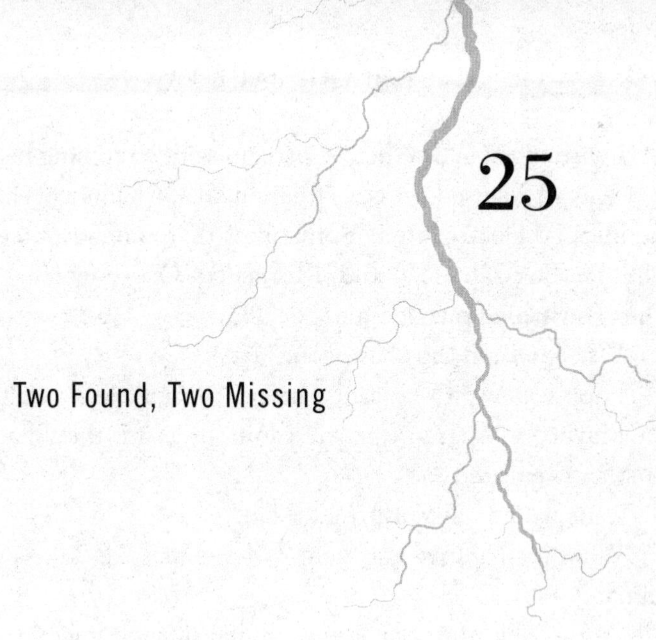

25

Two Found, Two Missing

I didn't know what time it was, though I'm sure it was well after midnight. Under the ceiling of branches and leaves, the jungle was nearly pitch-black, except where the moon's light occasionally pierced the canopy. Almost as thick as the jungle darkness were the sounds. A nocturnal symphony of Amazonian life had emerged with the nightfall, tree crickets and howler monkeys and the bad-tempered grunt of caimans. Occasionally a single voice would break through the cacophony with a shrill mating call or the tortured last scream of death.

We didn't dare use flashlights (or even McKenna) in the dark. Even though we were shielded by the thick jungle and rugged terrain, we were less than a half mile from the entrance where the displaced Chasqui were congregated. Still, there was light from our glow and the constant flash and buzz of insects burning off my skin.

"I wish my skin did that," Cristiano said, scratching his neck.

I was so focused on our situation that I hadn't even noticed all the bugs I'd electrocuted. "Sometimes there are advantages to being a human bug zapper," I said. I turned to Ostin, which I usually did when something puzzled me.

"Where would they have gone?"

"I don't know," Ostin said. I hated it when he said that.

"Maybe a Chasqui patrol came by, and they had to hide," Cristiano ventured.

"Zeus would have just fried them."

"What if an animal got them?" McKenna said. "Like a jaguar. Or a caiman?"

"Zeus is the most dangerous animal in the jungle," I said. "We're too far from water for a caiman, and I don't see any animal tracks."

"No," Ian said. "Neither do I."

"What are the Chasqui doing now?" I asked Ian.

"They're mostly still out in front of the cave. A few have moved over to the side entrance, but there's too much smoke."

"Are any coming from the plant yet?"

He looked out. "Yes. Dozens."

Our plan to draw more Chasqui to the cave was working, but now we faced a new dilemma. Did we hunt down Zeus and Nichelle, or stick to the plan and go after Jack? If we chose to go after Zeus and Nichelle, where would we even begin? On top of it all, I was past exhausted. What Johnson had warned me about not getting enough sleep, I was finding painfully true.

"So what do we do?" Ian asked.

"I don't know. To go after Jack, we'll need Zeus. And I have no idea where we would even start looking for them."

"We'd have to split up," Ian said.

"Not again," I said. "From now on we stick together." I breathed out slowly. "I need to think." I walked away from the others to sit alone near the edge of the forest. A few minutes later Taylor sat down next to me.

"I need to tell you something," she said.

I looked over at her. I could tell from her face that I wasn't going to like what she had to say.

"I had a dream last night."

"A dream or a nightmare?"

She hesitated. "A nightmare, I guess."

I was really starting to hate her gift. "What was it?"

"I saw Zeus and Nichelle surrounded by native tribesmen."

I just lowered my head into my hands.

"I'm sorry. There's more. I saw Jack. He had a hood over his head, and he was standing in front of a firing squad. The Chasqui were executing him."

I looked up. My heart was racing. "Where was he?"

"I'm not sure. Outside somewhere. Maybe the courtyard of the Starxource plant."

"Did you see him die?"

"No."

"What time of day was it?"

"The sun was just rising."

"Then we've got to get to the plant." I stood and walked back to the group. Everyone looked as exhausted as I felt. "I've come to a decision. I know you're all tired, but we need to hike to the plant to save Jack. We believe the Chasqui are going to execute him."

"That makes sense," Ostin said. "Amash is trying to make us pay for attacking his cave."

Everyone stood.

"Which way is the plant?" I asked Ostin.

He pointed. "It's that way. Northeast." As I was looking out into the jungle, I saw a sudden flash of electricity arc between two trees. I turned back. "Did you see that?"

"See what?" Ostin asked.

"There was electricity. Like lightning."

"It could be St. Elmo's fire," Ostin said. "When atmospheric—"

Taylor interrupted. "Maybe it was Zeus sending us a signal."

"Where was it?" Ian asked, walking toward me.

I pointed to where I'd seen the flash. At that very moment there was another.

Ian said, "It's Zeus and Nichelle and . . ." He turned to us. "And a tribe of . . . natives."

"But they're still alive?" I asked.

"Very."

"Are they being held captive?"

"If they are, they like it."

"What?"

"Zeus has his arm around one of the warriors, and they appear to be laughing. Nichelle is smiling."

"Nichelle is smiling?" Taylor said. "What did they do, drug her?"

"Zeus is waving us over," Ian said.

"Let's go," I said, walking over to Tara, who was still unable to stand.

"I can carry Tara," Ian said. "I'm not as tired as you."

"Thank you."

Taylor took my hand. "I'm really worried about you. Are you okay?"

"I'm just really tired. I haven't really slept since . . ."

"I surrendered myself to the Chasqui?"

I nodded. "Pretty much."

"You barely slept the night before," she said. I could see her eyes well up. "You really do love me."

"Did you ever doubt?"

"No. I know your mind. But you know how sometimes we believe things that aren't true?"

"Yes."

"Sometimes we *don't* believe things that *are* true. Especially things that seem too good to be true." She leaned over and kissed me. "You're a good man, Michael Vey. I don't know what I would do without you."

"I hope you never have to find out."

PART FOURTEEN

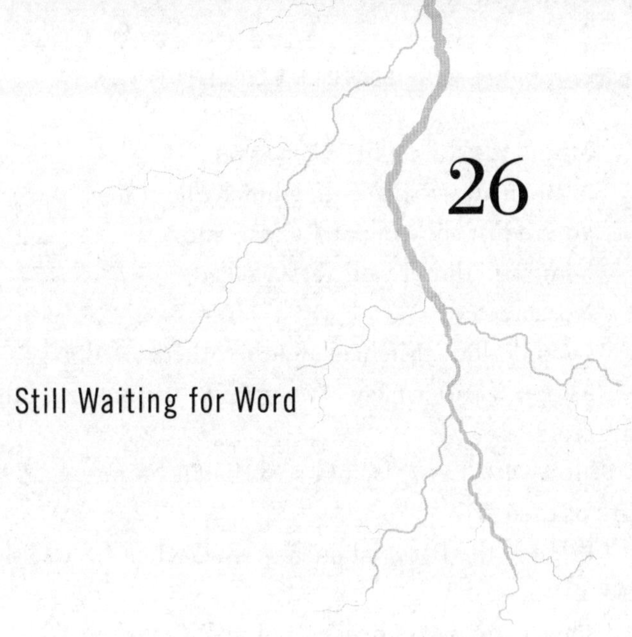

26

Still Waiting for Word

By the time Alpha Team had returned to the hacienda, the staff had a light dinner of soup and potatoes waiting for them. They ate quickly, then went to their rooms to sleep, after setting their alarms for six a.m. Johnson slept with the radio twelve inches from his head. The moment he heard from Jaime, they would move.

The next morning Johnson woke to the alarm. There was still no news from Jaime. He checked to make sure everyone else was up.

"Jaime didn't call?" Jax asked.

"Nada."

"He should have called even without seeing them."

"That was the plan," Johnson said. "Let's be ready to move in thirty. Breakfast is ready."

Within five minutes, the group was gathered around the table for breakfast.

"I think it's still night," Cassy said.

"In the field we'd be eating lunch about now," Jax said.

"You're just showing off," Cassy said.

"Jaime still didn't call?" Tessa asked.

"No," Jax said.

"I wonder how Michael and the others are doing."

"I hope Jaime is okay," Cibor said. "It's not like him not to communicate."

"He's with Lars," Jacinta said. "He'll be fine. Lars will take good care of them."

"What if the bat containers passed when he was sleeping?" Tessa asked.

"That's why we're headed out now," Johnson said. "Redundancy."

They finished eating, then drove back to the kill zone. After they were all settled in, Jacinta drove the van back to Puente Inambari. She found a place to park near the bridge, where she could keep a lookout. It was not yet ten a.m. when she called in to Johnson.

"I'm in position. Nothing can get by me."

"Very well."

"Still no word from Jaime?"

"Not a word. I just called him. But he didn't answer."

"That is not like Jaime."

"No. I'm afraid something might have happened."

"To him or his phone?"

"Either is possible."

"Then the cargo could have already passed him as well."

"That's possible. That's the thing about war. It's always a response to what you didn't plan for."

PART FIFTEEN

27

An Unexpected Reunion

Zeus, Nichelle, and the Amacarra were gathered in a small clearing about a hundred yards from where we had been. There were a couple dozen warriors. I remembered them from my first encounter with the tribe, and in the pale light of the moon I could see their painted faces—the top half black, the bottom half and jaw bloodred. Some of them had bones through their noses. They wore loincloths and headdresses of plaited leaves. They all carried weapons—spears or blow darts.

"It's about time you got here," Zeus said as we walked into the clearing.

"You have no idea what a relief it is to see you two."

"Yeah, thanks for the scare," Taylor said.

Nichelle grinned. "It wasn't really our idea. We would have left a note, but . . ." She raised her hands. "Nothing to write with."

"I see you got them," Zeus said.

"Yeah, we did."

"Good job. What about Jack?"

"We're working on that."

There was suddenly a lot of mouth clicking between the warriors. I looked over at the tribe. It seemed like it had been a lifetime since I'd last seen them. I didn't remember any of them individually, not that I would have anyway. Back then their faces had been covered with the same black-and-red war paint.

I bowed slightly. "I am pleased to see you again. Thank you for watching over our friends as you once did me."

There was no response.

"They don't speak English," Nichelle said. "Except him." She pointed to one of the Amacarra, who was emerging from the deep shadows.

I recognized him as the chief of the Amacarra. His face was easier to see than the others', since it was painted all white, with black lines around his mouth and eyes. He had a bone through his nose. He was bare-chested, and he wore a necklace of piranha teeth and jaguar claws. He was not wearing the parrot headdress I remembered from before but, like the others, a crown of woven banana leaves. He'd been old the last time I saw him. I was a little surprised that he was still alive, and more surprised to see him away from the village.

"Michael Vey," he said. "It is good to see you again. I remember you from the last time you came to our jungle."

"I remember you too, Great Chief. That was a long time ago."

"Many leaves have fallen since then. Much has happened in our jungle since you came. Unfortunately, much of it evil. The demons took the cave of our fathers. We fought them, but, as before, their weapons of war were too powerful. We lost many brave warriors. Then the *bai mwo gwei* tried to exterminate us, but they were unsuccessful. They do not know the jungle like we do. The jungle gods protect us.

"We have watched the white devils from the shadows since then. Lately they have been more active in our jungle, and we have fought to keep them from our home."

"Earlier today we saw three dead Chasqui soldiers on the trail," I said. "That is where we got our uniforms."

"Yes, the three devils were hunting one of our warriors."

"How did you find us?"

"We saw your friends. We thought they were Chasqui, since your friend, like you, is wearing one of their uniforms. The gods were looking out for you. It is fortunate that it was night and we saw the glow of his skin. We were confused. We did not know if our friends, the *gwang lyang ren*, the Glowpeople, had joined our enemy, so we took both to find out.

"We were very pleased to learn that we are still friends and you had gone into the demon cave to save your friends."

One of the warriors said something to the chief. The chief pointed at Cristiano, then said to me, "This one is recognized. He is a Chasqui soldier. Is he your prisoner?"

"No, he is a friend. He helped us against them. The Chasqui killed his brother."

The chief walked over and put his thumb between Cristiano's eyes, then closed his own eyes. He held it there for nearly a minute; then he stepped back. I don't know what he was doing, but he seemed satisfied that Cristiano was one of us.

"Were you successful in freeing your friends?"

"Yes," I said, gesturing toward the women. "These are the two we rescued, Taylor and Tara."

My introduction of them was followed by a lot of mouth clicking. The entire tribe looked astonished.

The chief looked surprised as well. "How are they the same woman? Do the Glowpeople make themselves into two people?"

"No. They are twins."

"I do not know that word, 'twins.'"

"It is when a mother has two babies at the same time."

"Two babies? Like the otter?"

"Yes. It is rare with humans, but it happens."

Another warrior said something to him in their tongue. The chief nodded. "Yes, I had nearly forgotten. Many generations ago an

Amacarra woman had two babies born to her. It was a sign from the gods." He stepped closer to Taylor. "She is beautiful like Hung fa. The one you call Tessa."

"Thank you," Taylor said.

"Tessa still breathes?"

"Yes, she's in Peru too. She is helping to battle the Chasqui somewhere else."

He nodded slowly. "Yes, she is a warrior too." The chief looked down at Tara, who was sitting on the ground where I had set her down.

"This one cannot walk?"

"Not now," I said. "The Chasqui hurt her."

His eyes narrowed. "*Bai mwo gwei.* They are evil." He knelt down next to Tara and put his hands on her legs. She looked up at us, unsure of what the chief was doing.

"It's okay," Taylor said. "He is a healer."

After a moment the chief took his hands off her. "Her bones are not broken."

"No. It's mostly her muscles. The Chasqui have a machine that hurts the Glowpeople."

The chief shook his head again. "We have medicine from roots that can fix her."

I remembered the mud-and-herb compress they had put on my broken ankle that had healed it in just one day. "Yes, you have powerful medicines."

"The jungle gods are healers," the chief said. He stood. "But perhaps it is not your wish to stay in the jungle. Your friend Zooz"—I figured he meant Zeus, but it's not polite to correct a chief—"said that you will be leaving to go back to your home."

"That was our plan, but the Chasqui have another one of our friends at the Starxource plant. We are going there to free him."

The chief frowned. "The plant is not safe. Do you not remember, there are many, many soldiers at the plant?"

"I know. But we have to try. We do not leave our friends behind."

He nodded. "It is our way too. How can we help you?"

"This is not your battle."

"We are friends, so it is our battle."

"You are most noble and good," I said. "If you would help, could you guide us through the jungle to the Starxource plant?"

"Yes, we will. The demons have made a trail that is clear, but it is not always safe. That is where they patrol."

"Yes, we can't use it right now. We have lured the Chasqui from the big plant to the cave so we could free our friend."

"You are very clever to confuse your enemy. And you speak the truth. Our warriors have been watching many soldiers come from the gray building to the cave tonight. That is why we are out at this hour of the moon. We thought the demons might be planning to attack our people again."

"No, it's us they want."

"We can help you. We have our own trails. I will send two warriors, Li and Kwai, to guide you." He looked over at Tara. "This one will not be able to travel. We can take her and give her medicine. We will keep her safe."

I looked at Tara. "You can trust them. Will you be okay if we leave you?"

She nodded. "I'd just slow you down."

"Do you need someone to stay with you?" Taylor asked.

She shook her head. "Saving Jack will take all of you."

I turned to the chief. "Thank you. We will accept your help."

"We are the same spirit," he said. "Our hearts beat together. If it is the gods' will, we will be victorious together."

I looked at the other tribesmen and put my hand over my heart. They did the same back, followed by more mouth clicking.

"You should get rest before you go to war," the chief said. "You are very tired. I can feel your weariness in my own bones."

"We are all very tired, but we are worried for our friend. We believe they will kill him when the sun rises. We need to go now."

He looked at me for a moment, then said, "You will not make it as you are. You are more tired than you know."

"We must try."

"If you believe you must go now, I have something to help you. It is a special water." He held up his hand and shouted words to the tribe. One of the warriors brought over a bulging waterskin and gave it to the chief. The chief offered it to me.

"We call this *li-shwei*. It comes from the *warana* plant. Anciently it was called 'the eyes of the gods.' It will awaken you."

"It's guarana," Ostin said. "It's twice as potent as caffeine." He smiled. "He's giving us the Amacarra version of an energy drink."

I took the skin. "Thank you." I was already thirsty, so I took a long drink. I could feel the effect of the drink almost immediately.

"That's really good," I said. "It tastes like lemonade."

"Yeah," Zeus said. "Nichelle and I already had some. The stuff rocks."

"I'm going to market it when we get back home," Nichelle said. "Power lemonade."

"I like that."

"I'll have some," Ian said.

"There are lemons in the Amazon rain forest?" I asked Ostin.

"Lemons, limes, oranges, pineapples, and thousands of fruits you've never heard of."

"We should all have some of this," I said.

"Do not give it to the girl," the chief said, pointing at Tara. "It will fight the medicine we have for her. She needs to sleep."

"Thank you," Tara said.

We passed the skin around. By the time it had gone through us, we'd pretty much emptied it. I immediately felt energized.

"That stuff is amazing," Zeus said. "I feel totally awake."

"I hope it lasts," I said. I turned to the chief. "Thank you."

"You are most welcome, Michael Vey." The chief ordered several of the warriors forward, and they lifted Tara.

"This is not so bad," Tara said. "These guys are handsome."

"Get better," Taylor said to her sister.

"Kwai. Li," the chief said. Two of the warriors walked forward from the others. The chief spoke in the Amacarra language, then said to me, "I told them to go quickly."

"All right," I said. "Where shall we meet you after?"

"We will meet here. We will be watching for you."

"Drop a pin," I said to Ostin. I said to the chief, "Take good care of Tara."

"She will be protected with our lives," he said. "Now go with the gods. We will burn oils to petition the gods' help for you."

"We are very grateful," I said.

He bowed to me slightly, then turned to our guides and gave a final command.

The two warriors started off, single file, into the dark of the jungle. I thanked the chief once more. Then we all ran off behind Kwai and Li.

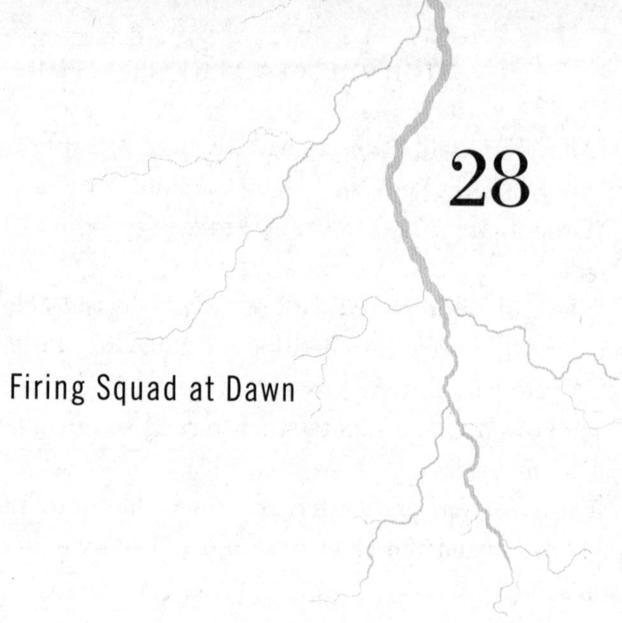

28

Firing Squad at Dawn

The way the Amacarra moved through the jungle at night, you would think they could see in the dark. Maybe they could. Or maybe it was just like walking through one's own home at night.

It was simple, of course, for Ian, who not only walked through the jungle with ease but kept us apprised of the frequent patrols of Chasqui making their way to the cave, counting them as he went. At last count he was up to sixty-nine.

It took us nearly three hours to make it to the outskirts of the massive Elgen compound. The first we saw of it was the tall metal fence posts surrounding their property, then, in the distance, the concrete curvature of the rat bowl. There was a plume of steam rising from the back side of it.

"Are they using the rat bowl again?" I asked Cristiano.

"Not like before. It is mostly used to keep the bats in."

Our Amacarra guides led us to where two large pipes emptied out from the plant.

"This brings back memories," Taylor said. "The Weekend Express."

"I never thought I'd go through that again," Ostin said.

"You probably won't," I said. "They sealed it shut."

Metal caps had been welded onto the ends of the pipes.

"No. It is not open anymore," Cristiano said. "The sovereign had it sealed off for good."

"Couldn't McKenna just melt the welds?" Nichelle said.

"Is there more than just the welds keeping it shut?" I asked Ian.

He looked for a moment, then said, "The other end of the pipe is sealed as well, and there are two rotting human corpses inside the pipe. There are also explosives inside and trip wires and mines at two other places."

Amash was clearly very serious about not letting anyone use these anymore.

"Then we go through the fence," I said. "Like we did before."

There was a tall electric wire fence that ran around the perimeter of the compound for as far as we could see. The wires were about a foot and a half apart, wide enough for us to slip through if they weren't electrified.

The first time we'd broken into the plant, the wires had been electrified as well, but I hadn't realized back then that I could touch them. Maybe I couldn't have. A lot of electricity had passed through me since then. Now the electricity didn't worry me anymore. After being struck by lightning, this fence's voltage was nothing.

As I walked up to the wires, the warriors started shouting, *"Bu yau tai jin! Bu yau tai jin!"*

"What did they say?" Ian asked.

"I think they're trying to warn me about the fence," I said.

One of them stepped ahead of me and pointed to the rotting carcass of a capuchin monkey lying on the ground at the base of the fence. *"Ting jr sho chu. Feichang wei syande."*

"Based on the dead primate, I'd say he's definitely warning you not to touch the wires," Ostin said. He turned to them. "Yes, we know they're electric."

The warriors didn't relax. I guess to further clarify their point, one of the men took a stick and tossed it onto the fence. An electric spark crackled from the wires.

"Yes, we know," Ostin said. "It's no big deal."

"That's pretty high voltage," I said.

I reached out to touch the wires, and the warrior grabbed my arm to stop me. *"Bu yau, bu yau. Jen hen wei syande!"*

"They must think we're idiots," Ian said.

"No," I said. "Just me." I turned to them. "It's okay. Really." I waited for them to take their hands off me, since I didn't want them close to me when I grabbed the wires. "You don't need to worry."

The Amacarra stepped back. Before they could move again, I turned around and grabbed a wire. A deafening zap of electricity filled the air, like a squirrel jumping onto a bug zapper.

It would have killed anyone else, but to me it was like drinking a cold soda—tingly and refreshing. My glow more than doubled in brightness. The Amacarra's expressions turned from fear to amazement, then, maybe, to admiration.

I shrugged. "What doesn't kill me only makes me stronger." I turned to Cristiano. "But it will definitely kill you."

"Thanks," he said. "So how do I get in?"

"Ever play the game Operation?" I asked.

"No."

"The point of the game is," I said, "don't touch the sides, or you lose." I put my foot on the bottom wire of the fence, grabbed the wire above it, and pulled it up as high as I could. "Can everyone get through that?"

"We can," Taylor said.

I was able to open the space nearly three feet, easily enough for each of them to straddle and get through.

"Let's go," I said. "Take your time. Be careful."

One by one, everyone passed through the fence except the two Amacarra.

"Are they coming with us?" Taylor asked.

"I don't think so." I looked at them and touched my chest. "Thank you."

They likewise touched their chests, then quickly disappeared back into the jungle's darkness. I let go of the fence. My exhaustion was gone and my body fairly hummed with energy.

"You're really glowing," Taylor said.

"I just got a good recharge," I said.

The compound grounds were still dark, though the first traces of dawn could be seen in the gradation of light on the eastern horizon.

"What's the fastest way in?" I asked.

"The cells were next to the old rat bowl," Ostin said.

"Ian, can you see Jack?"

He looked toward the bowl. "I can see the jail cells. But they're all empty." He paused for a moment, then said, "Something is going on in the courtyard. There's a lot of soldiers in there."

"We've got to get inside."

We crept behind foliage for about twenty yards to the end of the outer tree line. There was a magnificent two-story antebellum-architecture-styled mansion that looked more like it belonged in the American South than in South America. It was all white, with a gabled roof with a cupola, and huge Greek revival columns that framed the wide porch that encircled the house. The mansion was located toward the north end of the bowl and had its own roadway from the plant. There was a chain-link fence with a razor wire top around the property, which, despite its unwelcoming facade, was beautifully manicured.

"They've made some additions," Taylor said.

"Anyone want to bet that's the sovereign's place?" Ostin said.

"It is his mansion," Cristiano said. "When he is not in the cave."

There were three other new buildings to the side of the residence, one still under construction. The two finished buildings were luxurious and of Western design, though not as luxurious as the main mansion. All three of the buildings looked out of place against the stark industrial contrast of the concrete-and-steel architecture of the former Elgen Starxource plant.

"What are those other buildings?" Taylor asked.

"The far one is like a hotel for the sovereign's guests," Cristiano said.

"He has that many guests?"

"Not many. Drug traffickers, mostly. Sometimes foreign dignitaries. The other building is for the scientists. They are treated differently than the soldiers. They have much nicer quarters. I do not know what the third building is going to be. It was started after I left."

Each of the buildings was fenced in and had a guard booth. We continued hiking until we could see the entrance to the rat bowl. There was still a pen with cattle, but it was nothing like the last time we had been here. I could see no ranch hands, just a sentry post with guards. There were cameras everywhere.

"We could disguise ourselves as scientists," Ian said. "There are only two guards at their building. We could take uniforms and IDs."

"We don't have time for that," I said, looking at the horizon. "It's almost dawn. With all the cameras, we couldn't get anywhere near the building without being seen."

"We need some kind of distraction," Ostin said.

"We still have C4," Ian said. "We could blow something up on the other side of the compound."

"Then the whole compound would go on alert and lockdown," I said. "I was thinking something a little more nuanced."

"I have an idea," Taylor said.

I turned to her. "Let's hear it."

"Since you're in Chasqui uniforms, they'll think you're with them . . ."

"I'm not in uniform," Ian said.

"They will still require ID," Cristiano added. "The Chasqui have very strict routines and rules. They will want to know why you are there."

"But once we're that close, we could shock them," Ostin said.

"Let me finish," Taylor said. "We don't just walk up to them. You take Nichelle, McKenna, Ian, and me to them as prisoners. Each of you will have one of us, and we'll be struggling like we're trying to get away. That way they'll assume you were sent out to capture us, and their first concern will be the captive American girls, not the guards bringing them.

"Cristiano, you tell them that you caught us trying to get in and that we said we had an American friend being kept inside. They will think we mean Jack.

"After you give me to them, you can ask about Jack and where he's been moved. Even if they don't tell you where he is, I'll read their minds. Nichelle, if you'll enhance me, that will help."

"Of course."

"Then, after we've got everything we need to know, I'll do a heavy reboot on them, and Michael and Zeus will take them out. We'll go rescue Jack."

"That's pretty brilliant," Ostin said.

"Let's do it," I said. "Let's pair up. Make it real, ladies."

I took Taylor by the arm, Ostin took McKenna, and Cristiano took Ian, and Zeus took Nichelle. Nichelle immediately started acting like she was trying to get away and shouting at Zeus, "Let go of me. You can't treat me like this. I'll sue! I'll call the embassy!"

Taking her cue, Taylor, Ian, and McKenna also started carrying on. The commotion immediately caught the guards' attention. Two of them came out of the booth.

"Qué pasa?" one shouted.

We waited until we were closer.

"We caught them," I said.

"We caught the intruders," Cristiano said in Spanish.

The guard with the most stars on his uniform walked up to us.

"I'm *Sergeant* Bentley," he said, stressing his rank over his name. "What do you have here?"

"We caught the intruders," I said. "These Americans were outside the fence trying to sneak in. They say we're holding their friend. An American."

"We have no American women in here."

"Not a woman," Ostin said. "A man."

He nodded. "Oh, yes. The traitor." A slight grin crossed his face. "Tell them to wait an hour. We'll give him back."

His words sent a chill through me.

He smiled darkly. "They can save us the trouble of burying him."

Taylor pushed me away and ran toward the man. He grabbed her.

"Where do you think you're going, *Bonita*?"

"Get your hands off me!" she shouted.

"Why isn't she handcuffed?"

"I can handle her," I said.

"If you could handle her, I wouldn't be holding her."

"Where's Jack?" Taylor shouted. "What have you done with him?"

Taylor turned to me, her eyes wide with terror. "What did you do to Jack?" she asked again.

Between her dream and her reaction, I could guess what she had read in his mind.

"You don't need to worry about that," he said. "It's me you should worry about. I haven't seen a woman for a while."

It was all I could do not to fry him. I kept my cool.

"Did they do it yet?" I asked calmly.

"The execution is at sunrise. First light."

Cristiano said, "That is the tradition for traitors."

"'Shot at dawn,'" Ostin said.

"How long do we have until sunrise?" I asked. I was afraid of his answer, as the jungle was already in twilight.

Ian glanced down at his watch. "About fifteen minutes. You were right. Amash must have ordered Jack's execution after we attacked," he said, as if we weren't standing next to the enemy.

The sergeant looked at Ian with a confused expression, then shouted to his men, "Take these prisoners!" He looked at Taylor. "Lock this one in the first brig."

As the other guards started forward, I said, "Taylor, now."

Nichelle stepped forward with her hand out as Taylor rebooted them. One of them fell over. The sergeant blinked several times, then looked blankly at Taylor, then me.

"Where is this execution?" she asked.

He didn't answer. I turned to Taylor. "Can you see?"

"I just saw the same yard as my dream."

"Where is it?" I shouted.

The sergeant looked at me coolly. "If you were a Chasqui, you would know that."

I burst out with a powerful shock wave but pulled back just enough to not leave him unconscious. He yelled out with pain as he hit the ground. The other guards were, at first, startled. Then they reached for their weapons. Zeus sent a lightning bolt that daisy-chained through the men, blistering their hands and knocking them off their feet. It was as intense a lightning blast as I'd ever seen from him.

"Take their weapons," I said. "Lock them up inside the booth with their own handcuffs."

"On it," Ostin said. While he, Cristiano, and Ian took care of the other guards, I knelt down next to the sergeant.

"Who are you?" he asked.

"We're the ones who brought down the Elgen," I said. "And the Chasqui. Now, where is our friend?"

He tried to look tough. "What friend?"

"He's playing with you," Taylor said.

"We don't have time to play." I tapped his forehead with my forefinger. "I don't have time for this."

The man looked afraid, but he still didn't speak. I looked over to the horizon and the first streaks of dawn. We were running out of time. Jack was running out of time.

"Do you really want to die for the Chasqui?"

His eyes hardened. "You can't make me talk."

I turned back. "McKenna, give me a hand. Your hand."

She walked over and knelt on the other side of the man. "What do you need?"

"This man says we can't make him tell us where Jack is. I think you can."

"Gladly." She grabbed his fat cheek and pulled upward several inches. McKenna took a deep breath. Then, as she exhaled, the sound of sizzling skin was accompanied by the smell of burning flesh. The man's fat cheek sounded like bacon on a hot grill.

The sergeant screamed out in agony, but McKenna didn't flinch. He still didn't talk.

I leaned over him, close enough that he could feel my breath. "Have you ever seen an eyeball pop from heat? They do that, you know. I can't imagine how much that would hurt. You'll have to let us know.

"I hope that after you're blind, the Chasqui take good care of you. But I doubt it. I heard that they usually feed the helpless to the rats, but you probably already know that." I turned back to McKenna. "Go ahead and do his eyes. Slowly, though. One at a time."

Before McKenna could move her hand, he said, "I'll tell you where he is. Please, no."

I nodded to McKenna, and she released his cheek. The man groaned out in pain. One side of his face was bright red, his cheek charred and blistered.

I leaned into his burned face. "Let me be clear, Sergeant. You're taking us to our friend. This one can read your mind. If you lie to us, we'll know, and we will burn you to a crisp. If you think you can lead us into a trap, we'll know as soon as you think about it, and we will burn you to a crisp. Do you understand?"

"Yes, I understand."

"One more thing. If we're too late and my friend dies, so will you. Is that clear enough?"

"Yes," he said frantically. "The execution is about to happen in the courtyard. We must hurry."

I let him up. "Take us."

The sergeant practically jumped to his feet, holding his hand over his burned cheek.

"You're going with me," Taylor said, taking his arm.

"Come, come," he said. "We need to hurry."

"Looks like someone doesn't want to die today," Zeus said.

The sergeant led us to the former rancher entrance to the rat bowl. He tried to run his key through the lock, but he was shaking so badly, he had trouble making it work.

"Calm yourself," I said. "Give it to me." I took the key from him and unlocked the door and opened it.

"Come," he said. "We need to hurry."

Little had changed inside the bowl since our last visit. This was where I'd been held as I'd awaited being dropped into the rat bowl. It was one of a hundred memories I'd love to be rid of.

We jogged through the concrete feeding area, past the cells where we had rescued Tanner years before. Then we entered a hallway—the same hall where Hatch had released a million rats at us. The hallway wound nearly a quarter of the way around the complex, past the laboratories and what had been the rat breeding facilities. We passed a group of five scientists walking, their attention lost in their conversation.

"Don't even think about it," Zeus said to the sergeant.

"He didn't," Taylor replied. "He's focused on not dying."

My anxiety grew with each step. "Faster," I said.

"I'm hurrying," the sergeant said. "We're almost there."

We exited out the last set of doors into the wider outer corridor. The outer wall was lined with large windows, and in the growing dawn, we could see the open courtyard. Something was definitely going on, as there were at least fifty Chasqui soldiers, congregated together and facing toward the same thing. Closer to the building, there was a line of soldiers holding rifles. In front of them, next to the building, someone was tied to a wide wooden post with a hood over his head.

"It's Jack," Ian said. "That's him."

The post was scarred with bullet holes. It was the kind of thing that Hatch would have built to keep his guards in line. Sort of a monument to horror.

At the far side of the line, facing the riflemen, was an older officer in a dark blue formal military dress uniform with white cuffs and gold fringed epaulets. In his right hand he was holding a sword that was pointed to the ground, and he was looking at his watch on his left arm. Then he lowered his watch arm and looked up.

"It's a ritual execution," I said. "He's about to start."

The officer slowly lifted his sword. He shouted, *"Listo."*

The line of riflemen chambered a cartridge, then lifted their rifles.

"Apuntar . . ."

They lifted their rifles to their shoulders, pointing their guns at Jack.

"Taylor, reboot him now!" I shouted.

Taylor grabbed Nichelle's hand and put her hand against the glass. The man commanding the execution froze. He looked down at the ground, then around the yard with a blank expression on his face, like a man who had just woken up. The firing squad looked almost the same, all lowering their rifles.

Zeus, Cristiano, Nichelle, and I ran to the nearest set of doors. I kicked them open, then ran directly in front of Jack, pulsing to repel any possible bullets, though none came.

Zeus fired a lightning bolt at the commander. The commander was still holding his sword, which was an excellent conductor for Zeus's lightning, and the man was knocked off his feet.

Once I was in front of Jack, I turned around and blasted the riflemen, taking them all out in one pulse. One of the rifles went off, and Jack's body jerked in anticipation. He still had his hood on and had no idea what was going on.

Apparently, neither did the Chasqui soldiers in the audience, who looked as confused as the men Taylor had rebooted. They seemed unsure if this was part of an exercise or the show they'd come to watch.

I pulled Jack's hood off. After his eyes adjusted to the sun, he looked at me with disbelief. "Michael?"

He had been beaten so badly, I almost didn't recognize him. His face was cut and bruised, he had two black eyes, and dried blood covered most of his hair.

"Not your day to die, my friend." I went behind the pole, melted the vinyl rope he was tied with, and pulled it off him. "Nor mine. Let's get out of here."

"Where are we going?" he asked.

I looked back at all the soldiers, who were starting to move toward us. "Not totally sure," I said. "I didn't think we'd make it this far."

For one of the few times since I'd known him, Jack's eyes welled up. "And you came anyway."

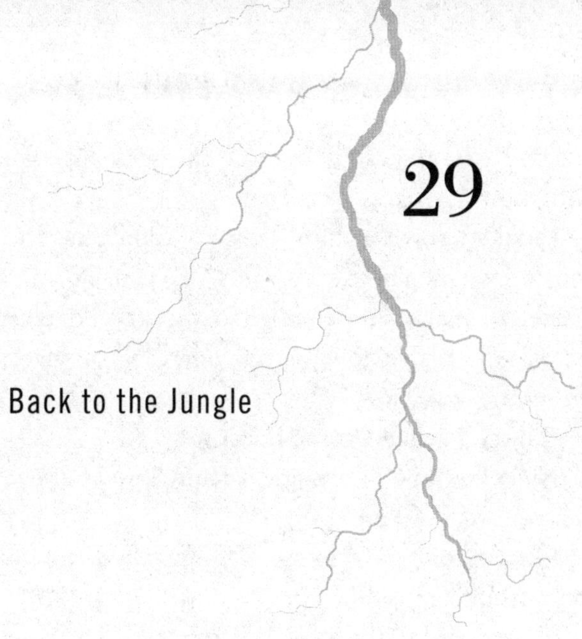

29

Back to the Jungle

I shouted to Zeus and the others, "Back the way we came." Jack, Zeus, and I ran to the building.

"Hurry," Nichelle shouted. She was holding the door for us. Cristiano stood there pointing the pistol we'd taken from the sergeant, but not firing. There were too many soldiers, and none of them were chasing us yet anyway.

"Hello, Jack," Nichelle said as he passed. "It's good to see you in one piece."

"It's good to be in one piece."

Zeus and Cristiano came in after us; then Nichelle shut and locked the door. Inside the corridor, the sergeant was lying on the ground with McKenna and Taylor standing above him. Taylor came over and hugged Jack.

"You saved my life," Jack said. "Twice."

"Then we're even," she said.

"Did you save your friend?" the sergeant asked eagerly. "This is him, right?"

I looked down at him. "Yes, you don't have to die today. Unless you follow us. The next time I see you, no mercy." I checked my pocket to make sure I still had the key I'd taken from him, then looked up. "We've got to go. Taylor, can you give the whole group a big reset?"

"I'll try. Nichelle, come boost me."

Nichelle came to her side. Taylor closed her eyes and reached out. "There."

I looked out the window. The mob was now just looking around the yard in confusion.

"Come on," I shouted. We retraced our steps to the rat bowl. There were still no sirens.

"Where are we going?" Cristiano asked.

"Back to the jungle."

"But the Chasqui are all over out there."

"I know," I said. "But they don't know *we're* out here. They haven't turned on their sirens."

Just then a siren went off, blasting over the entire compound.

"Never mind," I said.

We ran out of the rat bowl past the guard booth, then through the brush to the electric fence. I stepped on the bottom wire and lifted the one above it, the power again arcing between my fingers.

"Still high voltage," I said. "Everyone, be careful."

Once everyone was through the fence, I asked Ostin, "You got the GPS?"

He lifted it. "Right here."

"Let's try to take the same trail back to the Amacarra. We'll pick up Tara, then hike to the lodge. Ian, keep your eyes open. They'll be coming for us."

"Do you think they'll alert the Chasqui at the cave?" Cristiano asked.

"You can be sure of it," I said.

"Then we could be surrounded."

"Not completely. It's a big jungle." I turned back. "Lead us, Ostin."

We started back out into the forest. We moved quickly, powered by the adrenaline of being chased.

"Ian, is anyone behind us?"

"Not that I can see. But they had to go around the electric fence. We went through it."

"Hopefully they won't find our tracks."

"You can bet they'll bring the RESATs this time," Ian said.

"Let's just keep in front of them."

Even without our Amacarra guides, it was much easier moving in the daytime.

"I could use some of that Amacarra power water," Ostin said.

"Me too," Ian said. "That was good stuff."

"You guys came to Peru alone?" Jack asked.

"No. We came down with Johnson and Alpha Team."

"Johnson," Jack said. "I love those guys. I haven't seen them for months. Bentrude is my main man. Did he come down with them?"

The question stung. I stopped and turned back. "Bentrude was killed."

Jack was stunned. "Killed?"

"By the Chasqui." I turned back to the trail. "Don't think about it. We've got to keep going."

After a few more minutes, Jack asked, "Was anyone else killed?"

"Luther and Gunnar." I glanced back. "Really, there's too much to tell you right now."

Saying that only stressed him more. "Where's the rest of the Electroclan?"

I wondered if he was really just wondering about Abigail. This wasn't the time to tell him we didn't know where she was.

"Most of them are with Alpha Team. They're going to stop the Chasqui trucks carrying the electric bats."

"How did you know they were doing that?"

"Cristiano told us."

Jack glanced back at Cristiano, who was three people behind us. "Is that Cristiano, the Peruvian guy?"

"Yes."

"Where'd you find him?"

"He was a Chasqui."

Jack moved closer. "Michael, you can't trust a Chasqui. They're fanatical in their beliefs. It's a cult. Once a Chasqui, always a Chasqui."

"Just like you, Cristiano never joined the cult."

Jack was silent for a few more minutes, then asked the question that was really bothering him. "Where's Abi?"

I didn't answer. I wished he'd just be quiet.

"Michael?"

"She's not here," I finally said.

"I don't blame her for not wanting to come. After that fight we had about her going to school instead of coming with me. I was really an idiot."

By now everyone else was listening. I didn't say anything.

"That's why she didn't come, right?" He looked around at everyone else. "She's okay, right?"

"She's missing," Nichelle said.

"Missing? Where?"

"If we knew that," Nichelle said, "she wouldn't be missing."

"We think she was kidnapped from school," Ostin said.

"By whom?"

"We found some footage of her kidnappers," Taylor said. "We think they're electrics like us. And we think we saw Bryan with them."

"Hatch's Bryan?"

"Yes."

"I'm going to fry his—"

"Jack," I said. "Save it. We're not out of the woods ourselves."

"Literally," Ostin said.

After another ten minutes, Jack said, "Michael."

"Yes, sir."

"When I called you from the helicopter and told you I was one of them, did you believe me?"

"I don't know."

"Tell me the truth."

"The truth is, I didn't know. You were pretty convincing."

He walked a bit more, then said, "Would you have killed me if you had to?"

"I don't know how to answer that. Had to is *had to*."

"If the Chasqui had come at you, me with them, would you have killed me?"

"I don't know."

"Let me tell you something. If I ever pose a threat to my friends, you'd be doing me a favor to kill me. Do you understand?"

"My head does. But it's not that simple."

"Then get this into your heart and head. I'd rather be dead than be a traitor to you and my friends. Okay? You'd be doing me a favor. You never forget that."

"I understand."

"I love you, man."

"I love you too."

As we continued plodding through the jungle, I shouted to Ostin, "None of this looks familiar. Are you sure we're going the right way?"

"The GPS doesn't lie," Ostin said. "And I don't make mistakes."

"Of course not."

"It was night before. That's why nothing looks familiar."

"Are we there yet?" Nichelle asked.

"We've still got at least two hours," he said.

"I'd kill for some water."

"The Amacarra will have water," I said. I turned to Ian. "Still no Chasqui?"

"Not that I can see."

"Why does that make me nervous?"

"Me too. I like to keep my enemies close."

Fifteen minutes later a helicopter flew by us, followed a few seconds later by another.

"That's got to be Chasqui."

"Maybe it's just rich tourists," Nichelle said.

"It's Chasqui," Ian said.

"I wish Tanner was here," Nichelle said.

"Are they slowing down?" I asked.

"Not a bit."

"They just can't see us under the trees," Nichelle said.

"They have el-readers," I said. "That's how they tracked us the last time we escaped."

"Maybe they're not looking for us," Ostin said.

That seemed like a dumb thing for Ostin to say.

"Why wouldn't they be looking for us?"

"Because they're going after Alpha Team."

My chest constricted. "I hope you're wrong for once. How would they even know about them?"

"I don't know," he said.

I hated it when Ostin didn't know something.

PART SIXTEEN

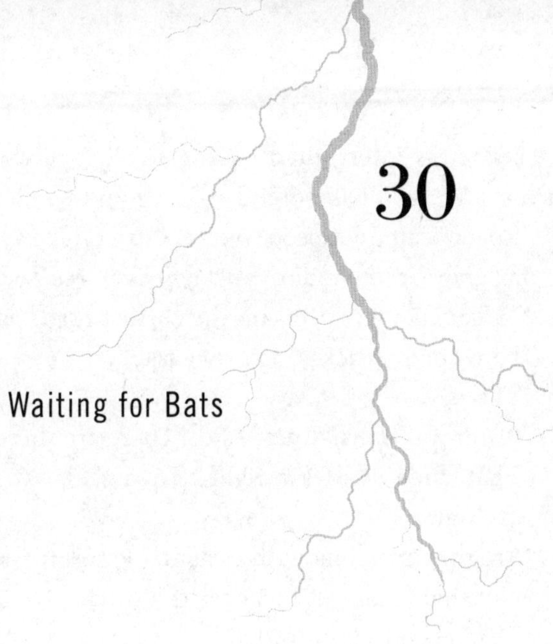

30

Waiting for Bats

In the first nest, Jax said to the women, "This is always the hardest part of battle for me. Waiting."

"I would think it would be when someone starts shooting at you," Cassy said.

"I'm not saying that's easy, but when you're in a firefight, you're so full of adrenaline, you don't really have time to think about fear. I've seen guys shot and not even know it until they slow down."

"I see that," she said. She turned to Tessa. "How are you doing?"

"I'm officially ready to go home."

"What will you do when you get home?"

Tessa smiled. "First I'm going to kiss Brummell."

"Brummell? Is that your boyfriend?"

"He's my Cavapoo. Then I'm going to take a very long bubble bath. Then I'll go to the spa for a pedicure and get my nails done. And, of course—"

Tessa was interrupted by the squelch of the radio, followed by Jacinta's voice. "Strikeforce Two, are you there?"

"Roger," came Johnson's voice. "Strikeforce One, are you there?"

Jax grabbed the radio. "Roger, Strikeforce Two."

"Target is in view. It is on the correct road," Jacinta told everyone.

"How many trucks?" Johnson asked.

"Three."

"Ostin was right," Cassy said. "There are three cargo containers."

"That dude is always right," Tessa said. "At least as long as I've known him."

"Are they traveling with escorts?" Johnson asked.

"Not that I can see. I just see the trucks."

"That's good," Johnson said.

"I am pulling out to follow them," Jacinta said. "I will keep you updated."

"Thank you," Johnson said. "Over."

"Over," Jax said. He turned to the two women. "So it begins."

Tessa lay back in the nest. "You're right. It's the waiting. I've got butterflies."

"That's a good thing," Jax said. "Butterflies keep you alert. But this mission is different from most."

"How's that?" Tessa asked.

"No one will be shooting back. It's just like shooting fish in a fishbowl."

"Isn't it supposed to be 'fish in a barrel'?" Tessa said.

"A fishbowl is easier. Smaller. Like this road."

"You mean the . . . *kill zone*," Cassy said sarcastically.

Jax grinned. "You really shouldn't be so flippant with your commanding officer. You could get written up for insubordination."

"What does that mean?"

"What does 'insubordination' mean?"

"I know what 'insubordination' means. What does getting 'written up' mean?"

"It means whatever they want it to mean."

"Then it could mean that I'm put in private confinement with someone, like, say, you?"

"I'm sure that could be arranged."

Tessa rolled her eyes. "Really, guys? Do you think about anything else?"

"She's right," Cassy said. "Save it for later. Besides, no one's writing me up. I'm a civilian contractor." She looked back out over the road. "How far out are they?"

"They just passed the fork, so about two hours."

"Two hours."

"So," Cassy said, turning to Tessa. "After you kiss your dog, have a bath and the manicure, then what?"

PART SEVENTEEN

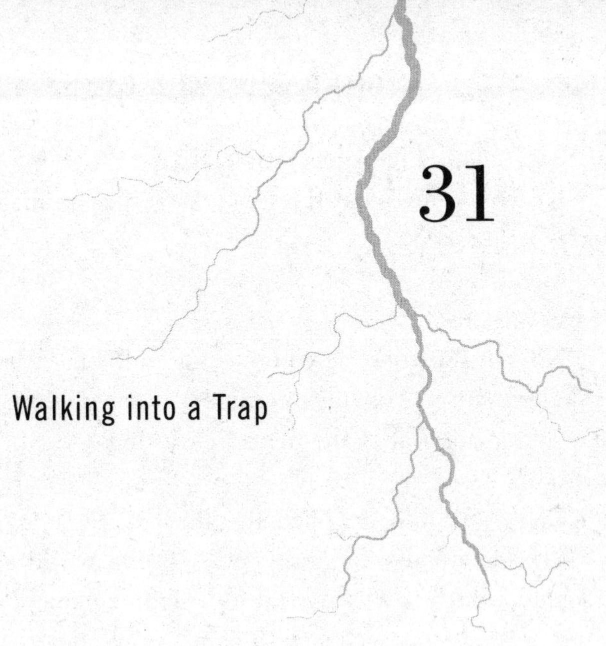

31

Walking into a Trap

"Look over there," Ian said. "There's a jaguar."

"Where?" McKenna asked.

"In that tree over there. It's hanging on the second-to-lowest branch."

"I see it," she said. "It's beautiful."

The cat was just lounging in the tree, watching us, its green eyes reflecting the ambient light. It looked more bored than threatening.

"Should I drop it?" Zeus asked.

"It's not bothering us," McKenna said. "Besides, they're a protected species."

"I wish we were," Taylor said.

"We were what?" McKenna asked.

"A protected species."

I glanced over at her. "I'll protect you."

She smiled. "I'll protect you back."

"Do you know what the most dangerous animals in the Amazon are?" Ostin asked.

"Man," I said.

"Besides us."

"No, but I'm guessing you're going to tell us," Zeus said.

"There are the obvious predators—the caimans, anacondas, piranha, and jaguars—but the more interesting ones you might not have heard of."

"Can't wait to hear," Nichelle said.

"The Brazilian wandering spider is the world's most venomous arachnid, which is why part of its scientific name, *Phoneutria*, means 'murderess.' Its bite can lead to paralysis and death.

"Then there's the bullet ant, which isn't as much deadly as it just makes you want to die. Its sting is thirty times more painful than your average bee sting, and the pain can last for twenty-four hours. And the thing is, it will sting you over and over until you get the message.

"They call it the bullet ant because soldiers who have experienced being shot by a bullet and being stung say its sting is at least as painful as the bullet."

"I wish someone would shoot me through the ears with a bullet right now," Nichelle said.

"The entomologist Justin O. Schmidt created a stinging pain index, and the bullet ant was ranked at the top. He described the pain as pure, intense, and brilliant—like walking over flaming charcoal with a three-inch nail in your heel."

"That certainly is descriptive," Ian said.

"But, ounce for ounce, the most dangerous animal is one you'd never suspect. It's the tiny poison dart frog. It's barely the size of a human thumb, but it carries enough toxin to kill ten adult men."

"Then I'm glad I'm not an adult man," Nichelle said.

"That's not what I—"

"I know," Nichelle said. "I know."

I was really feeling my fatigue. If it hadn't been for the Amacarra's power water, I likely would have already collapsed. We were about a half mile from where we had left Tara and the tribe, when Ian suddenly stopped. He had a frightened look on his face. He walked around in a circle saying, "It can't be."

"What is it?" I asked.

"The Chasqui are everywhere. They're armed to kill, and they have portable RESATs."

"Where do we go?" I asked.

He shook his head. "We're surrounded. They've completely encircled us. It's like they know exactly where we are."

"How far out are they?"

"About a quarter mile. They must have known where we were going."

"Or they've been tracking us," I said. "Like they did before."

"How?" Taylor asked. "We got rid of our disks."

I thought a moment, then said, "Jack. Check your clothing."

Jack reached into his pockets, then patted himself down. "Nothing."

"Show me your arm," Ian said.

Jack pulled up his sleeve and put out his arm.

"Both arms."

He held them both out.

"Right there," Ian said, pointing to Jack's left arm. "That lump is an RFID. It's like Hatch used on his Glows, but smaller. Amash was guaranteeing you couldn't escape."

Jack looked panicked. "I just thought it was a hematoma, you know? Just another lump after they beat me."

"That's why they weren't chasing us," I said. "They were letting us run into their trap."

"These guys are smarter than the Elgen," Ostin said.

"That's not encouraging," I said.

"Cut it out of me," Jack said.

Ian said, "It's too late for that."

"No, it's not," Jack said. "This ain't over."

"Jack's right," I said. "If we somehow escape, they'll still just track us with it."

"Cut it out," Jack said again.

I took the Chasqui knife from my belt. "I'll do it."

"It's subcutaneous," Ostin said. "It's just under the skin. You don't need to go deep."

I set the point of the blade against his arm, hesitated, then pulled it back. "I'm too shaky for this."

"I can do it," Nichelle said. "I have a lot of experience doing this."

I wasn't sure what she meant by that, but I handed her my knife.

"We'll need to sterilize the blade," she said. "Anyone have something?"

"I have heat," McKenna said.

"That will work."

McKenna grabbed the end of the blade and heated it up. "That will do. Let the blade cool."

"I got a little water left," Cristiano said.

"You've been holding out," Nichelle said.

"Yes." He poured some over the blade.

"All right," Nichelle said, waving the blade in the air to cool it off. She looked up into Jack's face. "I wish Abi were here."

"Me too," Jack said.

Nichelle took a deep breath. "Ready?"

"Just do it."

She inserted the blade about an eighth of an inch into his arm and made a straight quarter-inch incision. Jack clenched his jaw as blood streamed down his arm.

"You can push it out," Ostin said. "Squeeze it. Like a zit."

Jack pinched the skin on his forearm, and a dime-sized metal disk popped out. It was covered in blood. "That's the traitor."

He was about to throw it, when I stopped him. "Wait, let's do what we did back at the zoo."

"What's that?" Jack asked.

"You mean put them on the monkeys again?" Ian said. "Because that didn't work so well last time."

"That's because the monkeys wouldn't leave the zoo," I said. "We'll use a wild bird this time."

"There are macaws in that tree over there," Taylor said.

I looked over. About fifty feet from us, there was a colorful flock of birds in a tree. "Taylor, can you reboot them?"

"I'll try. They're pretty far away."

"I can help," Nichelle said.

"You'll have to catch the bird before it hits the ground," McKenna said. "So it doesn't break a wing or something."

They walked closer to the tree. "Here we go," Taylor said.

Her rebooting worked better than she'd thought it would, as all of the birds and a sloth fell from the tree. Ostin and Nichelle did their best to catch the birds but only caught four of them. McKenna caught the sloth. The two birds that hit the ground got up onto their feet, then flew back up into the tree.

"I wish I could keep you," McKenna said, setting the sloth on the ground.

"We only need one bird," Nichelle said, letting one of the birds go. It flew back up into the tree. Ostin still hung on to his two birds.

"Wait," Taylor said. "If Jack has a tracking device, maybe Tara and I do too."

"Do you remember them giving you a shot?" I asked.

"No. But neither does Jack. They had the RESAT so high, I was unconscious much of the time."

"Let me see your arm," I said.

Taylor held out her arms. I ran my fingers up them. There was nothing.

"They're not necessarily in her arms," Ian said. He looked her over. "Do you feel anything foreign on your body?"

"There's something on my hip." She pulled her pants down on one side, exposing a small lump.

"There it is," Ian said. "You have one."

Taylor winced. "I thought it was a bug bite. Hurry, cut it out."

"Nichelle?" I said.

Nichelle came over, wiping Jack's blood off the blade on the inside of her shirt. "McKenna?"

Nichelle held on to the knife as McKenna heated the blade again.

Then Nichelle crouched down next to Taylor. "I'm sorry."

Taylor gritted her teeth. I took her hand.

"This is going to hurt," Nichelle said. She poked the blade into Taylor's hip. Taylor squeezed my hand so tight, I thought she might break my fingers.

"Done."

"Will you take it out?" Taylor asked.

Nichelle pinched the skin around her hip. The disk, along with blood and tissue, came out. "Got it." Nichelle held the disk up in the palm of her hand.

McKenna came over and hugged Taylor. "I'm sorry."

"I'm okay," she said.

The blood kept streaming down her hip, soaking up in her underwear.

"We don't have any gauze, do we?" I asked. "Or a clean cloth?"

Cristiano looked inside the pack. "Nothing."

"Do you want McKenna to cauterize it?" Ostin asked.

"You can do it," Taylor said to me.

I put a single finger over the incision and slowly brought up my electricity. I could smell the blood burning. I took my finger away. The wound was yellow with red edges. The bleeding had stopped.

"What about you, Jack?"

His arm was covered with blood. "Go ahead." I put two fingers over his wound and pulsed. This time I could hear the blood sizzling. He jumped back from the jolt, then looked down at his arm. "That worked."

"Guys, we've really got to hurry," Ian said. "They're getting close."

Ostin was holding the macaws by their talons, like a farmer would carry a chicken. He handed one to me, then one to Taylor.

"Don't let them bite you," he said. "They can crack open nuts with that beak."

"I'm rebooting them again," Taylor said.

"How are we going to attach the disks?" Cristiano asked. "We do not have any tape or glue."

"Tree sap," Ostin said. "Give me your knife." He looked around for a moment, then said, "Perfect." He walked over to a tall mushroom-shaped tree. "The *sangre de drago* tree. Its latex sap is legendary. The natives use it as a liquid bandage." He stuck his knife into its trunk and cut off a swath of bark. The sap beneath was red, like blood.

"It's a very strong adhesive." He scooped out a glob of latex and brought it back to us. "We'll do Taylor's bird first." Ostin scooped a quarter-sized gob of the sap and put it onto the scarlet feathers between the wings in the middle of the bird's back. Jack handed Ostin the RFID, and Ostin pressed the disk into the goop.

"Now let it go," Ostin said to Taylor.

Taylor tossed the bird up into the air. It let out a loud screech, stretched out its wings, and flew back to the top of the tree with the other macaws.

"Now your bird, Michael," Ostin said. He did the same with the tree sap. Nichelle brought the disk over and pressed it into the sap.

"Fly away, little decoy," she said, throwing the bird up into the air. The bird likewise flew up to the flock.

"They're just sitting there," Nichelle said. "Like those stupid monkeys."

I threw a lightning ball up near the branch. The flock flew off.

"People, we've really got to go," Ian said.

"We need a place to hide," I said. "If they're chasing the disks, they'll walk right past us."

"Over there," Ian said. About a hundred feet from us was a massive lupuna tree. Its trunk was more than twenty feet in diameter, and its roots were more than eight feet high, providing an almost cave-like space to hide.

"That will do," I said. The cavity in the tree was nearly fifteen feet wide and spread out from the opening, so we could hide around the sides of the roots without risk of being seen.

About five minutes later Ian said, "Here they come."

We could hear the scuffling of boots through the forest's dense foliage as the line of Chasqui advanced. They were moving at a brisk pace when their advance abruptly stopped. The sound of their boots was replaced by shouting.

"What's going on?" I asked.

Ian said, "They've closed the ring. They just met up with the soldiers coming in from the other sides. I don't know what he's saying, but one of the captains is shouting and pointing at the other two soldiers. Man, he is, like, red in the face. Now he's pushing one of them."

"He is blaming the other soldiers for letting us slip by them," Cristiano said. "The other soldiers are defending themselves. They say no one went by them and something must be wrong with the trackers."

The Chasqui's shouting continued.

"Now what's going on?" I asked Cristiano.

"The most important Chasqui boss commanded one of the groups to go back and find us. He said that his soldiers and the other group will go after the other one."

"What does that mean?" Nichelle asked. "The other one?"

"What other one?" I asked.

Taylor said, "It's Tara. If we had trackers, she will too. She'll lead them to the Amacarra's village. The Chasqui will find her, then slaughter the tribe. We need to warn them."

Taylor was starting to leave the tree when I grabbed her.

"Not yet," I said.

"They're going to get Tara and the Amacarra."

"And we're outnumbered and outgunned. They'll kill us first, then slaughter the tribe, along with Tara. We need to let them divide up. Then we'll go after them."

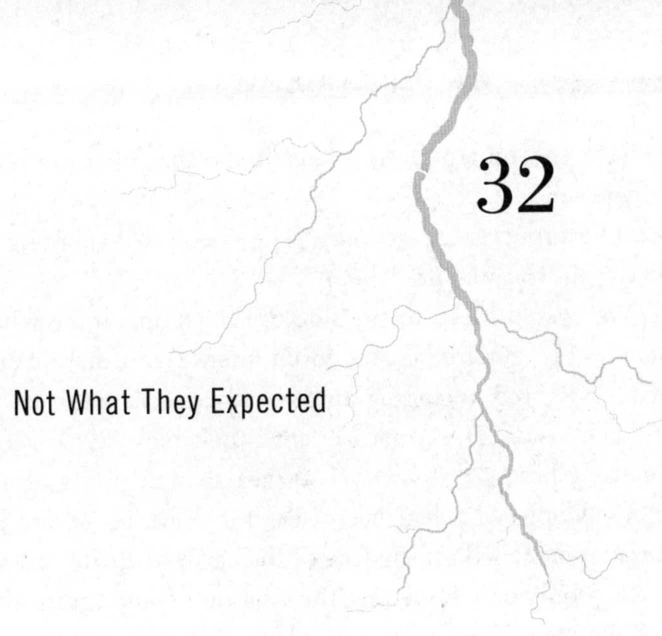

32

Not What They Expected

The soldiers divided into three groups. Two of the groups went off in different directions; the third, with the commander, just stayed in place.

"What are they doing?" I asked Ian.

"I have no idea."

Ostin said, "They might be planning to flank the tribe, so they're giving the other team time to get ahead."

About five minutes later the commander called his men to attention. Then they started off southwest toward the Amacarra camp.

"I think you were right," I said to Ostin. "Ian, can you see the other group?"

"They're too far," he said.

When the main group was out of sight to all of us except Ian, we came out of our hiding place and went out after them. We had hiked for about a half hour when, in the distance, we heard gunfire.

"The second group must have found the Amacarra," I said. "What do you see?"

"Our group is engaged now. They've started shooting too. It's too dangerous to go in after them."

We veered south to the side of the troops to see what was happening. The gunfire became more intense, and there were hundreds of rounds fired, including automatic weapons and machine guns. I felt sick inside. The Amacarra with their blow darts were no match for the Chasqui firepower. The idea that the Amacarra—an indigenous people who had been here for centuries—were going to be completely wiped off the face of the earth made my stomach sick.

We could only hope that the Chasqui would capture Tara instead of killing her. Then, at least, we'd have a chance to try to save her.

As we climbed the hill that overlooked the Amacarra village, the gunfire stopped. Tears welled up in my eyes. I figured we were too late. But when I came up over the pinnacle, I couldn't believe what I saw.

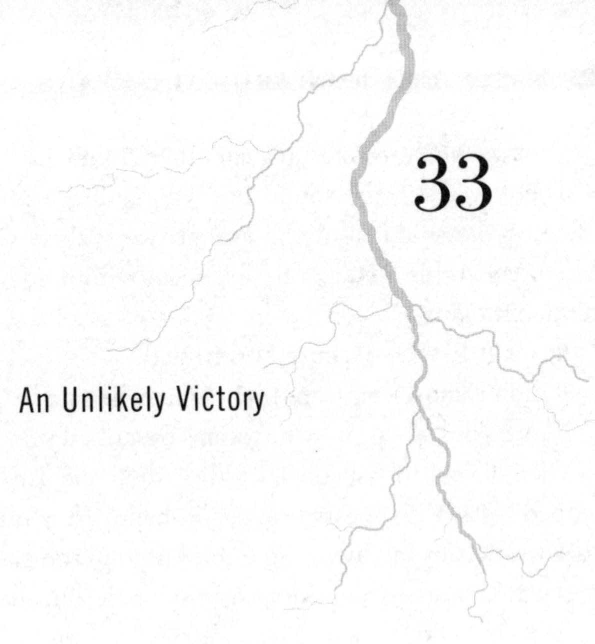

33

An Unlikely Victory

I hadn't seen the Amacarra village from this vantage point since the first time the tribe had brought me there. The thatch huts were still mostly standing, though several had holes blown into them, and straw and mud plaster littered the ground like a tornado had passed through. Two of the huts were on fire, and dark plumes of smoke climbed up through the jungle canopy. The astringent smell of gunfire still filled the air, along with the white lingering smoke of shells.

There were bodies scattered all over the ground. But they weren't Amacarra. They were Chasqui. The bodies, on both sides of the camp, were uniformed Chasqui soldiers lying in pools of their own blood. It was an unmitigated massacre. They had killed themselves.

"That makes no sense," Ian said. "It looks like they shot each other."

"Their argument was getting pretty heated back there," Jack said. "They clearly hated each other."

"Not so much to turn on each other," I said.

There was still the sound of crying and groaning, evidence that a few of the soldiers on the ground were alive. One of them was able to get to his feet, but he fell again within a few seconds. A few stopped moving.

"It looks like Gettysburg," Ostin said.

"I didn't know you were there," Nichelle said.

"I'm talking about how historians described it."

Then, from the shadow of the trees, the Amacarra tribesmen stepped forth with spears or clubs in hand. They quickly finished off what was left of the living Chasqui. Entering the clearing next to the chief was Tara. She was leaning against a pole, but she was on her feet.

"It's Tara," Taylor said. "She's walking."

"Oh, I see what happened," Ostin said. "Very clever."

"What happened?" I asked.

Ostin turned to me. "Tara made the Chasqui look like the Amacarra to each other. They thought they were fighting their enemy, but they were only fighting themselves."

"Brilliant," I said. "I'm going down."

"Just don't spook them," Ostin said. "They still have those blow darts."

We all walked out of the jungle into the clearing. The chief saw us first. "Michael Vey!"

"Tara!" Taylor shouted. She ran to her, and the sisters embraced.

The chief said, "Did you witness this amazing miracle?"

"Just now," I said. "It was Tara?"

"Yes. Her special power. She made them look to each other as they truly are, the enemy." He looked at Jack. "You have someone new with you. You saved your friend?"

"Yes. We saved him."

"I am very happy for you. This is a day for us to always remember, to share stories for our children's children's children. The day of the great miracle, when the magic of the Tara, the *lyang gwang*, prevailed against the demons. We will have a great feast this night to celebrate."

"We would like to sleep first," I said. "We are exhausted."

"Of course. You may sleep in the huts."

"We first need to gather their weapons," Jack said. "There is still a Chasqui group out there."

"Yes. He speaks truth. Our warriors are watching them from the trees. They are going away from us. If they come back this way, we must be ready. But for now you will sleep safely under our watch. Then we will celebrate this great victory."

PART EIGHTEEN

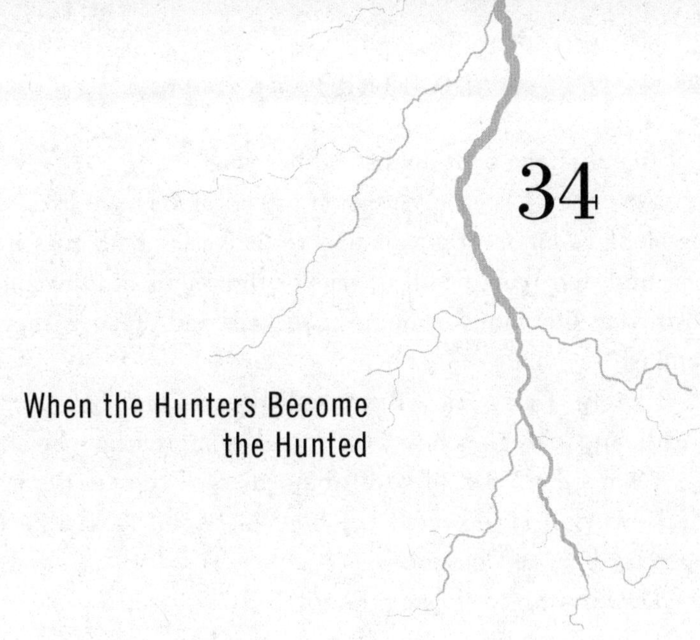

34

When the Hunters Become the Hunted

"Targets are six kilometers from the kill zone," Jacinta said.

"We're ready," Johnson said. "Strikeforce One?"

"We're ready," Jax repeated. He put down his radio. "That's about three and a half miles. We're five minutes from assault. Ready, ladies?"

"Yes," they said in unison. The mood had changed to extreme gravity as the reality of what was about to happen became more real.

"In five minutes, someone's life is going to end, and they don't even know it," Cassy said.

"That happens every day," Jax said. "It's not a big deal."

"It is to them," Cassy said. "And to me. I'm about to end someone's life."

"Technically a million of them," Jax said. "If you want to count the bats." He looked over at her. "Does that bother you?"

"I would hope so. It doesn't bother you?"

"Not when I keep my mission in context. These 'lives' are driving along as innocently as if they're delivering bath rugs instead of a painful, terrifying death to tens of thousands of innocent people, destroying thousands of homes and lives and dreams. They have it coming."

"I know," Cassy said. "But it still bothers me." She took a deep breath. Suddenly they heard the sound of approaching helicopters.

"What's that?" Jax lifted his binoculars. "I've seen those. They're Black Hawks." He lowered the binoculars and looked back at the women. "They're Chasqui."

"They must be following the trucks," Cassy said.

Jax lifted the binoculars again. Suddenly he shouted, "Get down. They've fired missiles." He threw himself over Cassy to protect her.

Their radio squelched, "Strikeforce One, Strikeforce One, there are—" The message never finished. Two of the helicopters' missiles were direct hits on the nest.

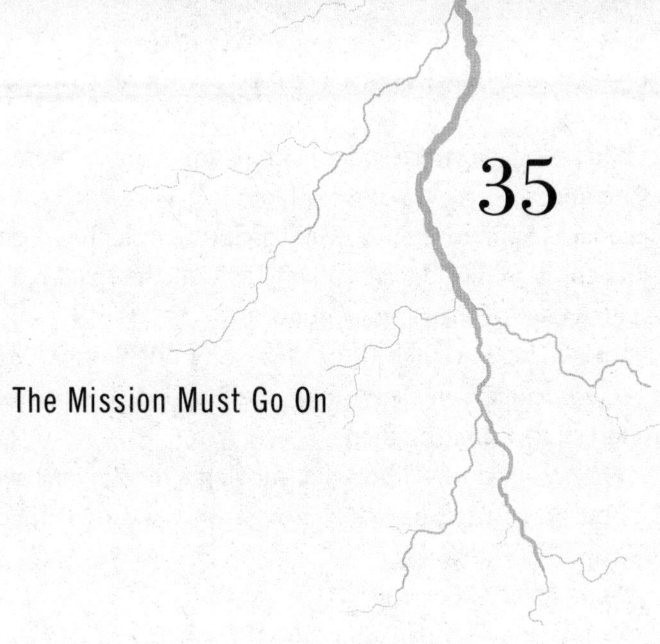

35

The Mission Must Go On

"Strikeforce One. Strikeforce One!" Johnson shouted. "Come in, Strikeforce One."

"The Chasqui knew we were here," Cibor said.

The radio buzzed; then Jacinta's voice came over. "Strikeforce Two, target is in the kill zone."

Johnson's discipline kicked in. "It's on us, team. Quentin, stop the first truck on my command. RPGs on target. Fire on my command. Cibor, prepare for detonation on my word."

"Got it."

The first truck careened around the corner into view. "Hold. Hold," Johnson said.

The second truck came around the corner.

"Quentin, stop truck one." The truck's engine stopped, but it continued to coast.

"Fire on truck one," Johnson shouted.

Both Johnson and Quentin fired direct hits. Johnson's grenade hit behind the truck's cab, exploding its gas tank, while Quentin's hit square in the cargo box. The truck tore in half and exploded into a fireball, flipping sideways off the side of the road and flinging the dead bats out of the cargo container.

Strikeforce Two picked up their second RPGs and fired, destroying the second vehicle. Above them a helicopter swung its tail around so it was facing them.

"He's spotted us," Cibor said, shoving a missile into his RPG.

Johnson pointed his RPG heavenward and fired. The helicopter blew up like a firework.

"Nice shot," Cibor said.

As Johnson was reloading his RPG, the third truck came speeding around the corner but was slowed by the scattered and burning wreckage of the second truck.

"Detonate!" Johnson shouted to Cibor.

"Roger," Cibor said as he flipped two switches. The truck exploded along with a side of the mountain, burying the road in a landslide of rock, earth, and trees. Above them the second helicopter veered off, then headed back in the direction it had come from.

Johnson picked up his radio again. "Strikeforce One, Strikeforce One, please respond."

There was nothing. Then Jacinta's trembling voice came over the radio. "They are gone, David. The nest was hit. I think they are gone."

36

The Ultimate Sacrifice

The highway was still burning with diesel fuel as Johnson, Cibor, and Quentin ran down the mountain and back up the road toward the Strikeforce One nest. They could see their van parked below and Jacinta climbing the mountain as well. There was no movement from the nest, and the trees around it were on fire.

Johnson was the first to reach the nest. His heart stopped at what he saw. Tessa had been thrown by the blast to the side of the nest. She was on her back, her eyes open. She was dead.

Jax's lifeless body was draped over Cassy's. His back was ripped open, and what could be seen of Cassy was spattered in blood.

When Quentin reached the nest, he screamed out, "Tessa." He jumped into the nest, and to her side. "Tessa, Tessa," he said, shaking her. There was nothing. Tears ran down his cheeks. He turned back to Cassy as Johnson pulled Jax's body off her. Her eyes were closed, and she was lying in blood. Johnson knelt and pressed his fingers onto her neck over her carotid artery.

"She's still alive." He looked up. "We've got to get her to a hospital."

"The only hospital is in Puerto," Jacinta said.

"We've got to make it there." He felt around her body for shrapnel, then lifted her in his arms. "Cibor, bring down our friends. I'll need Quentin and Jacinta to help me."

"Yes, sir."

Johnson carried Cassy down the side of the hill. Jacinta opened the back van doors, climbed in, then rolled out a blanket on the floor. "Lay her here."

Johnson laid her down. As Jacinta pulled her in, Quentin climbed into the back and pulled the doors shut. Jacinta grabbed the van's first aid kit. Johnson hit the gas and pulled a U-turn in the road, throwing both Quentin and Jacinta off-balance.

"We need to stop the bleeding," Jacinta said. "Her pant legs are soaked with blood. Raise her feet."

Quentin found a backpack and put it under Cassy's ankles.

"We need to take her clothes off," Jacinta said.

Quentin undid Cassy's shoes, then pulled down her pants, smearing blood down her legs as he did. Jacinta immediately pressed her hand against Cassy's thigh.

"She is bleeding too much. She will need a tourniquet."

Quentin looked around for a rope, then said, "We'll use her pant legs." He pulled out his knife, cut the left leg off, and handed it to Jacinta, who wrapped it around Cassy's thigh, then twisted it. The bleeding above Cassy's knee stopped.

"Hold that," she said to Quentin. Quentin grabbed the knot she'd made.

"The Puerto hospital is almost three hours away," Jacinta said. "We must keep her alive until then."

Looking at all the cuts and burns on Cassy's body, Quentin was glad that she was unconscious. He was also glad her eyes were closed. He could not get Tessa's cold, frozen stare out of his mind. He took Cassy's hand. "Don't leave us, Cass. Please. Stay with us."

He looked up at Jacinta, who was looking at him. "We should pray to Jesus," she said.

Quentin nodded. "You pray. I don't know how to."

"Jesus, please let this brave young woman live. She just saved many, many lives. Please save hers. Amen."

"Amen," Quentin said.

"Amen," Johnson said from the front.

Quentin squeezed Cassy's hand as he looked out the front windshield at the landscape flying by. He knew Johnson couldn't drive any faster. He just wished he could.

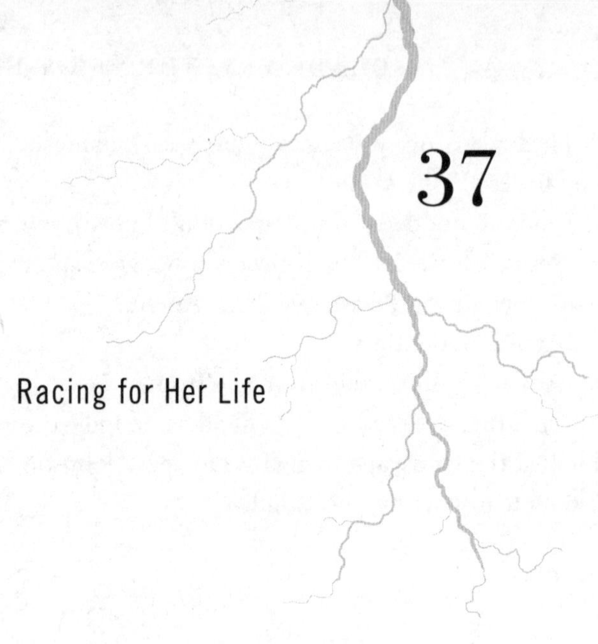

37

Racing for Her Life

Johnson looked over at the satellite phone next to him on the passenger seat. For more than twenty-four hours he had been waiting for a call from Jaime—a call that had never come—but now it was irrelevant. The moment of conflict had passed, and apart from his first call outside the lodge, Jaime hadn't contacted them at all. For the first time, he doubted Jaime was even alive. Or Michael and the rest. Of the two missions they'd set out on, Johnson had considered his the safest. Though they had been successful—they had stopped the Chasqui from destroying Arequipa—it had also been a personal disaster. It had seemed, from the beginning, that the Chasqui had always been one step ahead of them. Could he even hope that the others were still alive? He had no idea that, at that very moment, Michael and his friends were walking into a Chasqui trap.

It occurred to him that he could have Jacinta call her friend at the lodge to find out what was going on, but that would have to wait. For now, he pushed all thoughts of the others out of his mind. Right now there was only one life he had any hope of saving.

It was nearly three in the afternoon when they reached the outskirts of Puerto Maldonado.

"How is she?" Johnson shouted to the back.

"She has lost much blood," Jacinta said. "But she is still with us. It is a miracle."

He handed the phone back. "Call the hospital. Tell them we're almost there."

She took the phone and dialed. "*Aló?* I have an emergency. . . ."

Cassy's skin was turning waxy. She began to shake.

"Stay with us," Quentin said. "We're close."

Johnson drove the van up to the emergency entrance of the small hospital. In a larger city the Puerto Maldonado hospital would have been considered little more than a clinic, but it was the most equipped medical facility for hundreds of miles. A doctor and two technicians were waiting at the door as the van pulled in. They opened the back door of the van as Johnson jumped out of the cab.

"A su madre," the doctor exclaimed. *"Llévenla adentro."* The technicians pulled her body out onto a gurney. On the way to the intensive care unit, the doctor asked Jacinta in Spanish, "She is American?"

"Yes."

"What happened to her?"

"She was near an explosion."

"What kind of explosion?"

"A boiler," Jacinta said, making something up. "A metal boiler."

The doctor glanced at her skeptically but said nothing.

"Get a transfusion on her," he shouted as they entered the ICU.

"Her blood type is O positive," Jacinta said. "I'm a nurse."

"Then stay with us," the doctor said.

An ER nurse cleaned Cassy's arm and shoved a transfusion needle into it while another attached a bag of blood. A third put a blood pressure cuff on her other arm.

"She is very close," the doctor said, looking at the readings. "She has lost a lot of blood." The nurses began attaching electrodes to her body. The doctor looked at the monitor's readings. "Blood pressure sixty over forty-two. She is in hypovolemic shock."

Johnson and Quentin were standing outside the operating room looking in the window. The doctor glanced over at them, then back to Jacinta. "How long ago did this happen?"

"Three hours."

"And she is still alive? Where did this happen?"

"Out in the country. South toward Arequipa." Jacinta swallowed. "Is she going to live?"

"We hope," he said. "You can go out now."

"Thank you."

Jacinta walked out of the ICU. Johnson and Quentin met her in the hallway.

"What did the doctor say?" Quentin asked.

"He says she's lost a lot of blood."

"We know that. Is she going to live?"

"He says we can hope."

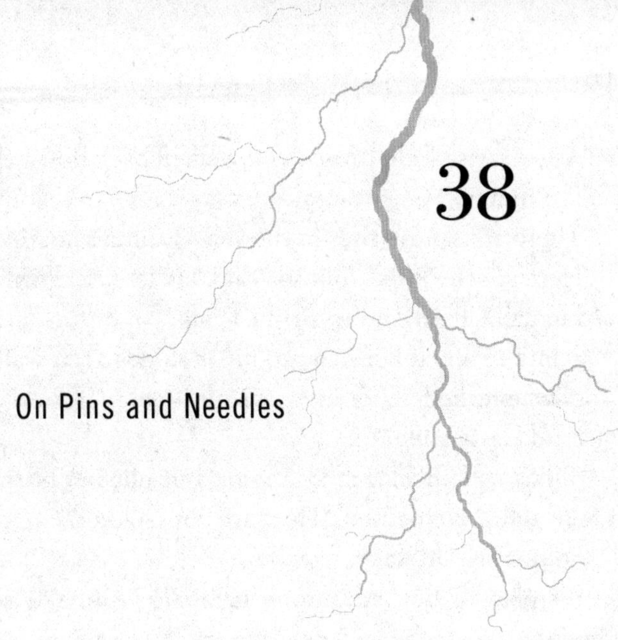

38

On Pins and Needles

The minutes passed like hours. Like a criminal waiting for the jury's decision, the group both anticipated and feared the verdict. Hour after hour passed, which Quentin decided was good, as it meant that Cassy was hanging in there. Around midnight the doctor came out to talk to them. All three of them quickly stood.

"How is she?" Jacinta asked.

"She is still bleeding internally. She is not stable yet, but she is strong."

"Thank goodness."

"I am off shift now. I will be back tomorrow morning. Dr. Flores will be taking over for me. I have gone over everything with him. He is capable. I do not expect that anything will change much in the next few hours. You should maybe get some sleep."

"We're okay," Quentin said.

"As you wish." He turned and walked back down the hall.

"I'm hungry," Quentin said.

"There are sandwiches in the van," Jacinta said. "I will get them."

"Here are the keys," Johnson said. He looked down at his phone. "I need to call Cibor. And try Jaime again."

Jacinta touched her hand to his shoulder, then walked out.

Johnson called Cibor first. "It's me," Cibor answered with a hoarse voice. "Is Cassy alive?"

"She is still alive," Johnson said. "But not out of the woods. She's in their ICU." He paused. "How are you, soldier?"

"Soldiering," he said.

"It's okay, Cibor. We are all heartsick. Alpha Team started with seven of us. As far as we know, we are the last two."

"Then Jaime is dead?"

"I don't know. We still haven't heard from him, but it's not promising."

"They could all be dead," Cibor said.

"It's possible. Where are you?"

"I'm at the hacienda. I have put . . . our friends in sheets. They are in a storage unit."

"If you want to come to the hospital to be with us, it is your decision."

"I would like to sleep a few hours," he said. "If you don't need me, I will come later."

"Get some rest."

"Good night, Johnson."

"Good night."

He hung up. Then he dialed Jaime's phone for the fifth time, but still there was nothing. "Where are you, Jaime? Where are all of you?"

PART NINETEEN

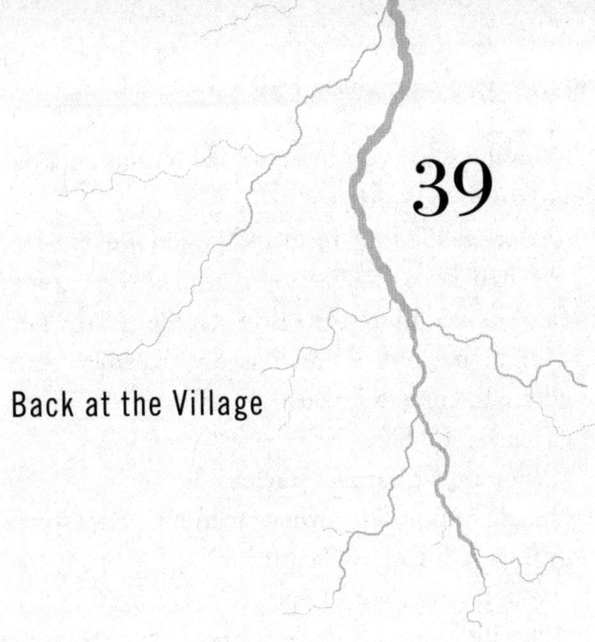

39

Back at the Village

It was dark when I woke. Taylor was lying next to me on the mat. She was already awake, looking into my eyes.

"How long have you been up?" I asked.

"A little while."

"What are you doing?"

"Looking at you."

"What do you see?"

She smiled. "Something beautiful." She sighed. "How do you think our friends are?"

"I'm sure they're okay. Johnson's smart. And there's no way the Chasqui know where they are. We don't even know where they are."

"I hope you're right." She touched a finger to my lips. "I'm wondering why you haven't gotten mad at me for surrendering to them."

"You did what you thought you had to do. I did what I thought I had to do. Same spirit, right?"

Taylor grabbed my head and pulled me into her. "I love you."

We had been kissing for a while when someone cleared their throat. I looked up to see Ostin standing in the doorway of the hut.

"Sorry," he said. "Dinner is on, or, whatever they call it. They asked me to come tell you."

"Thanks," I said.

"What are we eating?" Taylor asked.

"Jungle buffet. They have a wild boar on a spit, a baked anaconda, and a bunch of fruit and stuff."

"We'll be right out," I said.

"I'll tell them not to start without you." He went back out.

"Baked anaconda," Taylor said. "That sounds tasty."

"Snake is a delicacy in the jungle. The last time I was here, they fed me smashed grubs and bat guano."

Taylor made a face. "I'll stick to fruit."

40

A Celebration of Heroes

Around the fire were large wooden platters with different meats, including the anaconda, which had been sliced up into six-inch sections like a giant hoagie. It was dark, and the chirping of jungle cicadas filled the air. The village was lit by torches. The Chasqui bodies and weapons were gone. I don't know where the Amacarra took the Chasqui. Maybe somewhere the animals would find them.

The tribe and the rest of our group were gathered around a large fire. There were woven baskets filled with acai berries, bananas, mangoes, passion fruit, cupuaçu, avocados, and a few things I couldn't identify. The chief stood as we approached.

"Welcome, Michael and Taylor," he said with his arms extended. "Please sit next to me and eat." We sat on the right side of the chief, next to Ostin and McKenna.

Taylor lifted a cake and took a bite. "These are good."

"Do you want to know how they're made?" Ostin asked.

Taylor looked at him warily. "I don't know. Do I?"

"I'm guessing not," McKenna said.

"But you're going to tell me anyway, aren't you?" Taylor said.

"I watched them prepare it," Ostin said. "The women sat around a bowl chewing on yams until they were soft, and then they spit the yams back out into the bowl. They added some mustard and pepper, then formed them into little cakes and baked them."

"I'm going to throw up," Taylor said, taking the cake from her mouth. "Why did you have to tell me?"

"You said you liked it. I thought you'd like to know what you're eating. If you don't want it, I'll have it."

Taylor set the cake on the ground. Ostin picked it up and ate it.

"At least there's this stuff," she said. "It's pretty good." I looked at Ostin and shook my head. Taylor looked at me. "It's not something weird, is it?"

I didn't have the heart to tell her it was the same dish I'd mentioned earlier—live grubs ground in with taro root.

"Weird is a matter of perspective," I said. "I'm sure eating Jell-O pudding would be weird to them."

"This is kind of like Jell-O," she said.

"Go with that."

When the chief had finished eating, he raised his arms and said, *"Nigeb supmur layor eht tel!"*

Several of the Amacarra stood and left the circle. A moment later they came back carrying drums, which they set down on the ground, then sat behind, wrapping their legs around them.

"Oh, there's a program," Taylor said. "I like dinner theater."

I grinned.

The Amacarra began pounding their drums in a rhythmic beat. The chief said, "This is a dance of victory. We dance it in honor of the twines."

"I think he means 'twins,'" Ostin said.

Taylor put her finger to her lips. "Shh."

The dance went on for about twenty minutes. When it was over, the chief made a loud clicking noise, which the tribe members copied. Then he turned to me and asked, "Now that you have rescued your friends, what will you do?"

"We're going back to the lodge to get our other friend. Then we'll meet up with the rest of our friends."

"What is this lodge you speak of?"

"It's one of those Amazon eco lodges on the river. It's just a few miles from here."

His brow furrowed. "The lodge of the makisapa?"

"That's the one."

"No, Michael. You must not go to that place."

His response surprised me. "Why?"

"It is the demon's place. The demon Chasqui go there all the time. We see them."

"No, it belongs to our friend's friend. She says we can trust him."

"The man with the silver hair? He is tall and comes from the land of the yellow cross."

"That's him. The Swede."

"No, you cannot trust him. He has made an alliance with the Chasqui. He helps them to watch the river and warn them of anyone coming into the jungle."

I glanced over at Taylor, then back. "One of our friends is with them. He might be in danger. We need to go."

"The lodge is our concern as well. I will go with you," the chief said. "And my warriors."

"Thank you."

"It is late. You will need more of our water."

"All you can spare," I said.

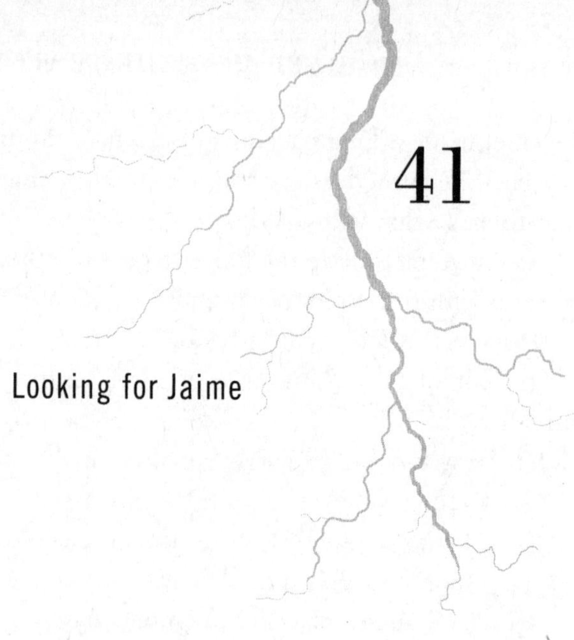

41

Looking for Jaime

Michelle, Jack, and Cristiano loaded up with Chasqui weapons. Then, after drinking our fill of their power water, we started off. The Makisapa Lodge was three miles from the Amacarra's village. We were able to make our way quickly along the Amacarra's trail, guided by their warriors, who knew the area well.

In just a little over an hour, we emerged from the lush jungle at the back side of the lodge, to a spacious, well-kept clearing. Directly behind the lodge there was a beautiful swimming pool, glowing bright blue. The area around it was dark and vacant except for a drunk couple sitting at the closed outdoor café. The only sounds were the jungle's billion bugs and frogs and the steady hum of the lodge's electric generator.

Ian immediately began looking around the lodge.

"Do you see any Chasqui?" I asked.

"Not so far."

"Do you see Jaime?"

"Not yet." A moment later he said, "There he is. He's in the back of the main lodge, behind the kitchen. There are slabs of meat hanging around him. It must be where they butcher meat."

"What's he doing in a meat locker?" I asked.

"He's tied to a chair." He shook his head with anger. "They've tortured him."

"How can you tell?"

"He has rope burns around his neck and waist, he has knife cuts, and he's been badly beaten."

"Is he okay?" Taylor asked.

"He's alive, if that's what you mean."

"Where's the Swedish dude?"

"He's in his bedroom, sleeping. I'm pretty sure that's him. There's only one bedroom behind the main office."

"How do you know he's sleeping?" Taylor asked.

"He's snoring."

"You can hear him snore?" Cristiano asked.

"No. I can see his lips flap."

"Let's rescue Jaime first. What's the best way?"

"There's a side kitchen entrance," Ian said. "There's no one around."

Our entire group moved to the side of the main lodge. The door was locked.

"I can kick it in," Jack said.

"Wait," Ian said. "There's someone in the kitchen."

"A guard?"

"No. It's just a guest grabbing some bottled water. And pie."

"I want some pie," Nichelle said, mostly to herself.

"Let him finish," I said.

We waited until Ian said, "Okay. He's leaving. He's going out the front door."

"I can open this door," McKenna said. "That won't wake anyone."

"Do it," I said.

McKenna put her hand against the door's hardware. Within a minute the metal was glowing bright red. McKenna pushed against the door with her foot, and the bolt bent with the door's opening. *"Entrez, s'il vous plaît."*

"Merci," I replied, walking in. There were lamps on all over the lodge, leaving it illuminated enough to walk through.

"It's that door right there," Ian said. "The room is dark inside."

"And they left the key in it just for us." I turned the key and opened the door. There was a switch to the side of the door, which I flipped on, filling the room with light. All of us except for two of the Amacarra warriors went inside the room, the Amacarra standing shoulder to shoulder against the walls.

Jaime was seated in a wooden chair in the middle of the room. His mouth and eyes were covered with duct tape, and around the sides of the tape we could see knife cuts. Patches of his hair were missing from his scalp, and his arms, which were also taped to the chair, had cigarette burns on them. Several of his fingers were bloody, and he was missing several fingernails.

"The chief is right," Taylor said. "They are demons."

"Demons and monsters," Jack said.

"I'll take the tape off," Taylor said.

"Take it off his eyes first," I said. "So he doesn't scream out."

"I wish Abi was here," she said.

"We all wish Abi was here," McKenna said.

"They're going to pay for this," Jack said. "Every last one of them."

"They already did," I said. "Back at the village."

When Taylor touched the tape over Jaime's eyes, he began violently shaking his head and body, making it difficult to remove the tape.

"Jaime, it's me. Taylor."

He continued jerking wildly.

"I'll help you," Jack said. "Jaime, it's Jack. Sorry, but I've got to hold you still."

Jack put him in a headlock while Taylor pulled the tape off his eyes. As soon as it was off, they both stepped back. Jaime grimaced and blinked his eyes. Then he looked up at us frightfully. His expression of fear turned to one of disbelief.

I crouched down next to him. "It's us. You're safe now."

Taylor struggled trying to get the tape off his mouth, until Jack stepped in, grabbed it, and ripped it off. Jaime let out a short gasp.

"Sorry, brother."

Jaime took in a deep breath. Then another. Then he said, "The Chasqui . . . run this place."

"We know," I said. "The Amacarra told us."

It was as if Jaime had just noticed all the Amacarra who were standing around the room. "What are they doing here?"

"Our paths merged," Taylor said.

"Thankfully," I said.

Jack took a Chasqui knife from his belt and cut Jaime's arms loose. Jaime stretched them out, then rubbed where his burns were.

McKenna said, "I'm going to see if they have any bandages or medicine for your wounds."

"Look for honey," Ostin said. "That works better on partial thickness burns."

"Come help me look," she said.

Jack got on his knees and cut Jaime's legs free.

"Thank you," Jaime said.

"Who did this to you?" Jack asked.

"The Chasqui soldiers. And Lars. Jacinta's *friend*." He said the word as if it hurt his mouth.

"I'm going to break him in two," Jack said.

"Jaime, why did they do this to you?" I asked.

"They wanted to know where you were going and where the others were."

I looked intensely into his eyes. "Did you tell them?"

His face twisted in anguish. Then he slowly bowed his head in shame. "I tried not to, Michael. I really tried. I'm so sorry. The pain was too much."

"We're not blaming you," I said. "I just need to know what you told them."

"I told them you were trying to save your friends."

"I'm sure they already guessed that. But it didn't do them any good. Did you tell them we knew about the bats?"

He nodded slowly. "I told them that the others had gone to blow up the road."

"Did you tell the Chasqui where Johnson's group was?"

"It was fortunate that I did not know where they were. I lied to the Chasqui. I told them the trap was just outside Arequipa. They said they would kill me if I lied. I thought you were them, coming back to kill me."

"You're very brave," I said.

"No. I am a coward."

I looked at his abused body—the cuts, bruises, and burns—and shook my head. "No, you are brave."

McKenna and Ostin returned carrying a small first aid kit, bottles of water, and a jar of honey. Ostin spread the honey over Jaime's burns with a butter knife. Then McKenna wrapped gauze over the burns.

"Here's some ibuprofen for pain," she said.

Jaime popped the pills into his mouth, then downed them with the water, which he drank until it was gone.

"Thank you so much," he said. He turned to me. "Jacinta's friend is not who she thinks he is."

"We know. We're about to pay him a visit. Would you like to join us?"

"Yes," he said, standing. His legs were wobbly, and he had to grab the chair's arms to steady himself. "My legs are still weak, but I would like to join you."

"We'll wait until you get your balance back."

"It's back enough," he said, standing up tall.

Jack took Jaime's arm to help steady him. "I'm here for you, brother. After what you've been through, I'm surprised you can stand at all."

Jaime looked at the bruises and cuts on Jack's face. "You've been beaten too."

"I took some licks, but not any more than my father used to give me."

"I am sorry for that," Jaime said.

"Ian, which way to the Swede?" I asked.

"We go through the kitchen, then left down the hall, all the way to the end."

On the way through the kitchen, I stopped and opened the freezer at the top of the refrigerator. There was, as I'd hoped, an ice pack. "Here," I said, handing it to Jaime. "This will help."

"Gracias." He pressed it to his shoulder.

I shut the freezer, then opened the refrigerator and took something out, then turned to Nichelle. "Here's your pie."

She grinned. "You kill me."

"I know." As we walked down the hallway, I asked Ian, "Are you sure it's him?"

"I am now," Ian said. "It's the same man we saw at the dock. He even has a Swedish flag above his headboard."

I tried his door. It was locked.

"I can melt it," McKenna said.

"I've got a better idea," Jack said. He walked up and fiercely kicked the door open, splintering the wood on the doorframe and smashing the door into the opposite wall. Lars lived in a studio apartment, and from the light of the hallway, I could see him spring up in his bed.

"Va' fan?! Va' fan?!"

"Hey, amigo," I said. "We heard about your hospitality, so we decided to come back after all."

Lars looked over at Jaime, who was fiercely glaring at him. "I can explain," Lars said.

"How could you possibly explain what you've done to him? Get out of bed."

He started pulling the sheets down, then suddenly lunged over to the closest nightstand.

I pulsed, slamming him against the bed's headboard. He dropped back to the mattress.

"He's got a gun in there," Ian said.

"I figured." I walked over to the nightstand and opened the drawer. There was a 9mm Glock handgun. There was also Jaime's satellite phone. I picked them both up, then handed the gun to Cristiano, who was closest to me. I said to Lars, "You weren't thinking of using that, were you?"

Lars just looked at me with wide eyes. "No."

"Liar. Stand up."

He stood. "I have my rights. I want to call my lawyer."

I snickered. "Where do you think you are? You don't have any rights."

"You should know that I—"

I shocked him. "Don't talk."

He pursed his lips.

"The only thing I want to hear from your lying little mouth are honest answers to my questions." I turned back. "Jaime, Taylor, come here."

Jaime walked over, glaring at Lars. Taylor looked at me. "Yes?"

"I'm going to interrogate our friend here. I need you to translate the truth to me."

"I'd be happy to." She took Lars's arms. "Ready."

"There are wounds all over Jaime's body," I said. "What do you know about this?"

"I don't know—"

I shocked him, and he screamed out. "I barely shocked you," I said. "For living in the jungle, you're not very tough."

He looked at me like he was going to burst into tears.

"And you're not even a decent liar. I didn't even need Taylor in order to see that one. So let's try that again. What do you know about his wounds?"

"The Chasqui wanted to know what he was doing here—what *you* were doing in the jungle, so they tortured him."

I looked at Taylor. She nodded.

"That was better. Which of these injuries did you do?"

"I didn't do any of them."

I looked at Taylor. She shook her head.

"Wrong answer." I shocked him harder. This time he fell.

"Get up," I said.

"Please, sir . . ." It sounded weird, since he was at least twenty years older than me.

I said, "Get up."

"I think he wants more," Jack said.

Lars struggled to his feet.

"Now answer my question. Which of these injuries did you do?"

"The Chasqui did them." I was about to shock him again, when he threw his hands up. "But I did those burns on his arm. The Chasqui made me."

"Where are the Chasqui now?"

"They went to find you."

"Yes, we know. And now they're dead. What about the ones who went to find our other friends?"

"They were supposed to be back."

"What were they going to do when they got back?"

"Nothing."

"Jaime, would you do us the honor?"

"Thank you." He slammed his fist into Lars's face, knocking him to the ground.

I crouched down next to him. "You're not a real fast learner, are you?"

He looked up at me with blood running from his nose.

"Jaime already told us what they were going to do. I just wanted to hear it from your evil mouth."

Lars swallowed. "They were going to kill him if he was lying to them. . . . But they were going to kill him anyway."

"When do you expect your friends back?"

"They're not my friends."

"Answer my question."

"They didn't say when. I promise. I assumed as soon as they found the others."

"Okay, I believe you. Get your shoes."

"Where are we going?"

"Outside."

"How come?"

"I want to show you something."

Lars shuffled his way out of his room wearing nothing but his shoes, white briefs, and an ABBA T-shirt. That's when he saw the line of Amacarra warriors standing in the hallway.

"What . . . what are they doing here?"

"Same thing we are. They're the ones who told us that you were with the Chasqui."

"How did they know that?"

"It's their jungle." I stopped walking. "Does Jacinta know you're with the Chasqui?"

He swallowed. "No. She hates the Chasqui. They killed her family. We wouldn't have been friends if she knew."

"Why would she want to see you?"

"We drank good wine together. She said I was the only civilization she had in the jungle."

I shook my head. "You really did have her fooled."

I led him out the front door of the main lodge. "Where do you keep the key to your boat?"

He swallowed. "It's inside my office. In the right top drawer of my desk on a key ring. The key ring has the Swedish coat of arms."

Ostin said, "That will have two lions and a whole bunch of crowns."

"Jack, go grab them."

"On it."

"The door's locked," Lars said.

"That won't be a problem," Jack shouted as he ran back to the lodge.

Lars looked at me expectantly as we waited for Jack to return. A few minutes later Jack came back with an entire ring of keys. "One of these should do it."

"I'll need those other keys," Lars said.

"No you won't," I said. "Cristiano, let me see Lars's gun."

Lars began shaking even harder. "Don't shoot me, please. I beg you."

I examined the gun. "I'm not going to shoot you," I said. "What do you think I am? A Chasqui?"

"Then what are you going to do with me?"

"What are *we* going to do with you? Nothing."

He breathed out in relief. "Thank you." He fell to his knees. "Thank you so much."

"Stand up."

"Whatever you say, sir."

"There's no reason to thank me. We're not going to do anything to you because the Amacarra felt it was their place to punish you. They said you had betrayed the jungle's code, and they have a special punishment for that."

Lars looked at me with wide eyes. "What punishment?"

"Have you ever heard of the tangarana tree? You must; you live here."

He didn't say anything.

"Hmm. Maybe you know it from one of its other names. The devil tree, the novice tree, and the justice tree."

Still no response.

"Really? Nothing? I mean, I don't even live in Peru, and I know what it is. All right, then, I'll tell you about it. The tree doesn't look much different from other trees. Kind of a dappled gray, with a smooth bark. Nothing spectacular.

"But you can always find it because it's the one tree nothing else grows around. It looks like a pole just sticking straight up in the jungle. They call it the devil tree because it's the home to a very special ant, called the tangarana ant. The tree and the ant have a rare symbiotic relationship. The tree provides a place for the ants to live and sap for them to eat. The ants, in appreciation, protect the tree. And they're good at it. They're an extremely aggressive and venomous fire ant. If an insect climbs onto the tree to eat a leaf, the ants immediately attack and kill it. If another plant or tree tries to grow anywhere near their tree, the ants kill it.

"They're small, but their venom is so potent and painful that just one bite on a human finger would cause the entire hand to swell up, and make red streaks up the arm. That's why people call it the 'novice tree,' because only a jungle novice would make the mistake of coming close to it. It's not a mistake they'd make again.

"The reason they call it the 'justice tree' is because people who commit crimes against the jungle are punished by being tied to the tree. Could you imagine having ten thousand of these aggressive, angry ants crawling all over you? Ten thousand venomous ants, biting and biting until the wrongdoer dies of pain or shock."

Lars looked over at the tribe, then said, "Shoot me. Please."

"Like I said, this gun isn't for you." I pointed the gun toward the river and fired it until it had no more bullets.

"What are you doing?" Lars asked.

"Waking your guests before I set fire to their rooms." I handed the gun back to Cristiano, then said, "McKenna, burn the place down."

McKenna walked over to the main lodge building. "Like this?" She lit up her hand, then touched it to the thatch that overran the building's roof. The thatch immediately caught fire. All around us, the lodge's guests began running out of their rooms.

I nodded to the chief, and four of the Amacarra warriors walked up to Lars's sides. Two of them took his arms.

"Please. Don't let them take me. I'm Swedish. We're peaceful people. We're civilized."

"Do you think Jaime would call you that?"

"I told you, the Chasqui made me do it."

"Just because your hands didn't do all the dirty work doesn't mean they're clean."

I said to the chief, "He's yours."

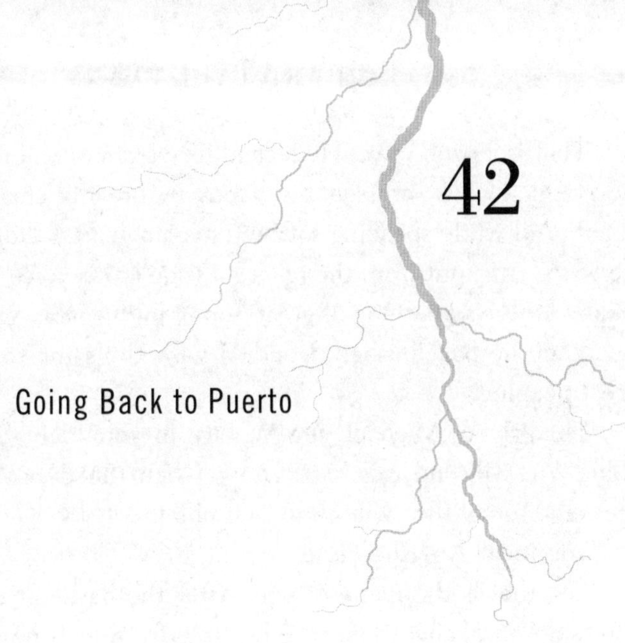

42

Going Back to Puerto

While the Amacarra warriors dragged Lars off into the jungle, the chief and two of his warriors stayed back with the rest of us.

Zeus had joined up with McKenna, and now every bungalow was on fire. The roof of the main lodge had already collapsed.

"That is a great fire," the chief said. "The gods will warm themselves."

"Indeed, they will." I turned to him. "Thank you for everything."

"Thank you, Michael Vey. You and your friends have saved our people. *Lyang gwang ren shr hau ren.*"

"And you have saved my people, my friend."

"Where will you go now?"

"We need to get out of here before the last of the Chasqui forces come after us. We're going to take the lodge's boat. The Chasqui don't know we've taken down their camp, so I think that taking the river will be the best way back."

"That is a good idea." He leaned forward and embraced me. Then he stepped back, crossed his hands before his chest, and bowed slightly, all while speaking softly in his language. I didn't know what he was saying, but from the reverent tone of his voice and demeanor, I knew it was something of great honor and veneration.

When he had finished, I said, "I wish the same to you and your great people."

"Thank you, Michael Vey. We are in your debt. Just one more thing. We will end this battle now, when the Chasqui are at their weakest. Tonight we will hunt their chief."

"You mean Amash," I said.

"Yes, that is the name of evil. After the battle at our village, his forces are weakened. The cave he stole from us is now empty. They are in our jungle. We will use the jungle against them. We will use their own weapons against them. Most of all, we will use their hubris against them.

"They think we are weak and backward. They mock our ways and our spirit guides. This will prove their downfall. Two nights ago, one of our wise seers, a great sage of many years, saw in a dream the demon ruler, on his knees with a spear through his side.

"Tonight, after our battle, one of our warriors said he had seen their sovereign this very night, that he had joined his men looking for us. We will hunt him as we do the wild pig. This will be his last night of doing evil. He will go to the land beyond the clouds to be judged by the gods."

"Be careful," I said. "He is very dangerous. I wish you the gods' favor."

"Thank you, Michael Vey." The chief turned and clicked his tongue several times, and the rest of his warriors came to his side. They all turned to me, touched their chests, then disappeared back into the jungle. I wondered if I would ever see them again.

"Hey, Electroclan," I shouted. "Let's get out of here."

We walked over to the boat. Zeus hopped in first and fired it up while the rest of us climbed in. While we were still at the dock, one of the Makisapa guests came waddling toward us, huffing loudly.

"What about us?" she shouted. "I demand to be taken back to the city this instant."

"You demand?" Zeus said. "Michael, this woman *demands* that we take her back."

"This is a private charter," I said. "I suggest you take it up with your host."

"Don't think I won't, young man. Where's Lars?"

"Probably sitting next to a tree somewhere," I said. "Take us out, Zeus. Let's get out of this stinking place."

PART TWENTY

43

Pondering a Deal with the Devil

"I got hold of Cibor," Johnson said. "He's back at the hacienda."

"What about the others?" Quentin asked.

"Still nothing."

"We might have to go into the jungle after them."

"With what army?" Johnson answered angrily. "That would be suicide. We couldn't defeat them with all of us on our own turf, and you want to walk into their fortress with what's left of us? We've lost enough friends already."

"We don't leave our people behind."

"We don't purposely lead them to their deaths either. This time we wait until we have the advantage. And I don't know where we'll find it. The Chasqui are powerful and diabolical on a level the Elgen didn't come close to."

"The Chasqui *are* Elgen," Quentin said. "They're just a mutant strain of the virus. They're a sickness."

"I will never understand why it is that people are always plotting to rule the world," Jacinta said.

"It's always been that way," Johnson said. "From Genghis Khan to Hitler. If they can't do it with swords, they'll do it with gold."

"So it is," Quentin said. He breathed out slowly. "I can't believe that less than two weeks ago we were having an Electroclan reunion in Boise. Now we're almost all gone."

"We don't know that yet," Johnson said. "I won't accept that until I have to. But I won't back another defeat. Next time I will not come undermanned and outgunned."

Quentin's expression suddenly changed. "I know who can help us. He has the weapons, the soldiers, and the motive."

Johnson's brow furrowed. "Who?"

"Torstyn."

"Your friend who's running a drug cartel?"'

"That's exactly who I mean."

"Not on my watch. You'll just trade one tyrant for another."

"Torstyn isn't in it for power."

"Everyone's in it for power. Why else would he help us?"

"He's a drug dealer. The Chasqui have been cutting off his supply lines and targeting his customers. If Torstyn takes out the Chasqui, he takes out his competition."

"And another drug smuggler wins," Johnson said.

"I wish it were that simple," Quentin said. "You know, when the Mexican marines captured El Chapo and broke up the Sinaloa cartel, drug trafficking and violence didn't decrease. It nearly doubled. All the smaller cartels saw an opportunity and stepped up the violence to take over the Sinaloa's place." He shook his head. "Like it or not, the drug smugglers are already winning." He looked down for a moment, then said, "If we help Torstyn defeat his enemy, nothing changes, except the Chasqui stop trying to take over the world. In that way, the world wins."

"Making a deal with the devil will never work," Johnson said. "It never has."

"But it has worked," Quentin said. "During World War II the US government asked the mafia to help guard the country's coast. Defeating Hitler and the Nazis was as much in the mafia's interest as it was in America's. War and politics make for strange allies, but an ally is an ally. Besides, there's another motive. Possibly an even more powerful one."

"What's that?"

"Torstyn always harbored a secret love for Tessa. She was here in the jungle with him. Alone. When she escaped from the Elgen, he was heartbroken. He never had another love after that. He carried that for years. And trust me, no one carries a grudge like Torstyn. He would come after the Chasqui for that reason alone."

Johnson sat down to think as Jacinta walked in carrying sandwiches and drinks.

"I am sorry that took so long," she said. "I thought you would like drinks. *Jugo de piña fresco.*"

"Where did you find fresh pineapple juice at two in the morning?"

"Where there is a will, there is a way," she said. She looked at them, and the sadness of her words sank in. "Sometimes." She set the food and drinks on the small table in front of the couch they were sitting on. "Has there been any word on Cassy?"

"No," Johnson said.

"Any word from anyone else?"

"I spoke to Cibor."

"How was he?"

"About as bad as you would expect."

She nodded slowly. "And the others?"

"Still nothing."

She breathed out slowly. "Please, eat."

Johnson picked up his sandwich. "I just wish someone would call."

PART TWENTY-ONE

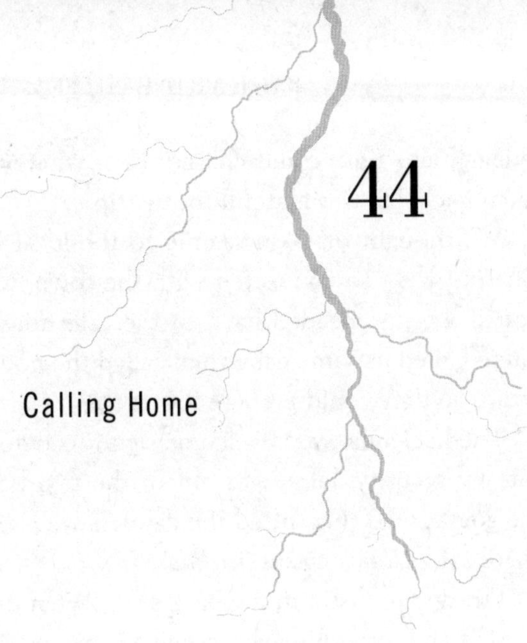

44

Calling Home

The ride back to Puerto was thankfully uneventful. I wanted to call Johnson to update him, but the satellite phone was dead. We didn't know where Johnson's team was or what they were up to. We didn't even know if the Chasqui had sent the bats upriver or not.

We passed only two boats on our way back to Puerto Maldonado. One was an old fisherman; the other was Chasqui. Ian saw the Chasqui boat long before they saw us, so we just stayed down (most of us were already on the floor of the boat sleeping), and Zeus and Nichelle waved innocently to them as they passed. The Chasqui soldiers ignored them, flying by us at full speed.

We arrived back in Puerto at sunrise, almost the same hour of day that we had left on our mission. We docked the boat at Jaime's friend's dock and handed him the keys. Jaime told him that there were a bunch of rich guests stranded at the lodge without food and lodging, and Kale could charge them whatever he wanted to bring them back. He was grateful for the tip.

We thought of taking Jaime to the local hospital, but since the Chasqui were so connected with the town, we decided it would be best if we just headed back to the safe house to rest and regroup. Jaime hailed us some cabs, then called the house to alert them to our return so they could prepare for us.

The hacienda was a welcome sight. As before, we were met at the gate by security. Jaime got out of the taxi behind us and talked to the guard, who then lifted the gate. As we were pulling forward, the guard said, *"Lamento sus pérdidas."*

I turned to Ostin in the back seat. "What did he say?"

"He said something about being sorry for our losses."

"What is he talking about?"

Ostin shrugged. "He probably heard about Luther, Gunnar, and Bentrude."

The taxis drove us up to the main house, and we piled out, relieved to be back. The first thing we did was get out of our filthy clothes—especially those of us still in the hated Chasqui uniforms. Jack wanted to burn them in effigy, but I figured that they could still come in handy, so we threw them into a pile in the laundry room.

I found some black cotton pants and a summer shirt that laced up the front. Not something I'd likely wear around Boise, but anything to get out of that Chasqui garb. Then I found the satellite phone charger and plugged the phone in to charge.

The staff fed us adobo arequipeño, a breakfast stew with marinated pork chop, cumin, garlic, and cloves; pork tamales; salchicha huachana, a sausage made from meat, pork fat, and achiote seeds; and scrambled eggs with onions and chilies.

The hacienda was well equipped with medical supplies, and one of the staff members was a former nurse from a Lima hospital. As the rest of us ate, she saw to Jaime's and Jack's wounds and gave Jaime pain pills so he could rest.

Taylor asked, "Is the satellite phone working?"

"It should be charged by now," I said.

"Can I use it to call my parents?"

"Of course." As I handed her the phone, I noticed there had been numerous calls from Boise and Johnson. "I'd better call mine too. You go first. Then we'll call Johnson."

Taylor sat down next to me on the bed and dialed her home. I lay in the bed. I could hear her mother's animated voice when she answered. Taylor didn't tell her that she had been held by the Chasqui, only that we'd rescued Tara and Jack. I guess she just didn't want to get into all that yet. About fifteen minutes later she said, "Thank you, Mom. I need to give the phone to Michael. He still hasn't called home. . . . Yes, I'm sure they are nervous wrecks as well. Okay, bye. I love you." She hung up the phone.

"How's your mother?" I asked.

"You know, relieved that I'm alive but now wants to kill me." She handed me the phone. "Your turn."

I sat up next to Taylor and dialed. She leaned over and kissed me on the cheek while I was waiting for someone to answer. It was my mother.

"Where have you been? We've been worried sick. Why haven't you called?"

"We've been in the jungle," I said.

"The phone works in the jungle."

"We didn't have the phone. It's complicated."

"What's going on?"

"More than I have time to tell you right now. But we got Taylor, Tara, and Jack out."

"Not Abigail?"

"We still don't know where she is. Just that she's not with the Chasqui."

"Wait, you said 'Taylor.' Taylor wasn't with them."

"The Chasqui captured Taylor too. They took them all to the Starxource plant, where we rescued you. But we got her back."

"And everyone else is safe?"

I hesitated. "No. You knew about Gunnar and Luther. We also lost Bentrude."

"Oh no," she said sadly. "I admired that young man. I'm very sorry. Let's get you all home. We'll send the jet."

"Not yet. We haven't talked to Johnson; he's still out."

"Out where?"

"We found out that the Chasqui planned to burn down the city of Arequipa with their electrified bats."

"Arequipa's a large city."

"It has about a million people. And if we don't stop them, thousands, maybe tens of thousands, will die."

"What do you need from us?"

"Right now, nothing. Like I said, we just got back from the jungle this morning."

"You sound tired."

"I haven't had a full night's rest in almost a week."

"I'll let you go so you can sleep. I'll pass your news along to everyone. You wouldn't believe how worried Mrs. Liss has been."

"Of course I would. She used to make Ostin wear a helmet to his clogging lessons."

My mother laughed. "I forgot about that."

"Ostin never will," I said. "He has PTSD. And Taylor already called her family."

"Good. They've been sick with worry as well." She sighed. "Thank you so much for calling. You have no idea how many prayers I've said for you. For all of you. Come home safe."

"We're trying."

"Call again when you can."

"I will. We will. Bye." I hung up the phone.

"How's your mother?" Taylor asked.

"Same as yours."

"Do you want to take a nap?"

"I need to call Johnson first."

I dialed the number. Johnson answered immediately. His voice was hoarse and as heavy as stone. "Michael. Where have you been?"

45

Sharing Bad News

"We're at the hacienda," I said. "Did you stop them?"

"We stopped them."

I breathed out in relief. "That is good news."

"Some of it."

I sensed the gravity in his voice. "What is it?"

"The Chasqui knew of our plan and sent attack helicopters." He hesitated. "Jax and Tessa were killed."

My chest felt like a bag of concrete had fallen onto it. "It can't be."

"There's more. Cassy was with them during the attack. She was hit too. We're in the ICU at the Puerto hospital right now. She's in critical condition. She's lost a lot of blood."

The news fell even heavier. "We're on our way."

"Michael, did you save the girls?"

"Yes. Jack too."

"Jack came with you?"

"Jack was only trying to save Tara."

"Is Jaime with you?"

"We have him, too."

"Why didn't he call us?"

"Jaime was captured by the Chasqui. He was beaten and tortured. That's how they knew about our plans to stop their bats."

"But Jaime didn't know where we would be. We didn't even know until the day before."

"They just needed a general idea. The Elgen had el-readers. They're machines that track us electrics. If the Chasqui still had them, the el-readers would have led them right to Cassy and Tessa."

"What about Jacinta's friend, Lars? Why didn't he help?"

"He did help. He helped deliver Jaime to the Chasqui. He's owned by them. He's a traitor."

"I'm going to kill that Swede with my own hands," Johnson said.

"We already took care of that," Michael said. "At least, the Amacarra did. Is Jacinta with you?"

"Yes. Just a moment." I could hear him walking. "I stepped outside to be alone," he said. "You're not saying Jacinta was in on it."

"No. She wasn't. I'm sure she doesn't know her friend is a traitor. You'll have to tell her."

"I'll tell her," he said. "What about the Chasqui? Are they hunting you?"

"We don't think so. At least what's left of them. After our last battle, most of the Chasqui are dead."

"How did that happen?"

"It was mostly Tara. I'll tell you about it when we get there. Just keep Cassy alive."

"I wish it was up to me," he said.

"I need to tell the others. I'll talk to you soon. Bye."

"Bye."

PART TWENTY-TWO

46

Jacinta Learns the Truth

Johnson hung up the phone and walked back into the room. Quentin and Jacinta were looking at him.

"Was that Michael?" Quentin asked.

Johnson nodded. "He's safe. They're all safe. They rescued Taylor, Tara, Jack, and Jaime."

"Jaime?" Jacinta said. "The Chasqui captured him too?"

"It turns out that your friend Lars is a Chasqui sympathizer. He set us up. They tortured Jaime until he told them what we were up to. That's how they found us."

Jacinta gasped. Then her eyes welled up. "I had no idea."

"I know. Michael assured me that you didn't."

Jacinta started crying. "It's all my fault. Their deaths are my fault. Their deaths are on my hands."

Johnson put his arms around her. "No. You couldn't have known. Their blood is on the Chasqui's hands."

PART TWENTY-THREE

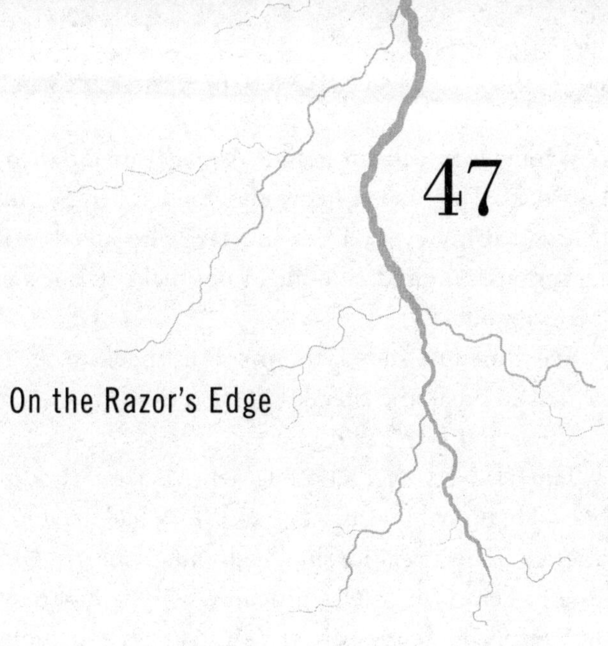

47

On the Razor's Edge

From my side of the conversation, Taylor knew that something bad had happened. Something horrific.

"What is it?"

"We need to gather everyone. Now."

"Can't you tell me?"

I looked at her dolefully. "I'd rather only say it once."

"I'll gather everyone," she said.

Taylor ran through the house calling everyone to the meeting. Within a few minutes, everyone had congregated in the dining area. The room was silent in anticipation of what I had to say. As hard as I tried to remain stoic, tears welled up in my eyes. I took a deep breath.

"This is really hard for me to say." I wiped a tear off my cheek. "The Chasqui knew about our plans to attack their cargo of bats. Those helicopters we saw fly over us in the jungle weren't looking for us; they were going to attack our friends. Alpha Team did their job and stopped the trucks. They saved many thousands of lives, but . . ." I stopped, then wiped my eyes. "Tessa and Jax were killed in the attack. Cassy was seriously injured. She might not make it. She's in the ICU at the Puerto hospital."

Everyone just stared, too much in shock to speak. McKenna was the first to break the silence. "Tessa is dead?"

"Tessa and Jax," I said.

Tara glanced over at Zeus, who looked almost paralyzed with shock. He probably was. Zeus and Tessa had been in love once, a long time ago. Their relationship had ended shortly after Hatch moved Tessa to Peru (which was probably why he had moved her to Peru), but I suspected that a part of Zeus had never completely let go of his feelings for her. Zeus said nothing, but I saw him furtively wipe tears from his face.

"This is my fault," Jaime wailed. "I killed them. I killed them all." He buried his face in his hands. "Why didn't they just kill me first?"

"You didn't kill anyone," I said. "The Chasqui did."

"If only I had kept my mouth shut."

"They tortured you," Ian said. "Any of us would have talked."

"It's true," Taylor said, putting her hand on his shoulder.

Everyone nodded their heads in sympathy. For the next minute the only sound in the room was sniffling and crying.

I had my own reasons for grief. Tessa had a way of climbing into your heart, and Torstyn and Zeus weren't the only ones who had felt something for her. I met Tessa when I was captured by the Amacarra. The tribe had called her "Hung fa" because of her red hair, something they saw as mystical and an omen of good luck. The first time they saw her in the jungle, they thought she was a goddess. I just thought she was pretty.

That was a terrifying time for me. I had just barely escaped the Starxource plant and the Elgen guard, only to be captured by these jungle warriors in red-and-black war paint. I was pretty sure they were cannibals and were planning to eat me. Instead, they brought me to their village and Tessa. Seeing another electric, one as brave as

Tessa, who spoke English and was also fleeing the Elgen, had been a huge relief. I hadn't realized at the time that she had probably saved my life. Had the Amacarra not already befriended an electric, they likely would have assumed I was just another "white devil" and shot me with their poisonous blow darts.

Tessa and I had spent days together in the jungle, and we got close during that time. After we were back with the others, she confided that she had feelings for me, which I probably would have been receptive to had I not already been with Taylor.

After that, things changed between us. We were still friends, but for the last several years we hadn't talked much. I felt bad about that, and I was looking forward to seeing her at the reunion in Boise. She always had a place in my heart.

I clearly remembered the last thing she said to me just before we left on this mission. She had come out to say goodbye, and she seemed especially anxious. She had put her arms around me, then said, "I just had this feeling." When I asked her what she was feeling, she smiled sadly, then said, "I'll tell you when we're all back." I wondered if she had a premonition that we wouldn't see each other again.

Remembering her last words broke my heart. *Be safe, Michael. I don't want a world without you in it.* Now I would have to live in a world without *her* in it. I couldn't believe she was gone.

It wasn't lost on me that Cassy had said something similar before we left, just after she kissed me. *If something happens to one of us* . . . Something had.

I just wanted to go to sleep and somehow wake up with a new reality. I had had enough nightmares lately. Why couldn't this be another one?

I took another deep breath, then said, "I'm going to the hospital to be with Cassy and the others. If anyone wants to come with me, I'm leaving now."

Everyone stood except for Nichelle.

"I'll pull up the van," Jaime said.

As everyone walked out to the front drive, I looked over at

Nichelle, who was sitting in the corner, crying. I walked over and crouched down next to her. "Nichelle."

She looked at me with swollen eyes. "Why did it have to be her, Michael? Why her? Why not me? Why not someone who doesn't matter?"

"Don't say that."

"Everyone loved her."

I sat down next to her. "They did. Just like everyone loves you." I held her as she shook.

When she could speak, she said, "Why did they have to die? It hurts so much."

"I don't know. My mother once told me, the only way to take pain out of death is to take love out of life. We hurt because we love." I lifted her chin. "You love her. Just like we all love her. And you. We're family."

She looked at me gratefully.

"Now let's go. Cassy and the others need us."

"Thank you."

I kissed her cheek. "You're welcome."

I stood, then took her hand and helped her up. We walked together out to the van. Jaime had pulled the van up to the front door of the hacienda. Taylor was sitting in the front passenger seat. Jaime got out when he saw me and got in the back so I could drive.

The best word to describe the ride into Puerto Maldonado was "solemn"—each of us dealing with the loss in our own way and praying that we wouldn't lose Cassy too. Several times Taylor took my hand to comfort me, then released it almost as if she'd touched a hot stove. I suppose the pain and intensity of my thoughts were too painful for her.

I parked the van near the hospital's emergency entrance, and we all went inside. Johnson, Quentin, Cibor, and Jacinta were sitting on vinyl couches inside the entrance. They all looked physically and emotionally drained. They stood as we entered.

I can't describe the feelings we had, such a bizarre mix of emotions—the joy of seeing each other alive, the anguish of loss, and the foreboding that we still might lose another one of us.

"It's good to see you all," Johnson said. His eyes were bloodshot and swollen.

"How's Cassy?" Taylor asked.

"She is not doing well," Jacinta said. "The doctor was just here. She has internal bleeding, but they are having trouble finding where she is bleeding."

"Have they scanned her?" Ostin asked. "Do they have a CAT scan?"

"They have a CAT scan, but it is not working. They only have one. This is a small hospital."

"Why can't they just bring one in from somewhere else?" McKenna asked.

"It is not that simple," Jacinta said.

"We don't need one," Ostin said. "We have Ian. Where's Cassy?"

Jacinta pointed. "The ICU is through those doors. But they won't let you just go back there."

"I got it," Ostin said. "Come on, Ian. Let's do this."

The two of them walked through the doors.

"You'd better go with them," Johnson said to Jacinta.

"To translate?" she asked.

"No. To buffer."

"I'll go too," I said. I walked through the emergency room doors with her.

Halfway down the corridor a nurse stepped in front of Ostin. "You cannot be back here," she said in accented English.

"This is an emergency," Ostin said. "I am Dr. Ostin Liss of Caltech. This is Dr. Ian Fleming. He is a trauma specialist from the Mayo Clinic. We are here on official hospital business for the American patient Cassandra."

The nurse suddenly looked confused. "Excuse me, doctors. I was not told you were coming. Let me get you some masks."

"Thank you," Ostin said.

She handed us all surgical masks. We put them on and washed our hands. Then she led us back to the OR. Cassy was lying on the table, as motionless as if she were dead.

"Doctor, the specialists from America are here," the nurse announced.

He turned toward us. "I do not know of any specialists."

"Her parents are very wealthy," Ostin said. "They sent the best from the States." He walked closer to the table. "I understand that our patient is bleeding internally, but you're having trouble finding where she's bleeding."

"Our imaging equipment is not functioning right now. Our EKG equipment isn't working either. I've never seen such an irregular reading before."

This was common with all of us electrics. There was no way to practically explain it to him, so Ostin just ignored the electrocardiogram problem.

"Dr. Fleming can find where she's bleeding," Ostin said. "Please give us some room."

The doctor seemed a little apprehensive, but he still stepped back, along with his two nurses and a medical technician.

"How much blood have you gone through?" Ostin asked.

"We have transfused six units of blood," the doctor said. "Her hemoglobin has dropped to six."

"That doesn't sound good," Ian said, having no idea what the actual number should be. He stepped up to the table and looked over Cassy's body. Then he pointed to a place just below her rib cage. "The bleeding is right there, but in her back. You'll need to roll her over to see it."

The nurses looked over at the doctor.

"You heard him," he said. "Roll her over."

The nurses and technician rolled Cassy over onto her stomach. In her back was a small puncture wound.

"That's it right there," Ian said. "That's where the shrapnel entered."

The nurse anesthetist administered a local anesthetic, and the doctor cut into Cassy's skin about two inches above her hip.

"Retractors," the doctor said.

A nurse handed him the retractor, and he opened the incision. A small but steady stream of blood squirted upward onto his face and mask.

"There is a perforation on the transverse colon," the doctor said. "Nurse, clamp." He applied the clamp, and the spurting stopped.

Ian kept looking through Cassy's body. "It's the only internal wound," he said.

The doctor worked quickly to close the wound. As he worked, he asked, "How did you know she was bleeding here?"

"Dr. Fleming is the author of a scientific breakthrough in diagnostic technique and imaging," Ostin said. "Have you heard of the MEI machine?"

"No."

"It's where his expertise came from. You will read his paper very soon."

The doctor finished suturing the colon, then closed his incision.

Cassy's blood pressure almost immediately started to climb on the digital monitor next to her. One of the nurses put a disinfectant and gauze over the wound.

"Dr. Fleming," the doctor said, "you just saved this young woman's life. It was an honor to work with you."

"Thank you," Ian replied. "It was my honor to work with you."

"How long until she wakes up?" I asked.

The doctor looked over at me for the first time. "I have her sedated on fifty milligrams of propofol, with a fifteen-milligram maintenance. But now we can begin emergence. She should be responsive in less than an hour."

"Our work is done here," Ostin said. "Please let us know when she's gained consciousness."

"We will let you know."

The four of us walked back out to the waiting room.

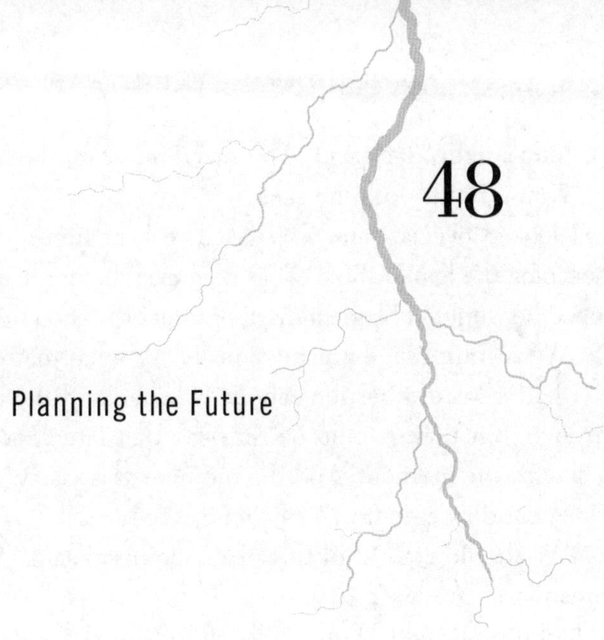

48

Planning the Future

"How is she?" Johnson asked as we emerged into the waiting room.

"Ian found the problem," Ostin said. "They've stopped the bleeding. Her blood pressure is rising."

"She's going to be okay?" McKenna asked.

"We think so," I said.

"Thank God something finally went right," Nichelle said.

Tara walked over and put her arm around her. "Nichelle, when I was in the cave, I had never felt such pain in all my life. I was sure I was going to die. I almost did. But you freed me. And you freed Taylor and Jack and Jaime. And we saved tens of thousands of lives by taking out those trucks.

"My heart is beyond broken for Tessa and Jax and Bentrude and the others. But it's also filled with gratitude. As much as we are hurting, I don't think we should forget how much has gone right. And how many lives have been saved."

"Tara's right," Jack said. "You saved me from the firing squad."

"Tara *is* right," Johnson said.

I looked over at him. I was glad to hear him say this. He'd been mourning the loss of three of his men even before this latest loss. I had hoped he wouldn't blame himself or forget the good that had happened.

"We accomplished our mission. That's what matters."

I had a lot of questions about what he and the others had been through, but there would be time for that later. For now we had to deal with the moment. And the moment was Cassy.

"What do we do now?" Nichelle asked.

"We should get out of this place," Johnson said. "As soon as Cassy is ready to leave, we go."

"Johnson is right," I said. "I'll call for the plane now."

I walked out to the van for the satellite phone. I sat inside and called my parents. This time my father answered.

"Michael, are you okay?"

"I'm alive. Most of us are alive."

"How is Cassy?"

"They've stopped the bleeding. She should be fine."

He exhaled in relief. "Thank goodness."

"We're ready to come home. All of us. Including Cristiano and Jacinta, if they'll come."

"Who are they?"

"They are friends who have been fighting with us. It's not safe for them here anymore."

"We should pull out anyone who has been involved. How many is that?"

I had to count. "Sixteen. And two bodies."

"I'll send the jet immediately. It will be there by morning. Will Cassy be ready to travel?"

"She should be."

"What about Abigail?"

"We still don't know where she is."

"Keep your phone with you. I'll have the pilots contact you when they're close."

"Thank you."

"Son, I'm sorry for all the losses. I know how much that hurts. But I'm glad you're safe."

"Thanks. Good night." I walked back into the hospital. Everyone turned to look at me.

"The jet will be here in the morning to take us home."

"All of us?" Johnson asked.

"Everyone. Including Cristiano and Jacinta. We have room for you too."

"Peru is my home," Jacinta said.

"I know. But we've stirred up a hornet's nest, and it's not safe for you right now. It would be best if we let things settle."

"He's right," Johnson said. He turned to Cristiano. "What about you?"

"I'm good with going back," he said. "I don't have a green card, but I'll figure something out."

"Neither of you needs to worry about a thing," I said. "You'll be taken care of. Just as you've taken care of us. Whenever you want to come back to Peru, we'll take care of that, too."

Jacinta slowly nodded. "Okay. I will come back to the States with you. At least for a little while."

Johnson reached over and took her hand.

"I know a good Peruvian restaurant in Boise," Ostin said. "In case you were wondering."

"Thank you."

About an hour later a nurse walked out into the waiting room.

"Your friend is awake now. She asked to see three people." She looked down at a paper she'd written the names on. "Jax. Michael. Tessa."

Taylor looked at me. "She doesn't know."

I exhaled slowly. "How could she?"

"I'd better go with you," Johnson said.

"So will I," Tara said. "Cassy and I are close."

Taylor squeezed my hand. "Good luck."

The three of us walked back to the room. It was good to see

Cassy awake. She was now clothed in a cotton hospital gown, with a white bedsheet pulled up to her waist. As we walked in, her eyes darted back and forth between us. We walked to her side.

"Where's Jax and Tessa?" She looked at Tara. "Taylor?"

"It's Tara," she said, taking Cassy's hand.

"Tara," Cassy said softly. "They got you out."

"They got all of us out," Tara said.

"Where's Jax and Tessa?" she asked again.

"Cassy, what do you remember?" I asked.

"It's still a blur. . . . There was a helicopter. Jax shouted something. Then he jumped onto me to protect me. That's all I remember." She looked into my eyes. "Is he okay?"

"It was a Chasqui helicopter Jax saw," Johnson said. "Your position was hit by a missile. Jax saved your life. But he lost his. So did Tessa."

Cassy stared at Johnson in disbelief. "You're saying they're dead?" She looked around at us. When no one answered, she said, "Don't tell me they're dead." She turned to Tara. "Tara? They're not dead, right? Tell me they're not dead."

"I'm sorry, Cass."

"No!" she shouted. "Don't say that!"

"I'm sorry, Cassy," I said. "We're all sorry."

"You're all wrong. It doesn't end this way." She broke down crying. "It doesn't end this way. Oh, dear God." She yanked a PICC line from her arm, and one of the monitors' alarms started beeping loudly.

A nurse rushed into the room. "What is wrong?"

Tara said, "She just learned that her friends who were with her didn't make it."

The nurse asked Cassy, "Would you like something to help calm you?"

"I want my friends back," Cassy said, crying.

Tara put her arms around her. I nodded to the nurse. She walked over and prepared a shot.

Cassy was sobbing so heavily, she could barely speak. "Why do things keep happening to us? What did we do to deserve this?"

"Not a thing," I said.

I wished more than anything else that Abigail was with us. Abigail could always bring peace, not just physically but emotionally as well.

After a few more minutes, Cassy asked, "Michael, will you hold me?"

"Of course," I said. "Will you let them give you a shot?"

She nodded. I put my arms around her. She wept until the shot put her back to sleep.

49

Splitting Up Again

The three of us stayed at Cassy's side for another hour or so. Then Johnson said, "I think we should get everyone back to the hacienda. This town isn't safe for us anymore."

"We can't leave Cassy alone," Tara said.

"No," he said. "Someone needs to stay with her."

"I'll stay," I said.

"So will I," Tara said.

"I want Ian to stay with us," I said. "And Cristiano to translate. We'll need someone who can talk to the staff when it's time to check out."

Johnson nodded. "Let's go out and tell the others."

Tara leaned over Cassy and kissed her forehead. Then we all walked back out to the waiting room. The others looked at us with anticipation.

"Cassy's doing well," I said. "At least physically. She's taking the deaths really hard. We think it's best that everyone goes back to the hacienda. Tara and I are going to stay. Ian and Cristiano, I'd like you to stay if you're not too tired."

"I'll stay," Ian said.

"Whatever you need," Cristiano said.

"I'd like to stay," Jack said.

"Thanks," I said.

Johnson said, "Okay, that's you five. Cibor and I will drive the van and Hummer back. Michael, you keep the car you came here in. You know the way back to the hacienda?"

"I know the way," Ian said.

"So do I," Cristiano said.

"Then we're good," Johnson said. "Let's go."

As everyone got up, Taylor sidled up to me. "If it's okay with you, I think I'll go back with them. McKenna isn't doing well. I'd like to stay with her."

"Of course," I said. We kissed.

"Don't stay too late," she said.

"That's up to Cassy."

"Michael," Quentin said. He was standing next to Zeus. "Do you need us?"

"No, we're good. Get some rest."

"Thanks, brother," he said. "I could use some sleep."

Zeus gave me one of his man hugs. "Night, man."

"Night."

"Good night, Michael," Ostin said. He had his arm around McKenna. She looked hammered. Her eyes were swollen.

"Get some rest, buddy," I said.

"Roger that," he said.

I grabbed Johnson before he left. "Keep an eye on Jaime," I said. "I'm worried about him. He's blaming himself for Jax's and Tessa's deaths."

"I'll tell him to get in line."

"That's not what I meant."

"I know," Johnson said. "Don't worry. I've had this talk before. I'll handle it."

"Be safe," I said.

"You be safe."

"We're in a hospital," I said. "What could go wrong?"

50

What About Abigail?

Cassy woke briefly around midnight, then fell back to sleep. The nurses came in every half hour to check the monitors and throw around some medical jargon about HCT and hemoglobin levels. I think a few of them just wanted to practice their English.

Every time I asked if we could go, they said they wanted to keep Cassy hydrated a bit longer and get her HCT level to thirty. I figured they'd tell us when she was there.

The hospital was quiet at night. They had transferred Cassy to a small private room. Cassy continued sleeping, which I was grateful for, while we just sat quietly around her trying not to fall asleep.

"What are you going to do when you get back to the States?" I asked Ian.

"Well," he said, yawning, "after I sleep for a week, then get some good Thai food and sushi, I've got a contract for another shipwreck hunt. I've got these producers who want to shoot a pilot for a streaming series. About treasure hunters."

"I'd watch that," Tara said. "That documentary on the *Titanic* was cool."

"If they can make a documentary about catching crabs," I said, "yours is a shoo-in."

"What's a shoe in?" Cristiano asked.

"It means you made it," Tara said. "Don't bother learning it. You'll never use it."

"Shoe in," Cristiano said, looking perplexed. "What is the shoe in?"

No one answered him.

"How about you, Tara?" I asked.

"My plan is to spend as much time with my sister as I can before you get the idea to marry her and take her away."

"You can always move in with us," I said.

"If you think that," she said, "you don't know my sister."

"I hope I do. What else are you going to do?"

"My basic plan is to finish school and stay away from people who want to kill me."

"That is a sound plan," Ian said. "I'm adding that to my life goals."

"What about you, Cristiano?"

"I don't know. Starting over in a new country. I have no money. I will get a job somewhere to earn money. I have worked in a restaurant."

"You gave up your old life to help us. Your reward is a new life with us helping you. Let me ask, if you could do or be anything you want, what would it be?"

"I would like to be a doctor. A brain surgeon."

"That's not ambitious," Ian said.

"How are your grades?" Tara asked.

"I have a four-point-seven at ASU so far."

"Those are . . . good," Tara said.

"I have one more year. Then I would like to take the MCAT."

"We can help you," I said. "Our company has scholarship programs and clout to get you into a good school."

"Really?"

"Really," I said. "We'll talk more later. What about you, Jack? You've been quiet this whole time."

Jack didn't move.

"I think he's asleep," Tara said.

Jack looked up. "I'm not asleep. I'm thinking."

"About what?" Tara asked.

"Michael's question." He cleared his throat. "A week ago, I thought I knew exactly what I wanted to do with my life. But now that's changed." To my surprise his eyes looked like they were welling up. "I've been given a horrible but amazing gift. I got to face my death.

"When I was tied to that post waiting for those bullets to end me, all I could think about was Abi. She was the only thing on my mind." He wiped his cheek. "I don't know where she is, but whatever it takes, I'm going to find her. I'm going to ask her to forgive me. And then I'm going to ask her to marry me.

"I don't know how long I'll live, but starting yesterday, every day is a gift. I want to spend every day of the rest of my life with her."

I looked over at Tara. She was wiping a tear from her eye.

"Anyway, that's my plan," Jack said to me. "I don't know where I'll start looking for her, but I'm hoping you'll give me a hand."

"We'll give you more than that," I said. "And McKenna will. She and Abi were in Purgatory together. I've never seen a closer bond. And if McKenna goes, Ostin goes."

"If you go, Ostin goes," Tara said. "Ostin will follow you anywhere."

"The fool," I said.

"Then you've got another fool," Ian said. "Because I'm with you. Don't forget, those are my girls too. I was in Purgatory with them. Besides, those ships have been down there for hundreds of years. A few more months isn't going to hurt anything."

"Don't leave me out of this," Tara said. "Or Taylor. We're in. Abi's our girl."

"What about your plan of staying away from people who want to kill you?" Ian asked.

"That can start after we find Abi."

"I never doubted any of you," I said. "That's what the Electroclan does." I looked at Cristiano. "You still think our loyalty is our weakness?"

He grinned sheepishly. "I'm sorry. That was a very stupid thing for me to say."

"Not stupid," Tara said. "Just not . . . smart."

Ian laughed. "What about you, Michael? You and Taylor have plans?"

"I love her."

"Technically, that's not really a plan," Jack said.

"Technically, that's the best plan," Tara said. "Love is the destination *and* the journey. If you've got that down, the rest of life is just commercials."

"Commercials?" Jack said.

"If you had known that before," Tara said, "you wouldn't be hoping a certain girl would take you back."

"That stings," Jack said. "It's true, though."

"That's why it stings," Tara said.

"I just want to be a mom," Cassy said.

We all turned to look at her. We hadn't known she was awake. Or listening.

"Welcome back," Tara said.

Her voice was soft. "I've always wanted to be a mom. I want a little boy and a little girl."

"Where do you want to live?" I asked.

"Maybe I'll go back to Switzerland. I loved living in Switzerland. But then, maybe somewhere on the ocean. Maybe both. I'm young."

"How are you feeling?" Tara asked.

"Sad."

"I meant your body."

"My body is sad too. But I don't feel like I'm dying anymore. I think I could walk now."

"Are you ready to go?"

"I'd like to go home," she said. "Someplace soft that doesn't smell like rubbing alcohol."

Just then there was a loud commotion outside Cassy's room. Loud shouting echoed down the hospital's tiled corridor.

"What's that?" Tara asked.

I turned to Ian, who was looking intensely toward the wall facing the emergency entrance. "What do you see?"

"Chasqui soldiers. Two helicopters just landed in the parking lot."

Jack and Cristiano immediately stood.

"They found us," Jack said. "I knew someone here was a snitch."

Cristiano looked pale with fear. "They'll torture and kill me. I'm not going with them alive."

"Calm down," Ian said. "They're not looking for us. They're carrying someone on a stretcher. They have an IV on him."

"Who?" I asked.

He looked at me. "I think it's Amash."

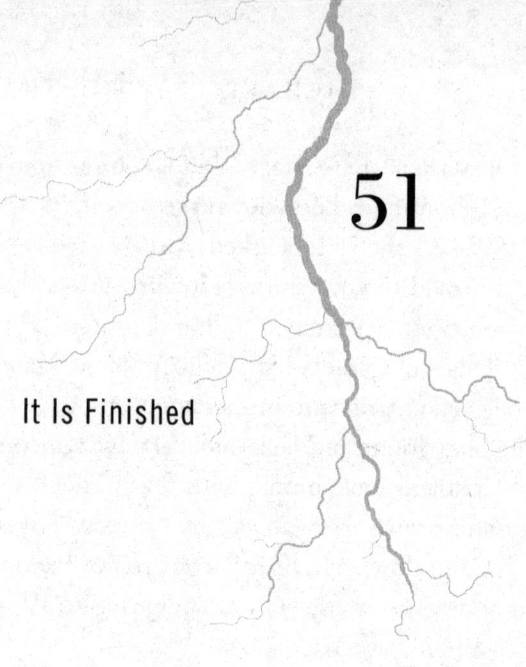

51

It Is Finished

"Amash is out there?" Cassy asked.

"Maybe," Ian said. "It's a little hard to tell."

"Are the guards wearing Chasqui patches with purple and gold?" Jack asked.

"Yes, they are."

"That's Amash, then. Those are Amash's special guards. They're the only ones with those patches."

"The chief told me that the Amacarra were going after him last night," I said. "He said their tribal seer had a dream that Amash was kneeling before the Amacarra with a spear through his side."

"Not a spear," Ian said. "A bullet. They must have used the Chasqui's guns they collected."

I turned to Cristiano. "I thought you said the Chasqui had their own medical facility."

"In the cave they do, but we locked them out of their cave."

"What about the Starxource plant?"

"They have an excellent medical facility there, but they do not have sophisticated equipment. Amash must be hurt badly for them to bring him here."

"How bad is it?" I asked Ian.

"They've got him on the table, and they've started a transfusion. The bullet is lodged near his heart. He has internal bleeding."

"Can they save him?"

Ian's brow furrowed. "Cassy's puncture was bigger, and they saved her. I think they should be able to save him."

"No, they won't," Cassy said. She closed her eyes, then reached out an open hand, her palm facing up toward the ceiling. We all watched her in silence. After a moment she said, "There it is." She very slowly closed her grip, like she was squeezing a ball, crushing it.

Suddenly the sound of alarms went off. Then, over the hospital's PA system, came the words *"Codigo azul. Codigo azul."*

"Code blue," Cristiano said. "Someone is in cardiac arrest."

I looked over at Cassy. Her jaw was clenched, and the anger on her face told me everything I needed to know. The code continued for another few minutes, then stopped. Cassy put down her fist and exhaled loudly.

We were all quiet for a moment. Then Cassy said, *"Tetelestai."*

"What?" I asked.

She slowly turned to look at me. "I'm ready to go home."

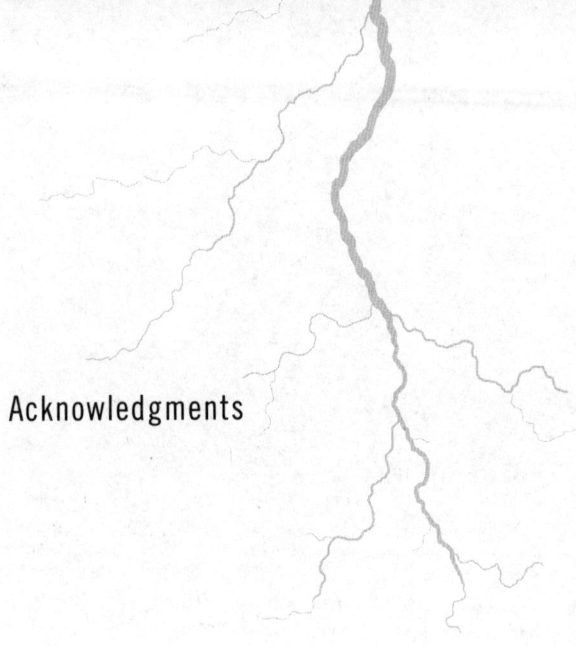

Acknowledgments

As an author, Michael Vey has not only been an amazing writing and literary journey, but it has also demonstrated to me that despite the borders drawn on maps, we earthlings are not as different from each other as we might think we are. As I hear from fans, male and female, young and old, from the US, Iran, Syria, Pakistan, Taiwan, France, Italy, Australia, South Korea, and dozens of other countries, they all share the same concern and hope for the Electroclan and their struggle to overcome evil.

I wish to thank Veyniacs around the world for making the Michael Vey series such a remarkable success. Shock on—there is more to come.

Join the Veyniac Nation!

For Michael Vey trivia, sneak peeks, and events in your area, follow Michael and the rest of the Electroclan at:

MICHAELVEY.COM

Facebook.com/MichaelVeyOfficialFanPage

Twitter.com/MichaelVey

Instagram.com/RichardPaulEvansAuthor

RICHARD PAUL EVANS

is the #1 *New York Times* and *USA Today* bestselling author of more than forty-five novels. There are currently more than thirty-five million copies of his books in print worldwide, translated into more than twenty-four languages. Richard has won the American Mothers Book Award, two first-place Storytelling World Awards, the Romantic Times Best Women's Novel of the Year Award, the German Leserpreis Gold Award for Romance, and is a five-time recipient of the Religion Communicators Council's Wilbur Award. Eight of Richard's books have been produced as television movies or feature films, including the Netflix movie *The Noel Diary*, a #1 international hit.

In 2011, Richard began writing Michael Vey, a #1 *New York Times* bestselling young adult series that has won more than a dozen awards. Richard is the founder of The Christmas Box International, an organization devoted to maintaining emergency shelters for children and providing services and resources for abused, neglected, or homeless children and young adults. To date, more than 140,000 youths have been helped by the charity. For his humanitarian work, Richard has received the Washington Times Humanitarian of the Century Award and the Volunteers of America National Empathy Award. Richard spends his time at his Timepiece Ranch in southern Utah, or at home in Salt Lake City with his wife, Keri, and their five children and two grandchildren. You can learn more about Richard on his website RichardPaulEvans.com.